SHIFTER ACADEMY: YEAR THREE

JODY MORSE

JAYME MORSE

PROLOGUE

It was strange to think there had ever been a time I hadn't believed in magic—a time when I'd thought monsters weren't real and that the supernatural existed only in TV shows and movies.

If only I had known then that magic would one day consume every aspect of my life. And that my future—and the future of the entire shifter world as we knew it—completely rested in the hands of a psychic and her ability to see into the future.

But I would worry about talking to her later. Right now, I had to locate my mates... but I couldn't seem to find them.

As I headed out into the grassy courtyard, I nearly stumbled over the lion's body that lay before me.

His golden body looked so strong, yet so... *lifeless.*

His blonde mane was splayed out all around him. It didn't look like he was breathing; I didn't see his chest moving up and down.

Crouching down on my knees on the ground next to him, I felt for a pulse.

Nothing.

A lump formed in the back of my throat, making it difficult to swallow or even breathe. Tears sprang to my eyes.

This wasn't supposed to happen.

CHAPTER ONE

Last Fall

I *had* survived my first shift.

I'd been waiting for this moment for so long, but it didn't even feel real now that it was finally happening. It felt like something out of a dream—a really *bad* dream. That was all I could seem to think about as I stood on Rafael's bedroom balcony.

I stared at myself in the sliding glass door. How the hell had this even happened? How had I shifted into *that?*

Before I had the chance to take it all in, I heard movement inside the room. Shifting my gaze away from my reflection, I watched Rafael climb off the bed.

Well, it was Rafael's *body*, but he wasn't actually in there. Shere Khan had somehow taken over—a startling realization I'd had moments before shifting for the first time ever. I wasn't sure what to do about Shere Khan stealing my mate's body, but one thing was for sure: I had to figure out a way to get him out of there.

As much as I wanted to help Rafael at that very moment, I couldn't. I needed to escape from Shere Khan.

Honestly, I was confused as hell. Just hours earlier, Shere Khan had given me such good advice for when I became the next Queen of the Shifters. I didn't want to believe Shere Khan was capable of hurting me—or anyone, for that matter. But since he was currently in my mate's body, it was clear he couldn't be trusted.

All I knew was I needed to get the hell out of dodge... and *fast.*

As Shere Khan began to make his way towards the sliding glass door, I did the only thing I could think to do.

I jumped off the balcony, tumbling onto the sandy ground below.

Ouch. No one had warned me that landing on my shifter ass would be so painful.

There was no time to slow down. I had to get away from Shere Khan; I had a feeling he would be hot on my tail.

I began to run on all fours then, realizing I could move at a lightning-like speed. I was actually shocked by how fast my feet —or should I say *paws?* —could carry me.

I headed for the beach. I had to get as far away from the castle as possible. I couldn't allow myself to forget I was in the Tiger Kingdom. I wasn't sure how Queen Bria or any of the other tiger shifters would have treated me if they knew my shifter race.

I was still so surprised by it myself. I had really expected to be a tiger shifter... not *this.*

I heard the sound of padded feet hitting against the sand in the distance. Glancing over my shoulder, I saw Rafael's tiger form running towards me.

I quickened my speed.

Was it even *possible* for me to outrun Shere Khan? I knew I was about to become the next Queen of the Shifters, but let's face it. He was *Shere* freaking *Khan*. He was a Legend for a reason. I knew there was no way I would ever be able to live up to his abilities, even if he wasn't in his own body.

Sure enough, Shere Khan caught up to me even quicker than I'd expected.

As he ran alongside me, Rafael's emerald green eyes locked on mine for a few seconds too long.

I half-expected Shere Khan to attack me or something. But to my surprise, he began to run in the opposite direction.

Relief passed through me, but it was short-lived. Where the hell was he taking Rafael's body?

Part of me wanted to follow him. But the stretch of beach that he was running along was so out in the open—so *exposed* —that I knew I couldn't. Following him was too risky. I couldn't chance being seen by the tigers. My mates needed to find out the truth about me first.

And honestly? I was afraid to follow him. I was afraid of what Shere Khan was capable of. I needed a plan. I would devise one with the rest of the Alpha Brotherhood later, once they came to the island and I shifted back into my human form. And after I figured out what to do about clothes, since I hadn't thought to bring any out here with me.

I would cross that bridge once I got to it. Right now, the goal was to stay hidden. So, I headed for the jungle—the same jungle Shere Khan had told me he'd lived in when he was King of the Shifters, long before the Royal Palace even existed.

I had just entered the jungle when I heard a male voice say, "Did you hear that?"

"I heard nothing," a second, obviously irritated, female voice responded. I recognized this voice immediately.

It was Queen Bria, Rafael's mom.

Shit.

My heart pounded. This wasn't supposed to happen. If there was anyone who couldn't find out about my shifter race yet, it was her.

I thought about sneaking out of the woods again, but I didn't want to draw even *more* attention to myself. So, I ducked behind a bush, hoping its large leaves were enough to conceal my body.

Peering out through the leaves, I saw Queen Bria standing in a large clearing. She was wearing a knee-length dress. The burnt orange satin material looked striking against her sun-kissed skin, which took on an almost supernatural glow in the moonlight. Her long, black hair was pulled into an elegant bun. She looked so different than she had at the dinner party earlier that night.

My gaze shifted over to the guy who stood to her right. He had dark brown hair and sun-kissed skin. He looked familiar for some reason, but I couldn't seem to put my finger on where I recognized him from.

"Anyway, back to what I was saying," Queen Bria continued. "Rafael seems to be completely taken by her. I've never seen him look at anyone the way he stares at this girl. It's as if she's the only one in the room."

A knot in my stomach twisted. She must have been talking about Anastasia or one of the other bachelorettes she had invited to the dinner party. Had her meddling actually worked on Rafael? Was he really smitten with one of those girls?

I tried to shake the thought away. He was *my* mate. That was supposed to mean he only had eyes for me.

Maybe Rafael had just put on a good show at the dinner party to get his mom off his back.

"Bria, darling. Is Rafael falling for this girl really the worst thing?" the man asked.

"No, it's not. The worst thing would be if he actually *marries* this girl. Fortunately, it hasn't gotten to that point yet. We can still stop this in its tracks, before she ruins his life."

"But Rafael needs to choose a wife. What if he thinks she's the one? In fact, what if she *is* the one? She could be his mate, for all we know."

"There's no way in hell this girl is our son's mate," Queen Bria said.

I realized she was talking to Rafael's dad, King Roman. It made sense now why he had looked so familiar. His build reminded me of Rafael's: slender, yet strong. Very tiger-like.

"How can you be so sure?" King Roman questioned.

"Well, for starters, she doesn't even know what type of shifter she is yet."

Holy. Crap.

She wasn't talking about Anastasia or any of the other girls at all. She was talking about *me*.

"How doesn't she know her shifter race?"

"Strange, isn't it? Rafael says she's a late bloomer, but she's in her second year," Queen Bria replied. "She should have already shifted for the first time by now."

"How do we even know she's even a shifter at all? She could be an imposter," King Rafe suggested.

I suppressed an eye roll.

If only they knew the truth.

Not that it would have mattered. If anything, it would have only made things worse. They never would have accepted that I wasn't a tiger shifter. I doubted it would have even mattered to the Queen that I could have made Rafael the next King of the entire shifter world.

The Khans wanted Rafael to end up with another tiger

shifter so that the Royal tiger bloodline wouldn't end up "tainted." It was the entire reason they had been trying to push Anastasia Brink on Rafael. Anastasia was the only tiger shifter who came from a bloodline the King and Queen had deemed "worthy enough" to marry their son.

"Imposter?" Queen Bria's voice snapped me out of my thoughts. "Are you saying you think Lena could be *human*?"

"It's certainly possible, isn't it?" King Roman replied.

"Hmm." She hesitated, clearly deep in thought. "No. I don't think she's human. There's just something so otherworldly about Lena. You'll understand when you meet her. I believe she is a shifter, but I'm not entirely convinced that she doesn't already know her shifter race. I think she's lying."

"Why would she lie?"

"I'm pretty sure she doesn't want me to know what she really is. I don't think she's a tiger shifter... or any type of cat shifter, for that matter. Nothing about her seems cat-like."

"What type of shifter do you think she is?"

"She has an unusually small build. That rules out the werewolves and werebears." Queen Bria hesitated for a long moment. "I get the sense that she's very sneaky. *Secretive.* She's hiding something. She might be a serpent."

Oh, hell no. Anger flooded my veins. How dare she compare me to the snake shifters?

There was only one shifter race I absolutely hated, and it was the serpents. I mostly hated them because the King of the Serpents had murdered my parents. There was nothing good about the serpents. Serpents were known to be sneaky, untrustworthy, and just all around snaky—and there wasn't anything remotely snaky about me.

"Rafael cannot marry a serpent." King Roman sounded horrified at the possibility that his son had fallen for a snake shifter.

Honestly? I couldn't say I blamed him.

"Do you think Rafael knows the truth about her?" Queen Bria asked.

"No. Rafael would not lie to me," King Roman replied.

"We have to get rid of her, Roman," Queen Bria insisted. "It's for his own benefit. She's no good for him."

"How do you propose we get rid of her?"

"We should tell her to slither away from our kingdom before we *make* her leave..We should tell her to leave right now."

"My love, you know we cannot do that. Rafael has brought this Lena Falcone to stay with us for National Felidae Day. Telling her to leave right now would only make him angry at us. Let's just put on some fake smiles and get through the holiday. Afterwards, we'll stage an intervention."

"And how, exactly, will we do that?"

"We'll sit Rafael down for a long conversation about the importance of preserving our bloodline. But I think there's a chance that this whole crush might fade away entirely on its own."

"What leads you to that conclusion?" Bria didn't sound even the slightest bit convinced.

"You know our son and what a hopeless romantic he is. He's always been fascinated with the idea of falling in love with his mate, despite knowing what marrying a girl from a powerful bloodline could do for him and the rest of the Tiger kingdom. Rafael has never cared about our kingdom's place in the hierarchy. It's fate, destiny, and the idea of true love that's always motivated him. It's always been his downfall. So, if this girl *isn't* his mate and I highly doubt that she *is*, if she truly is a serpent —there's zero chance of this evolving into something everlasting."

"Hmm. Maybe this is nothing more than lust." Queen Bria

paused. "She is very pretty—perhaps one of the most beautiful girls I've ever seen."

"Then I am certain that lust is the entire reason our son is so fond of her," her husband assured her. "Relax, Darling. She'll be out of his life in no time."

"I hope so. Because if an intervention doesn't work, then we're going to have to figure out another way to take care of the problem for good, if you know what I mean."

"Are you actually suggesting we *kill* Lena Falcone?" King Roman asked in a voice that was so low I wouldn't have heard it in my human form. Thankfully, being in our shifter forms heightened our senses so I now knew how desperate they were to get rid of me. And here I'd thought Ella Gray was going to be the worst of my mate's moms. *Two of them were bad so far.*

I felt like I was in the middle of a really bad dream—a dream where I had a target on my back from different angles.

"That's exactly what I'm suggesting."

"Bria, I don't know..."

"Roman, listen to me. Our son cannot marry this girl. I would rather die than let that happen."

"This is such an extreme measure," he replied. "I cannot believe this is our only option. I'd rather not have it come to that."

"I just need you to trust me on this. I know what's right for our son, and Lena Falcone isn't it." She tilted her head, staring up at him. "You're my husband. Are you on my side, or aren't you?"

"Of course I'm on your side, my love, forever and always. If killing Lena Falcone is what we must do, then so be it. But let's try our hardest to get rid of her another way first. Lena's death must be our very last resort."

"Yes, well. If she knows what's best for her, she'll leave on her own accord," Bria said.

I felt my heart race as the reality of the situation started to set in.

If Shere Khan hadn't taken over Rafael's body or I hadn't shifted for the very first time tonight, I never would have overheard his parents plotting to kill me. I was lucky to have eavesdropped on this conversation at all.

"We should probably get some sleep," Queen Bria said then. "Tomorrow is going to be a long day."

"You're certainly right about that. I have to tell you everything Ricky and I found back in the human world."

"Where is Ricky, anyway? I haven't even seen him since the two of you have returned," Queen Bria said as she and King Roman began to make their way out of the trees.

Watching them through the curtain of leaves that shielded me, I saw them head in the direction of the Royal palace.

Once they were out of sight, I took a deep breath.

My heart continued to race as I tried to process everything I'd just learned.

Queen Bria hated me. No, she *more than* hated me. She wanted me dead… just like Ella Gray.

Were Damon and Harden's moms going to put me on their hit lists after meeting me, too? I wasn't having good luck so far in the future mother-in-law department.

Suddenly, a weird sensation came over me. It felt like I had been in one place for too long, and I had this strong urge to move.

I realized that it was some sort of shifter instinct.

Climbing out from behind the bush, I began to walk deeper into the jungle.

As I came to a pool of water, I leaned down to drink from it.

The human side of me thought about how gross it was to drink water in the wild, but the animal within me was satisfied.

I stared into my reflection in the water, taking a real good look at myself for the first time. I couldn't tear my eyes away from my light brown snout. The silky black fur that surrounded it and coated the rest of my body was even more shocking. The most surprising part was my paws. My paws were freaking huge.

How the hell had this even happened? I was supposed to have been a cat shifter or maybe even a werewolf. Those had seemed like the most likely scenarios, anyway. And yet, I was none of those things.

I was the one thing I hadn't expected to be, the one thing that would only complicate everything.

I was a werebear. And I wasn't sure how to feel about that.

CHAPTER

TWO

When my eyes fluttered open, streaks of sunlight were streaming into my face. Glancing up, I saw the canopy of trees that hung above me.

I was still in the jungle.

I slept outside all night.

Almost immediately, I noticed that my senses were heightened. I heard the sounds of birds chirping and frogs croaking all around me. A waterfall was burbling off in the distance. I picked up on floral notes in the air, along with the scent of saltwater.

The reality of my current predicament hit me. I had somehow fallen asleep outside and shifted back into my human form. And I was completely naked.

I knew it was going to be a challenge to get back to the palace without clothes on. But that was *before* I knew I was going to be doing it in broad daylight.

FML.

"*Lena, is Rafael in the jungle with you?*" Ezra's familiar voice asked.

"Ezra?" I scanned the area for him, but I didn't see him. "Where *are* you?"

"*I'm in Rafael's bedroom,*" he answered. "*His mom let us all inside the palace.*"

"I'm so confused. If you're in Rafael's room, then how can I hear your voice?" I asked out loud. Almost as soon as the words slipped out of my mouth, I realized the answer on my own.

Mind-speak. Most shifter mates could hear each other's thoughts. It was an ability that I didn't have with any of my mates—until now, apparently.

"*You can hear my thoughts?*" I thought to him.

"*Yeah, completely out of nowhere,*" Ezra replied.

"*Me, too,*" Harden's voice filled my mind.

"*They're not the only ones who can hear your thoughts,*" Damon chimed in.

How the hell was this even happening? And why hadn't anyone bothered to mention how confusing it was going to be to hear not just one but *three* of my mates through my thoughts?

"*That's because we didn't know how confusing it would be. Historically, you* are *the first shifter to have more than one mate,*" Harden pointed out.

"*Crap. You just heard my thoughts? I wasn't even directing them at you.*"

"*We all heard them,*" Ezra answered.

Talk about lack of privacy.

A realization hit me then. "*I shifted for the first time last night. That must be why we can hear each other now.*"

"*You shifted? Lena, what type of shifter are you?*" Damon asked. The tone of his voice told me he was nervous to hear the answer.

In fact, I was pretty sure they were *all* nervously awaiting my answer if the intensity of their heartbeats was any indication.

"*I want to talk to you guys about it face-to-face,*" I explained. "*But first, I need your help. Raf's in danger.*"

"*What type of danger?*" Ezra questioned.

"*It's going to sound crazy. I'm not sure if you guys will even believe me.*"

"*What is it, Lena?*" Damon pressed.

I took a deep breath. "*Shere Khan swapped bodies with him. At least, I assume Rafael is inside Shere Khan's body, since Shere Khan is in Raf's. That's how it always seems to work in the movies.*"

"*I don't get it. What would Shere Khan even want with Rafael's body?*" Harden asked.

"*I haven't figured that part out yet. All I know is we need to save him.*" I paused. "*But first I have a favor to ask of you guys. I'm in a slightly embarrassing predicament.*"

"*You know you don't need to feel embarrassed with us, Lena,*" Damon replied. "*What do you need?*"

"*Clothes. I might be kind of, sort of naked.*"

If Rafael was able to communicate with me through mind-speak like the others, I knew he would have cracked a joke at that moment. The fact that he didn't say anything told me he didn't have access to my thoughts like the others did, and that made me nervous. I hoped that, wherever he was, he was okay.

"*Where are you?*" Ezra asked me.

"*I'm in the jungle near the ocean. It's northeast of the Palace.*" I wasn't even sure how I knew that last detail, but I *did*. I wondered if having an inner compass was a part of my new shifter abilities.

"*My clothes are in a pink duffle bag in Rafael's room,*" I added.

"*Okay, we're on it,*" Harden told me.

"*Thanks.*" Swallowing hard, I scanned the area for a place to hide. Ducking behind a tree, I hoped no one would find me standing there naked before my mates got to me.

I waited there for a few long, *breezy* minutes. Finally, I heard the sound of footsteps crunching.through leaves.

What if it wasn't them?

"*It's us,*" Harden confirmed.

"*We're here,*" Ezra added.

"*Lena, where are you?*" Damon asked.

Peering around the tree, my heart skipped a beat when I saw the three of them walking towards me.

Ezra's striking blue eyes locked on mine first. His dark brown hair was shorter than it was the last time I had seen him, and I couldn't help but think that he looked stronger than usual, too.

"*Found her,*" Ezra said.

Damon stood next to him. His dirty blonde hair fell into his forehead. His golden-brown eyes, which popped against his sun-kissed skin, caught on mine.

My gaze shifted to Harden. As his eyes met mine, I noticed that his naturally violet eyes resembled amethysts under the sunlight. They popped against his caramel skin.

They had never looked sexier before. Don't get me wrong. I had always been incredibly attracted to my mates. But something about them was even *more* attractive to me now. I knew it must have been because I'd shifted for the first time. It made me feel more drawn to them than ever before.

"So, here are your clothes." Ezra held up a pile of my clothes and a pair of flip-flops.

"Thanks." I glanced around at my mates.

"Should we bring them to you?" Damon asked.

The last thing I wanted was for all three of them to see me naked at once. Having all three pairs of those gorgeous eyes on my naked body would have been too much for me to handle.

"Put them on that rock." I pointed at the one I meant.

Ezra set my clothes on it and then backed away.

"And can you, uh, all turn around?" I twirled my finger in a clock-like motion.

All three of my mates turned around without saying a word.

Stepping out from behind the tree, I pulled on the pink dress and undergarments they'd brought me as fast as I could and then cleared my throat. "Okay. You can look now."

"Lena, you look beautiful in that dress," Ezra murmured. "I like you in pink."

"Really beautiful," Harden agreed with a nod.

"Stunning." Damon's eyes scanned my body up and down before landing on mine. "So, tell us, Lena. What type of shifter are you?"

"We're so curious," Harden said.

"*Dying* to know," Ezra agreed.

I took a deep breath. How did I just break this news to them? It wasn't what *any* of us had been expecting, and honestly? I wasn't entirely sure how any of them were going to react.

I glanced around at my mates, who were all staring back at me, waiting expectantly for my answer.

I wondered if they already overheard me thinking about it just now.

The looks on their faces remained unchanged, so they must not have.

"I'm... a... werebear," I managed to squeak out once I worked up the nerve.

"A *werebear*?" Ezra looked surprised.

I nodded.

"Are you sure about that, Lena?" Damon didn't look even the slightest bit convinced by my shifter race.

"I'm positive I'm a werebear. I saw my reflection and my gigantic paws. I'm a bear shifter. There's no doubt about it."

"But you're so... tiny," Harden blurted. "Sorry, Lena, I don't mean that in a bad way. But usually, werebears are really tall. You're like a peanut—no offense. You're the cutest little peanut I've ever seen."

I smiled. "No offense taken. I know what you mean. The last thing I ever thought I would be is a werebear, but I am."

"Well, there's one good thing about your shifter race." Damon's golden-brown eyes met mine. "We all have an equal shot at ending up with you now."

Shit. I hadn't even thought about that. My shifter race had completely ruined the way I was going to choose my King.

Since the idea of choosing only one of them completely broke my heart, I had been planning to choose the mate who I shared a shifter race with. Instead of choosing one and hurting three of them, I planned to let fate be the determining factor. Since the Shifter High Court would have to approve a Royal marriage between different shifter races, it had felt like the easiest option... and the option that would be completely out of my hands.

But since I didn't share a shifter race with even *one* of my mates, that idea had gone out the window. So, Damon was right. I was going to have to actually choose one of them now in the end, even though that would mean breaking three other hearts in the process (or four hearts, if you counted my own).

"So, we should probably try to find Rafael, or Shere Khan." Ezra's voice snapped me out of my thoughts.

"You're right." I couldn't let my emotions sidetrack me from what was really important—and that was getting my mate back from whatever shady thing Shere Khan had in mind.

"I still can't figure out why Shere Khan would want to take over Rafael's body," Harden said, shaking his head.

"I figured it out," Damon said.

As I glanced over at him, his golden-brown eyes caught on mine. "What is it?"

"The Legends can live for up to one year in their own bodies. At the one-year mark, they have to return to the Ancient Tombs—the place where their bodies were originally buried—to 'die' all over again, or they'll turn to dust. They can't be brought back to life again for the next one-hundred years." He paused. "But there is one way around all of this. As long as their bodies are returned to the Ancient Tombs, their souls can survive in a host body."

"Wait, so what you're saying is..." I trailed off, swallowing hard as the realization of what he meant hit me.

"That Shere Khan might be trying to permanently take over Rafael's body."

"What does that mean for Rafael?" I asked, even though I was pretty sure I already knew the answer.

Damon's golden-brown eyes caught mine. "If we don't figure out a way to get him back, Rafael's soul will be buried in the Ancient Tombs with Shere Khan's body for at least the next one-hundred years."

CHAPTER
THREE

We spent the entire day searching the island high and low for Rafael and Shere Khan. We searched the jungle, the beach, and even the water. But there was no sign of *either* of them anywhere.

It was frustrating, to say the least.

It also scared me. I had this feeling deep in my gut that the longer it took for us to find Rafael's body, the less likely it was that we ever would.

"We need to tell Rafael's parents about what's happened," Damon said as we stood in front of the Royal palace, debating our next move.

I narrowed my eyes at him. "You're joking, right?"

He shot a confused glance in my direction. "Why would I joke about that?"

I realized that I hadn't gotten the chance to tell them about what happened with Raf's parents the night before.

"What happened?" Ezra's blue eyes darted over to meet mine.

"What *didn't* you tell us?" Damon asked, concern all over his face.

I was really going to have to get used to them being able to listen in on my thoughts 24/7. So far, I wasn't a fan of it.

I took a deep breath. *"We can't talk about this out loud. I don't trust either of Rafael's parents, but especially not his mom,"* I told them through mind-speak.

Even though Bria and Roman weren't around, it still felt weird to shit-talk them on their island. Who even knew if they had ears around the palace? They probably had loyal servants.

"Why don't you trust them?" Harden's violet eyes met mine.

"I overheard the two of them talking. Long story short: Rafael's mom is planning to kill me if I don't leave Raf alone for good. King Roman didn't seem too thrilled by the idea, but he agreed to go along with it if that's what it takes to get rid of me."

Ezra's eyes dropped to the ground, and I knew he was probably thinking the same thing as me.

His mom wasn't the only one who wanted me dead.

"This really pisses me off," Damon told me. *"But as angry as it makes me, we need all the help we can get right now. We can't let ourselves forget that we're dealing with Shere Khan. The four of us may be strong, but we're up against a Legend—arguably the most powerful Legend there is. This is a whole lot bigger than all of us. We need help from Bria and Roman, and maybe even the rest of our parents, too—if that's what it takes to get Rafael back."*

When his golden-brown eyes caught on mine, I noticed the look of fear in them. He was just as afraid as I was that we would never see Rafael again.

Even though I didn't want to ask Rafael's parents for help, I was going to trust Damon on this. He had been in this world for far longer than me, and he'd been raised to rule the entire shifter world someday. Obviously, he was better at making these kinds of decisions than I was.

"Damon's right. We'll all just have to be really careful around

Rafael's parents. We'll keep an eye on you, Lena," Harden said reassuringly. *"We won't let them hurt you."*

"Okay," I agreed. I knew they *were* right. We needed to do this for Rafael. "Let's tell them."

As we began to move closer to the castle, I stared up at the sky above.

The sun had already begun to make its descent into the evening sky. We had to hurry. When darkness was completely upon us, it was going to be even more difficult to find Rafael. We needed all the daylight hours we could get.

The worst possible scenarios began to circle around inside my mind.

If Damon was right and Shere Khan's plan really *was* to use Rafael's body as a host, there was a good chance he had already taken him far away from the Tiger Kingdom.

What if we never saw Rafael again?

Or what if something happened to him? We couldn't let ourselves lose sight of the fact that we were in the middle of a shifter world war.

We were climbing up the steps to the Royal palace when I heard a familiar voice call out, "Lena! We've been looking all over for you."

I glanced over my shoulder. I was surprised to find my two best friends, Katerina Kordova and Alexis Brunswick, standing behind me.

"What are you guys doing here?" I asked.

The Tiger Kingdom was hosting National Felidae Day, which was Independence Day for cat shifters. Considering Katerina was the Princess of the Bears and Alexis was the future Queen of the Foxes, I was surprised they were here.

Then again, Ezra was a werewolf and *he* was here for the holiday. And for that matter, my werebear ass was also here when I didn't necessarily 'belong'.

"Queen Bria invited all the Royals," Alexis explained.

"Except for my parents, of course," Katerina added quietly. I didn't need to question why; her parents were the ones who had started this shifter world war. It was surprising *Katerina* herself had been welcomed to the palace.

Alexis met my gaze. "You seem disappointed that we're here."

"No, of course I'm not disappointed. I'm really glad to see you guys." The truth was that I was so relieved to see them. It was the first time I had seen or even talked to them since the Legends had rescued us from the bootcamp we'd all nearly died in. "I've been meaning to call or text you both, but there's so much going on right now."

"What's wrong, Lena?" Katerina studied my face. "You seem entirely out of sorts."

"Rafael is missing."

"*Missing*? What happened?" Katerina's dark brown eyes widened.

"*Should I tell them?*" I asked my mates through mind-speak, darting my eyes around at them.

"*It can't hurt to have more people looking for him,*" Harden replied.

"*I agree,*" Damon added with a nod.

"He's actually more than just missing," I told my friends. "He was kind of, sort of kidnapped."

"*Definitely* kidnapped," Ezra corrected me.

"Kidnapped?" Alexis's dark brown eyes widened.

"Shere Khan somehow switched bodies with him and then took off. We can't find either of them. They're both just *gone.*"

"What in the world would Shere Khan want with Rafael's body?" Katerina questioned. "Don't get me wrong. Rafael looks far more fit—and more ravishing, I suppose—than Shere Khan.

But he's *Shere Khan*. Why wouldn't he want his own body? He's a Legend, after all."

"We're pretty sure it's because Shere Khan needs to find a host body for his soul. If he doesn't, he'll have to die all over again at the Ancient Tombs or turn to dust in one year's time," I explained. "And that means the real Rafael will get buried at the Ancient Tombs, if we don't find him."

"Oh, shit." Alexis cupped her hand over her mouth. "This is not good."

"It isn't good at all. We absolutely must find him," Katerina said. "Do we have a game plan?"

"We just spent the entire day searching the island. Now, we're going to tell Rafael's parents about what's going on," I explained. "They don't have a clue yet."

"What can we do to help?" Alexis asked.

"Are your mates with you?" Damon questioned.

"Yeah. They're playing cornhole or some silly garden game with Ricky," Katerina replied with an eye roll.

I was surprised that Sean and Patrick were playing a game with Rafael's twin brother. I hadn't even met Ricky yet, but I couldn't stand the asshole—and for good reason. Ricky was three minutes younger than Raf was, and he'd spent his entire life hoping that Rafael would die just so that he could become the next King of the Tigers.

"Well, why don't you guys go round them up? Actually, keep them on standby," Damon said. "We'll see what Rafael's parents think we should do, but we might need to go back out there with a larger search party."

"Okay," Alexis agreed with a nod. "Just come find us when you're ready for us to help."

"We will," I said.

Katerina shot me a sympathetic glance. "I'm sorry, love. I

know how much Rafael means to you. Some way, somehow, we *will* find him. I promise."

"Thanks." I shot her a small smile, hoping that my inner defeat wasn't obvious.

As they descended the palace stairs that led to the back courtyard, I heard the sound of laughter from somewhere nearby.

Glancing over my shoulder, I spotted Queen Bria standing on a rooftop patio that overlooked the ocean. Surrounded by guests, she was donning a black mermaid-style gown. She had a champagne flute in hand, and her head was tilted back in laughter.

"Time for us to be the bearers of bad news," Damon muttered under his breath.

"Actually, why don't you guys stay here? I'll go talk to her." As much as I couldn't stand Bria, I was the last one who had seen Rafael before Shere Khan had taken over his body. It only seemed right for me to be the one to tell her what had happened.

"Are you sure, Lena?" Damon met my eyes.

I nodded. "Yeah. I'll be back."

As I climbed up the steps that led to the rooftop, I tried not to think too hard about her plans to murder me.

This wasn't about me. It was about getting Rafael back. And maybe, just *maybe*, I could win her approval if I helped get her son back. But I knew that was probably a stretch; Bria seemed pretty firm about how she felt about me.

As I approached her, she was mid-conversation with a short burly man who I was pretty sure must have been a lion shifter. With his long, blonde mane-like hair and his round face, he just *looked* like a lion.

I stood to the side, waiting for a pause in their conversation.

Finally, Queen Bria turned to me with an annoyed expression on her face. "What is it you want, dear?"

"Can I talk to you in private?" I asked her.

She glanced over at the man. "Please excuse me, Peter." Then she led me about ten feet away from where they were talking, towards the edge of the rooftop.

I saw the ocean ahead of us. I wasn't sure what it was, but something about its rolling waves felt angry.

"What was *so* urgent you felt the need to interrupt my conversation, Lena?" There was an angry look in her eyes.

"Rafael needs your help."

"With what?" Queen Bria asked.

I lowered my voice. "I know this is going to sound crazy, but Shere Khan and Rafael somehow switched bodies. It happened late last night, and Shere Khan took off with Rafael's body. The Alpha Brotherhood and I spent the whole day searching the island for them, but we didn't come across either of them. I think Shere Khan may have taken him far away from here. If there's any chance of us ever finding him again, we need your help."

When I finished speaking, I couldn't help but notice that she didn't look even the slightest bit fazed by anything I'd just said.

No, in fact, she looked even *more* annoyed, if anything.

"Well, you've got one thing right. All of this *does* sound crazy," Queen Bria replied. "And the reason it sounds crazy is because both Rafael *and* Shere Khan are here at this party as we speak."

"They are?" My eyebrows lifted questioningly.

She nodded. "Rafael is right inside there." She pointed at a door about twenty feet away from us. "And Shere Khan is in the main castle somewhere, mingling with our guests." She leaned in closer to me, embracing me in a tight hug, and whispered, "You might think I'm going to let you create dramatic, fictional scenarios like this one just for attention, but you have another thing coming to you if you think you can get away with that around here."

Pulling away from me, she winked.

Then she walked away from me and rejoined Peter, leaving me to wonder what the hell was going on.

CHAPTER
FOUR

"I'm so confused. *Rafael is* here?" Harden's voice filled my thoughts.

"*I don't know, but I'm about to find out. You guys stay put,*" I answered as I headed through the door that Queen Bria claimed would lead me to Rafael.

Even though I hoped she was right and he was actually in there, I had my doubts.

As I entered the room, I glanced around. From its white marble floors to the ivory stone walls and white décor, everything about this room was breathtaking. There was a gray stone bar on the far end of the room, and light gray velvet chairs scattered throughout.

Apparently, this part of the castle was a lounge.

Scanning the room, my eyes fell on Rafael. He was sitting on one of the chairs with a drink in hand, and he was talking to someone sitting to the left of him. A *girl.*

She was wearing a short burgundy dress. Her light brown hair was done in loose curls. Even though she didn't turn her head, it didn't matter. I would have recognized her from any angle.

Anastasia Brink.

Anger soared through my veins.

This was the absolute last thing I had been expecting, but I wasn't sure why. It wasn't the first time I had caught him talking to Anastasia behind my back.

A thousand possibilities entered my mind as my feet began to carry me in their direction.

"*Lena, don't hurt anyone,*" Ezra's voice filled my mind. He was clearly worried I would.

I wasn't sure where this was all going to lead and I wasn't about to make any promises I couldn't keep, so I ignored him.

As I approached them, they were in the middle of a heated conversation. Anastasia giggled in a high-pitched tone and reached out to touch his knee.

I didn't even try to suppress my eye roll. Her hand was on *my* mate.

"Ahem." I cleared my throat, trying to get Rafael's attention.

He didn't even look at me.

I cleared my throat again, to no response *again.*

"Hi."

That got his attention. His emerald green eyes flitted over to meet mine.

There was a soft but confused look behind his gaze.

"Can we help you?" he asked.

"Are you kidding me? That's your response after everything that's happened?"

"Everything that's happened?" He stared at me with a blank expression.

"Oh, come on, Raf. You've been back for who knows how long and you didn't even *try* to get ahold of me?" I just glared at him, trying to control my inner werebear. The last thing I needed was to change right here, right now, in front of *everyone*

—especially in front of Anastasia Brink. But Bear Lena *really* wanted to come out and destroy things.

I took a deep breath to calm myself.

"I'm sorry. I don't mean to be rude, but... I don't know who you are." There was a genuinely puzzled look on his face.

My eyebrows shot up. "What do you mean you don't know who I am?"

His eyes held mine for a long moment. "I feel like I might have seen you before. What's your name?"

When I glanced over at Anastasia, I noticed that even *she* looked surprised by the way Rafael was responding to me.

"*He's lost his memory,*" Damon's words filled my mind. "*Shere Khan must have done something to cause this.*"

Anger flowed through my veins.

Harden's voice came next. "*I wonder how much of his memory is gone. This is really bad, you guys.*"

"*No shit it's bad. It's all bad,*" Ezra thought.

"My name is Lena Falcone," I informed Rafael.

"Lena Falcone," he murmured, continuing to stare into my eyes.

"Can I speak to you for a moment?" I asked, shooting a pointed glance at Anastasia. "*Alone?*"

"Why?" he asked.

I got the feeling that he wouldn't *let* me get him alone, and that only made me even more angry.

I wanted to tell him I was his mate, but there was no way I could do that in front of Anastasia. She would just go tell Queen Bria.

So, instead of telling him everything right then and there, I simply said, "Never mind. It can wait. Excuse me."

Rafael nodded as I turned to walk away from him.

How had it come to this?

31

When I approached the door to leave the tower we were in, I glanced over my shoulder at him one last time.

His green eyes lingered on me. There was a flicker of recognition behind his gaze. It was as if he recognized me, but he didn't know who I was.

It made my heart break. We had to get him back. We had to restore his memories. I couldn't live in a world where Rafael had forgotten me.

I wondered if it was just me he'd forgotten. I wondered if he didn't remember the whole Alpha Brotherhood.

I descended the spiral staircase that led to the ground floor, and then I began to run.

I didn't care who was watching me or what they thought. I was infuriated by everything that was happening.

I ran as fast as my legs could carry me to the main palace.

As I stepped inside, I looked around for Shere Khan. I spotted him near the refreshments.

He was talking to the other Legends.

I made a beeline for them.

"There is so much we must do in so little time, all beginning with conjuring the others," Lycaon of Arcadia was saying to the rest of the Legends.

"Excuse me," I interrupted them.

They all stopped talking and glanced over at me, with annoyance written all over their faces. I doubted that any of the Legends had ever been interrupted back when they were alive, let alone since they had been conjured from the dead.

Well, there was a first time for everything.

"What is it, Lena?" Shere Khan's emerald green eyes slid over to meet mine.

A thought crossed my mind. How did I know for sure that this was the real Shere Khan? What if Shere Khan was actually in Raf's body, pretending to forget me? What if I was talking to Rafael right now?

"May I have a word with you?" I glanced around at the others and added, "In private?"

"Excuse me, my dear friends. We'll resume this conversation when I return. Don't let me miss a single thing." Shere Khan followed me out to the balcony overlooking the sand below us. "What is it, Miss Falcone?"

"What did you do to him?" I asked through gritted teeth.

His deep emerald green eyes pierced straight through mine. "You're going to have to be more specific. What did I do to *whom?*"

I rolled my eyes. "Rafael."

"Who says I've done anything at all to him?" There was an obvious look of amusement swirling around inside his eyes.

So, he was going to play *that* game.

"You really aren't going to own up to it?" I asked.

His eyes danced with amusement. "Own up to *what*, exactly?"

It took everything in me to keep my cool. I wanted to swear at him. I wanted to punch him. But I knew that neither of those things would accomplish anything. *But they would make me feel a little bit better.*

As much as I didn't want to admit that I needed help from Shere Khan, the truth was that I *did*. I needed to know what he had done to erase Raf's memories so we could reverse it—if reversing it was even possible. There was a part of me that worried he was gone for good.

I swallowed hard, trying to control my anger. "I know for a *fact* that you switched bodies with him last night. That whole iced tea comment was a dead giveaway. And now, suddenly, Rafael doesn't remember me. What did you do to him?"

"Iced tea comment? Whatever do you mean?" Shere Khan questioned.

"You're the *only* one who ever says, '*It's hot in here. I need some iced tea.*'"

The trace of a smile hit his lips. "Well, there is simply no denying that I certainly *do* love a nice cold glass of iced tea. However, the accusations you're making are rather... extreme. I haven't done anything to the young Rafael Khan. His memory is really gone?"

Any doubt in my mind about this not being the real Shere Khan completely faded away with his response. His sugary sweet sarcasm was enough to convince me.

"You're lying," I said. "You *know* his memory is gone because you're the one who *did* something to him. But what I can't figure out is why. Why couldn't you have just left him alone?"

Tears welled up in my eyes, but I refused to allow them to fall.

Damon's theory had gone out the window now. Shere Khan must not have been trying to take up permanent residence in Rafael's body after all. There had to have been another reason he'd done it. Because if Shere Khan had been trying to use Raf as a host, he would have still been in his body.

"*Unless something didn't go according to plan,*" Damon's voice filled my mind. "*My theory still works. There's just got to be more to it. Things we don't know.*"

Before I had the chance to respond, Shere Khan continued. "As for Rafael being unable to remember you, you should give him this potion." He reached into his pocket and then handed me a small vial containing a bright pink liquid. "It can help revive one's memories."

I just stared back at him, even more confused. If he had wiped Rafael's memories, why would he help us try to get them back? What was even more odd was that Shere Khan just happened to be carrying around a potion that could revive memories.

I narrowed my eyes at him suspiciously. "How do I know this potion won't just complete whatever thing you did to him?"

He let out a deep laugh. His green eyes danced excitedly. "Dear girl, don't you realize that if *I* wanted Rafael to drink this potion, he would have already? Life is about trust and learning who to give yours to. If you can't find it within you to trust me, I'll take the potion back from you. It won't be *my* loss. You're the one who wants him to have his memories back."

"No. I'll keep it," I told him, holding the potion close to my chest. I'd discuss it with the Alpha Brotherhood, but what if this was our only chance to help Rafael?

"*It's worth a shot*," Ezra thought.

"*I don't trust him*," Damon said next.

"*Three against one. We're in*," Harden spoke next.

Damon sounded annoyed that we'd all voted against him. "*Guess we'll worry about the consequences later.*"

"You'll want to make sure he drinks that potion sooner rather than later," Shere Khan added. "Time is of the essence."

"Thanks," I muttered under my breath.

"Well, now that we've resolved that issue, I should tell you that I'm glad you're here. I was planning to come find you." He leaned in closer to me. "Have you heard the news yet?"

I narrowed my eyes at him. "What news?"

"Shifter Academy will be reopening on Monday. All students are expected to return."

"Wait. *This* Monday?"

He nodded. "Yes."

"But there's a shifter world war going on. It isn't safe," I protested.

"You needn't worry about the war. A magical shield will be

in place to protect Shifter Academy's campus. It will be one of the safest places in this whole realm."

The truth was, I didn't feel ready to go back after everything that had happened in the past week. We had all nearly died in boot camp. I had shifted for the first time. And now, we had to figure out this whole thing with Rafael's memory. What if this potion didn't even work?

"I have spoken to the Royals and the other Legends, and we all believe it's necessary for you to return to campus," he continued. "With the Royal Change of Hands happening in less than a year, we think it's pertinent for all of you to continue your education so you'll be prepared for what's to come."

Of course, it made sense. The truth was that I didn't feel even the slightest bit ready to rule the entire shifter world in a year from now. How could I be the next Queen of the shifters when, so far, I had only ever shifted once in my life?

Not that any of that changed the fact that the idea of going back to school was a horrible one.

"But Headmistress Gray—" I started to argue, but Shere Khan interrupted me.

"Has been removed from her position as Headmistress. We would never allow any of you to return under her watch, considering the number of students who have died as a result of her wrongdoings. We can't even currently locate her. We suspect that she's hiding out in the human realm because she knows she's about to face some serious reprimanding once we do figure out her whereabouts." He paused for a moment. "That said, a new Headmaster has already been established." His eyes danced with amusement. "And you are currently staring him right in the face."

I swallowed hard. "*You're* the new Headmaster?"

"*Holy fuck,*" I heard Harden say in my mind.

"*Holy fuck is right,*" Damon agreed.

Shere Khan nodded. "Yes. I was the most suitable candidate for the position. I will also be acting as a professor. In fact, *all* of the Legends will be teaching this year. We're going to conjure several other legendary figures from the dead so they can assist us in our efforts."

"*Imagine being brought back from the dead just so you can be a teacher?*" Harden sounded amused.

"*We should all feel lucky to have them on board. We're going to be taught by the* Legends," Ezra replied.

"*I just feel bad for them. Talk about a bad afterlife,*" Harden joked.

"I see." It was all incredibly overwhelming. We weren't even going to have our regular professors. We were going to have famous professors who had risen from the dead just to prepare us.

It made me realize one thing. *We couldn't fail them.*

"This will also count as your third year as a Shifter Academy student," he continued.

I frowned. "But what about my second year?"

We had gotten in about a month of virtual classes before Ella Gray had dragged us to bootcamp. It wasn't that I hadn't learned anything during my sophomore year, but I didn't feel prepared. There was so much about this world that I still needed to learn. I felt like I'd missed out on so much.

"To be frank with you, we have our work cut out for us. Given the current state of affairs and the upcoming Royal Change of Hands, we felt it absolutely pertinent for you to learn from the best. And I can assure you that I *am* the best—along with the other Legends. You have much to learn and only a short amount of time to do it in." His feline-like lips curved upwards into a smile. "I look forward to seeing you in the class-room on Monday, Miss Falcone. Don't be late." He winked and then began to walk away from me.

I tried really hard to keep it together, but it wasn't easy. I was really pissed off.

Not only did we have to go back to Shifter Academy in the middle of the war, but we had to do it with the Legends as our professors.

A year ago, the idea of being taught by Shere Khan would have been completely enthralling. After all, he *was* a Legend—and quite possibly the most powerful one. There was no denying that.

But after everything that had happened, I didn't trust him. Not even a little bit. He might have given me a potion to recover Rafael's memory, but I knew what I had witnessed the night before.

Shere Khan really *had* been in Rafael's body. I wasn't sure what he had been doing in it or why he had switched back to his own, but I was determined to find out.

CHAPTER
FIVE

Once I finished talking to Shere Khan, I headed over to my mates, who were waiting for me by the stone staircase that led to the rooftop where Queen Bria was still entertaining guests.

"Well, *that* wasn't how I was expecting it to go," I said with a sigh as I approached them.

"At least he gave you the antidote," Harden pointed out, motioning to the vial I still held in my hand.

"If we can call it the antidote," Damon replied. "I'm skeptical about it."

"We know," Ezra said with a sigh.

"I have to believe it's real." Shere Khan didn't *have* to give it to me. "But I can't deny that he gave me weird vibes. There's no doubt in my mind he was in Rafael's body at some point. I just can't figure out why he's not *still* in it."

"And I can't be the only one thinking it's weird that Shere Khan and the other Legends are going to be professors this year," Harden said.

"I also think it's weird we're going back to school. It's so spur of the moment," I replied.

I couldn't put my finger on what it was, but something about the whole thing just felt... *off*.

"I think we should probably go talk to Rafael's mom," Ezra said. "I know she didn't take you seriously, but she needs to know Shere Khan can't be trusted."

"Well, you guys can talk to her. I'm not going with you. That woman hates me." I didn't think any of my mates' moms could hate me as much as Ella Gray did, but Bria Khan was definitely up there. I couldn't help but wonder what Damon and Harden's mothers were like. Would their moms want to kill me too? I dreaded meeting any more parents.

"Come with us, Lena." Damon's golden-brown eyes locked on mine.

I wasn't sure what it was about him, but one look into my eyes could have convinced me to do just about anything. It must have been our mate bond. I found myself agreeing without hesitation.

"Okay." I nodded.

As we all began to climb the staircase, I noticed something.

Out of nowhere, I could feel all of my senses kicking in even stronger.

Suddenly, I could hear... well, *everything*: Bria laughing to the guests above, glasses clinking, the sound of the waves crashing against the shore below, the sound of a gentle breeze.

I could even *taste* the saltwater, even though we had to have been at least a thousand feet away from it.

My sense of smell was stronger than ever before. I had already been able to smell the food and liquor, as well as the saltwater and damp sand.

But there was something new about it. Now, I could smell *shifters*. I could pick up on my mates' odors; their scents were overwhelmingly intoxicating. But my sense of smell went beyond my mates. It was as if I could smell *everyone*. Mostly, what I picked up on was the scent of cat shifters, probably because there were so many of them. I could also smell a few werewolves, fox shifters, and werebears, too. There was also a horse shifter somewhere within the palace. I could smell it.

I wasn't sure how I could tell all of the different shifter races apart by their scents, but somehow, I just *could*. The odor was most overwhelming from the tiger shifters. They smelled like jasmine and orchid, with notes of watermelon and mango weaved in.

Werebears, on the other hand, had more of an earthy scent. They smelled like pine trees, fresh mountain air, a crisp stream, and dirt.

Damon's scent was the strongest to me, which I knew had to have been due to the bond we had that I didn't have yet with my other mates. He smelled like... well, a lion. His odor was a mix of sunshine, citrus, and fire.

I smelled my own skin and frowned.

It was completely odorless.

That was strange. I would have thought that I should have been able to smell my own scent better than anyone else's.

"*Normally, we can,*" Harden informed me through our thoughts. "*It's kinda weird that you can't.*"

"*It's possible that shifter ability may kick in later,*" Damon added. "*Clearly, your shifter senses are just now being awakened.*"

I hoped Damon was right. Maybe it was like my ability to shift, which had taken forever to kick in.

As we reached the rooftop, we began to head over to Queen Bria. That was when I spotted Rafael walking towards us.

He smiled and waved at the rest of the Alpha Brotherhood.

I might have been wrong, but it looked like he actually *remembered* them. But how could that be?

"Hey, what's up?" Rafael asked as he approached us.

Damon shot a glance in my direction before turning his attention back to Raf. "Do you remember us?"

Rafael gave him a funny look. "Of course I remember you, Damon. I've known you since we were in diapers. Why *wouldn't* I remember you?" The tone in his voice told me he was genuinely confused by the question.

"Well, what about me?" Harden asked. "You remember me?"

"I remember you, Harden. What's with all these questions?" Rafael questioned.

What the hell.

Why was it only *me* he didn't remember? It didn't even make sense, considering *I* was his mate. Shouldn't I have been the first one he remembered?

There had to have been a reason Shere Khan wanted him to forget me—and *only* me.

At that moment, I heard the sound of a voice over a loud-speaker. I followed everyone's gaze. The crowd was looking at King Roman.

"Welcome, ladies and gentlemen," King Roman spoke into a microphone. "Queen Bria and I would like to thank each and every one of you for attending our National Felidae Day celebration. Before the festivities begin, there are a few things I would like to say. First of all, I want us all to welcome the Legends." He pointed to where the Legends were standing. "Please give a round of applause to Shere Khan, Leo, Lycaon of Arcadia, and both of the Jaguar Knights."

The crowd clapped as he introduced each of them.

"The Legends have risen from the dead thanks to Ella Gray's terrible scheme to murder our children. Fortunately, the Legends arrived just in time to save our kids. Now, the Legends will be heading off to Shifter Academy, where they will be joined with other legendary shifters, to help prepare our students for the Royal Change of Hands, which will be happening later this year." King Roman glanced around at the crowd. "Most of us already know it, but the Royal Change of Hands is going to be huge for the future of every Kingdom. It's important for our children to learn as much as they possibly can so they can rule our kingdoms effectively."

"There's something else we would like to announce," Queen Bria announced into a second microphone. "Since our son Rafael is next in line to rule the Tiger Kingdom, we have officially opened the Marriage Lottery. To enter, please submit your application through the House of Tigers' website. Thank you."

I noticed Bria's emerald green eyes move in my direction. Her lips curved upwards, into a taunting grin.

"*What is the Marriage Lottery?*" I asked my mates through mind-speak.

"*The Marriage Lottery is exactly as it sounds. The King and Queen of any shifter kingdom can decide they want to marry their son or daughter off,*" Damon explained. "*They open the lottery to anyone who's interested, and the winner—in this case, the Queen of the Tigers—is selected at random.*"

"*Does the Prince or Princess have to agree to this?*" I questioned.

"*Yes, he does.*"

I glanced over at Rafael. I wondered if he had known that his parents were planning this. He looked completely unfazed by it—and also fairly unreadable to me.

Then again, why *wouldn't* he have been open to this? It wasn't like he even *remembered* me. He had no idea he even had a mate. So, what did he really have to lose?

"*Once a winner to the lotto has been chosen, he can't change his mind,*" Damon continued. "*Well, technically, he could, but it would be very dishonorable of him — and not something the King and Queen would let him forget about any time soon. They likely wouldn't allow him to back out of it. Once a lottery winner has been chosen, he will have no choice but to go through with it."*

"Shit," I murmured as the full gravity of the situation hit me.

If Rafael married someone else, the entire prophecy would fall through.

I would never get to be Queen of the Shifters, let alone the most important queen in history.

The war would continue.

I would never be able to unite the shifter races.

I had to make Rafael remember me—and *fast*—or our entire destiny would change.

And it would be entirely his parents' fault.

I stood on the sand, watching as the fireworks shot off all around us. With every crackle that sounded as an explosion of colors hit the sky above, it felt like a piece of my heart was breaking.

"It's going to be okay, Lena."

I glanced over my shoulder to find Damon standing behind me.

"I'm sorry," he went on. "I didn't mean to intrude on your thoughts. It's just that I could feel your sadness. It's overwhelming. It's making *me* feel sad. But I really meant what I said. It is going to be okay." His gold eyes locked on mine.

I felt bad because I knew he really was trying his hardest to reassure me, but it just wasn't working.

I sighed. "That's easy for you to say. Rafael actually remembers *you*. And the rest of the Alpha Brotherhood. And his mom.

And Anastasia Brink." I rolled my eyes. "It seems like he remembers everyone... except for me. His mate."

"It almost seems like Shere Khan *wanted* him to forget you," Damon said.

"I know. But I can't figure out why he would want him to forget me—and *only* me? What did *I* do?"

He shook his head. "I still haven't figured that part out yet."

I sighed. "This has been the week from hell. First nearly dying in boot camp and now this." I glanced down at the potion I held in my right hand. "At least there's a way to restore his memories."

"Lena, I'm still not sure that I trust this potion," Damon commented.

My eyes slid over to meet his. "I know. But it's the only option we have, so we're going to try."

"Just hear me out." He held up a hand. "Let's look at the big picture. Shere Khan and Rafael switched bodies. When they switched back, some of Rafael's memories—including any memory of *you*—were completely wiped away. Shere Khan doesn't own up to having anything to do with this, and yet he's somehow able to magically produce a potion that will help restore Rafael's memories. And we're supposed to just trust that this potion does exactly what he says it does?"

I shrugged. "We're going to have to."

"I'm just not sure if we should give this potion to Rafael. What if it has nothing to do with his memories at all?"

"What type of potion do you think it really is?"

"I don't know, honestly. But what if whatever it is does more harm than good?" Damon's fearful golden-brown eyes met mine.

I thought about it for a long moment. The alternative to not giving Rafael the potion was risking the possibility that his memories of me would be gone *forever*. Every touch, every kiss, every moment we'd shared over the past two years could have been lost to him for an eternity. And that scared the hell out of me.

But I knew that the alternative was far worse. What if Damon was right? What if this potion really *did* do something completely horrible to Rafael? Something irreversible?

What if the potion killed him? A tiny voice at the back of my mind wondered.

I didn't even want to consider the possibility. But after everything that had happened, I didn't trust Shere Khan. Not even a little bit.

"You're right. We shouldn't give him this." I glanced down at the vial for a moment. Part of me was tempted to toss it out onto the stretch of sand that lay before us. But I didn't want to lose it—just in case we were able to somehow figure out what the potion really was.

"Go ahead and toss it. Throw it into the sea. We don't need it," Damon said.

"We don't?" My eyes flicked up to meet his.

"We can try to find a way to revive Rafael's memories *without* the potion, Lena. There must be another way," he said softly.

I shot an unconvinced glance in his direction. "Like what?"

"I don't know. I've never dealt with anything like this before. But when we get back to Shifter Academy, I'll go to the library and see what I can dig up." His eyes met mine again. "I promise I won't give up until we figure out a way."

"Thanks." I forced a smile. I doubted the answer to our problems could be found in a library book.

"It's not only for you, Lena. I need him as much as you do." His golden-brown eyes locked on mine. "I need you, too."

"And I need you." It was hard for me to admit; I hated the idea of needing *anyone*. But it was true; I did need him. I needed all of the Alpha Brotherhood, but right now, I needed my connection with Damon more than anything.

He leaned in closer to me then, wrapping his arms around my waist.

Staring up into his eyes, I pressed my lips to his—allowing myself to forget, for the first time, about everything else that was going on in our world.

It was just me and him. The fireworks exploded above us, and the waves crashed near our feet, but I was fully consumed by his kiss and intoxicated by the scent of sunshine, citrus, and fire on his skin.

It may have only been a moment in time, but it was just enough to make me forget everything... *for now.*

CHAPTER

SIX

On Sunday night, we all arrived on Shifter Academy's campus. I walked with Damon's arm draped around my waist and Ezra holding my hand.

Every student who passed us by did a double take. I knew it looked strange to outsiders for me to be so close to two guys.

If only they knew I was mated to the entire Alpha Brotherhood.

Rafael walked ahead of us with Harden by his side. It was hard to look at him, knowing he might never remember me.

It made me sad to think about how bad the holiday weekend had gone. Things had gotten so rocky and Raf didn't even know it. I couldn't confide in him, either. He had been so excited before we arrived. He couldn't wait for me to meet King Roman and Ricky, but I hadn't even gotten the chance to meet either of them.

Not that I was going to complain about that. After I'd overheard King Roman talking to Bria about killing me, I hadn't *wanted* to meet him.

A thought occurred to me then. Was the Marriage Lottery a way to avoid killing me?

They had another thing coming to them if they thought I

wouldn't try to ruin it. I *would* put my neck out on the line to make sure they didn't ruin the prophecy.

"I guess this is where we say goodnight," Damon commented as we approached the stone building that housed the dorms.

I didn't want to part ways with them, but I was missing my friends.

"Yeah," I agreed with a nod. I knew I would end up spending a lot of nights at the Alpha Brotherhood's penthouse, so I wanted to spend my first night back in my dorm with Alexis and Katerina, just like old times. It was our tradition.

Damon leaned in closer to me and pressed his lips to my cheek. "Goodnight, Lena."

I smiled. "Goodnight."

Harden kissed me on my other cheek. "Sleep well, Lena."

"You, too."

Ezra caught me off guard when he pressed his lips to mine. It was the first time he had kissed me since bootcamp.

"*It's been too long, Lena,*" he said to me in mind-speak. His lips lingered on mine for a long moment.

"Sweet dreams, Lena," he whispered as he broke our kiss.

"Sweet dreams," I replied, meeting his blue eyes.

Rafael didn't say a single word to me before he walked away. It was enough to break my heart all over again.

I didn't think I would ever get used to this. And I didn't *want* to get used to it. We had to get him back.

I walked over to my friends, where they stood waiting for me so we could all head to our dorm room together.

Alexis glanced over at me. "I don't know how you do it, Lena."

"Do what?" I asked.

"Juggle *four* mates," she whispered. "I can barely handle Sean."

"And while I *can* handle Pattie, I'm not sure that I would even *want* more than one mate," Katerina added. "He's enough for me."

"It isn't easy," I admitted. "But I can't imagine it any other way. It's my reality."

"Do you have any idea yet of who you'll choose in the end?" Alexis's dark eyes darted over to meet mine.

I shook my head. "I don't even want to *think* about having to choose only one of them. The idea of not having all of them completely breaks my heart."

As we entered the part of the castle that housed the girls' dorms, Katerina shot a sympathetic glance in my direction. "I'm sure you'll figure it out in good time, love."

I hoped she was right. But two years had passed, and I still didn't have the slightest clue of who I would end up choosing in the end.

"Home sweet home," Katerina commented as she entered our dorm room and flicked on the light. She glanced around. "What the bloody hell happened in here?"

I took in the dorm room. Some of my belongings were still strewn across the floor from when our room had been ransacked. The room looked exactly the way I'd last seen it. Since we had to leave campus ASAP when the war first broke out, I hadn't gotten the chance to pick everything up.

"Right before we left campus, someone ransacked our room and left behind this mess," I explained. "I'm pretty sure they were looking for something, but I'm still not sure what it could have been. I didn't have time to clean it up because we had to leave campus so abruptly."

"Who would *do* such a thing?" Katerina sounded completely horrified by the idea.

"Whoever it was left behind this really cryptic note." Alexis glanced over at me. "What did it say again, Lena?"

"It said, 'Come be our Goldie Locks.' It was signed by the three bears," I explained as I knelt down to pick some pens and loose papers off the floor.

"Goldie Locks? The three bears? Are we stuck inside some sort of fairytale?" Katerina asked with a little laugh, but I couldn't help but notice the concern on her face. "Did these 'three bears' ever reach out to you again, love?"

"No. I almost wonder if the note was meant for someone else. It doesn't make sense. I don't even have blonde hair." But even as I spoke the words, I knew I was wrong. Gretta had made it very clear that I needed to watch out for the three bears; it was my only proof that these bears really had been targeting me.

"Maybe the note was meant for *you*." Alexis glanced over at Katerina.

"Me?" Katerina let out a little laugh. "What would the three bears want to do with me?"

"Well, you do have blonde hair," Alexis pointed out. "It happened right after the war first broke out. And you *are* a werebear."

"Actually, you guys... I'm a werebear, too," I confessed.

"You are?" Alexis glanced over at me in surprise.

"Wait, what?" Katerina glanced over at me, completely shocked. "*You're* a *bear*?"

"Yup." I nodded. "I shifted for the first time the night before National Felidae Day."

"Unbelievable. I never would have guessed." She stared me up and down, as if laying eyes on me for the very first time. "You're just so tiny. You're unlike any other werebear I've ever seen."

"You're like a shrimp," Alexis agreed. When she saw the look on my face, she added, "The cutest little shrimp, of course.

I always just assumed you were going to be a fox shifter. Are you, like, a koala werebear? They're tiny."

I laughed. "No. I'm a black bear."

"I can't believe we're the same type of bear. This is bloody brilliant." A smile hit Katerina's lips.

I breathed a slight sigh of relief. I hadn't been sure how she would react to the fact that we were both black bear shifters, but I was glad she was excited about it.

～

"Our schedules are here," Alexis announced the following morning as she took down the three gold envelopes that someone pinned to our dorm room door.

She handed me mine, and I tore it open.

My eyes poured over the schedule.

Lena Falcone
Junior
Shifter Type: TBD

Ancient Royal History (Elective)
Instructor: Shere Khan
Castle, Room 41
8:30 to 9:30 a.m.

Advanced Weaponry (Gen. Ed)
Instructors: Leo and Lycaon
Castle - Gymnasium
9:30 to 10:30 a.m.

Ancient Mating and Marriage Rituals
Cat Tower, Room 117
10:30 to 11:30 a.m.
Instructor: Byakko and Bagheera

Lunch
11:30 to 12:30 p.m.

Advanced Dark Magic
Cat Tower, Room 120
Instructor: Leo
12:30 to 1:30 p.m.

Ruling a Kingdom
Castle, Room 14
Instructor: Shere Khan
1:30 to 2:30 p.m.

Poisons and Potions
Castle, Room 12
Instructor: Kaa
2:30 to 3:30 p.m.

Advanced Werebear Studies
Werebear Tower, Room 13
Instructor: Baloo
6 to 8 p.m. (Tues-Thurs)

When I glanced up from my schedule, I found that both of my roommates looked just as baffled by their schedules as I felt by my own.

"There are *so* many classes," Alexis commented.

"*Too* many classes," Katerina agreed. Cupping a hand over her mouth, she exclaimed "Oh my gosh! Baloo is one of my instructors. I'm going to be absolutely starstruck."

"He's going to be one of mine, too." I paused. "Are *all* of the characters from The Jungle Book legendary shifters?"

"Pretty much," Alexis replied with a nod.

I supposed that it probably shouldn't have surprised me, considering I had already known about Shere Khan and Kaa. But for some reason, seeing Baloo and Bagheera on my schedule had caught me off-guard.

Katerina peered over my shoulder at my schedule. "Hey, we have Advanced Werebear Studies together! And Ancient Royal History."

"Do you guys have Ancient Royal History at eight thirty?" Alexis asked. "If so, we all have it together."

"Yes." Katerina continued to read through my courses. "It also looks like we must all have Ruling a Kingdom together." She paused. "So many of these classes have multiple instructors. Isn't that kind of odd?"

"It is really weird," Alexis agreed as she read through her own classes.

"Oh my gosh. We have Byakko together!" Katerina's eyes slid over to meet mine with excitement.

"Who the heck is Byakko?" I asked. She was obviously another Legend, but I had never heard of her until this very moment.

"Byakko is a Japanese tiger shifter. She was really well-known in Asian history. In fact, you know the Chinese zodiac calendar and the animals that represent each lunar year?"

"Yeah." I'd always thought it was really cool when Chinese restaurants printed the animals on their placemats. Based on my birth year, I was a horse. Thankfully, that hadn't carried over to my shifter race.

"Well, it's a really long story, but the way the animals were chosen to represent the Chinese zodiac was through a race," Alexis explained. "Each of the shifters who participated in this race had to cross the deadliest river in our land. Byakko was the tiger shifter who won and now represents the icon behind the Year of the Tiger."

"Wow. I had no idea the Chinese zodiac signs had anything to do with our kind," I murmured.

"Almost everything involving animals in human myths and legends involves shifters," Alexis said with a shrug.

"This is really exciting. Byakko was a bloody legend," Katerina added. "I simply can't believe they resurrected her to teach us."

"Well, to teach *you guys*, since I'm not fortunate enough to have her as an instructor," Alexis said in a pouty tone. "But I have a lot of other legendary professors. I have a feeling it's going to be a great year."

I hoped she was right. As the soon-to-be rulers of all the shifter kingdoms, there was no doubt that we *needed* a great year.

But I had this weird feeling deep in my gut that I just couldn't seem to shake. It took me a few moments to put a finger on what exactly the feeling was, but then it hit me.

Impending doom.

SEVEN

"It feels so strange to be back on campus," Alexis commented as we headed to the Dining Hall for breakfast.

"It is weird," Katerina agreed. "But nice. I'm glad to have the chance to finally have a social life again."

As a few girls walked past us, they stared at Katerina a few moments too long and then began whispering to each other. I knew it was because Katerina's parents had started the Shifter World War. It hadn't done her any favors when it came to her social life.

Katerina had clearly noticed it, too. She glanced over at us with a sad smile. "Not that I'm sure I'll even *find* a social life here, but at least I have you guys."

"And at least we're no longer in that hell we called boot-camp," Alexis added.

"Amen to that," Katerina agreed.

As we entered the Dining Hall, I grabbed a blueberry bagel and a mini tub of strawberry cream cheese and then headed to our usual table. I glanced around the room. There was only one thing missing.

My mates.

The table they usually sat at was empty, even though all I could picture was each of them sitting at it. It was strange to think that this was the first place I had ever laid eyes on them—well, all but Ezra, that is.

So much had changed since I'd first met them.

Out of the corner of my eye, I noticed a familiar flash of long, honey brown hair.

I did a double-take at first, but then I shook my head. There was just no way she was here. It couldn't have been her. It must have just been a lookalike. But then the girl began to head in my direction with recognition in her eyes, and I knew there was no way I was only imagining it. She *was* here.

"Lena!" she called out.

"Rachel?!"

Her eyes widened. "It *is* you. I wasn't sure."

"What are *you* doing here?" I asked as she approached me. I hadn't seen her since the night of the carnival—the night Ezra had kissed me the first time. It was the same night I had disappeared from the human world without a trace.

"What am *I* doing here? I should really ask *you* the same question," Rachel said loudly, narrowing her eyes at me.

"Excuse me. I'm a little confused. The two of you know each other?" Katerina interrupted from where she sat across from me. I could tell from the look in her eyes that she didn't like the tone of Rachel's voice. She was ready to jump in and defend me if this took an ugly turn.

"Yeah." I nodded. "This is Rachel, my best friend from the human world."

"*Ex*-best friend," Rachel corrected. "I sent you a million text messages, and you never answered me. Everyone else thought you were dead. I held out hope that maybe, just maybe, someone was holding you captive and you'd figure a way to escape their basement or dungeon someday. But nope. You were just here the whole time, living your best life and completely ignoring my texts. What the fuck, Lena?"

I swallowed hard as I glanced away from her. She wasn't wrong. I knew I had let her down. "I'm sorry. I wanted to tell you so many times, but what was I supposed to say? 'Hey, don't worry about me. I'm just off at a boarding school for shifters because I might be a werewolf or something'?" My eyes flicked over to meet hers. "You would have thought I was crazy."

"You're right. I would have thought you were completely batshit, but at least I would have known you were alive!"

"Rachel, I'm sorry—" I started to say, but she interrupted me.

"Don't bother apologizing, Lena. You had two years to figure out a way to contact me, but you didn't. Your apology isn't genuine so it means nothing to me. *You* mean nothing to me." Rachel blinked away tears. "I'll see you around."

Without saying another word, she walked away from the table. I stared after her, feeling like complete and utter shit.

I wondered if this was what my bad feeling was about, but honestly?

I was pretty sure it was just the beginning of a series of bad events that were about to unfold.

As my roommates and I headed out of the Dining Hall, I couldn't stop thinking about Rachel. She was a student at Shifter Academy. How bizarre was *that?*

We had been best friends for years, and I'd never known she was a shifter. I couldn't seem to wrap my head around it.

But then again, I hadn't even known *I* was one either, so maybe Rachel had been just as in the dark about her real identity as I was.

I tried not to think about our interaction. I needed to focus on the first day of classes. This year was going to be a critical one. Somehow, I would figure out a way to make things right with Rachel. *Later*, when I had more time—whenever that would be. As much as I didn't want to push it off until a later time, I knew I had to devote myself to my schoolwork.

As we crossed the courtyard, I was surprised to find Harden sitting on a bench. His violet eyes locked on mine, and I realized he'd been waiting for me.

"Hey!" I called out as I approached him.

He rose to his feet. "Good morning, Lena."

"Good morning." A knot tightened in my stomach. "Is everything okay?"

My first thought was that he was waiting for me because something had happened with Rafael.

He nodded. "Yeah, everything's fine." His violet eyes slid over to meet mine. "Is it so strange for me to want to walk my mate to our homeroom class?"

My eyebrows lifted. "We have homeroom together?"

"Ancient Royal History?" Harden asked.

"Yeah." I paused. "How did you know we're in the same homeroom? Shifter intuition?"

He laughed. "No, not this time. The rest of the Alpha Brotherhood is in this class, too. We think *all* of the soon-to-be Kings and Queens of each shifter kingdom are going to be in this class."

"Katerina and Alexis are in it, too, so you must be right," I agreed.

I realized what this actually meant: I would have class with all *four* of my mates. I wasn't going to lie. The thought made me sort of nervous.

How the hell was I supposed to pay attention?

"*We* all *have to pay attention, Lena,*" Ezra told me through mind-speak, reminding me for the first time since we'd set foot on the Shifter Academy campus that my mates were still able to hear my thoughts. Shifter Academy *hadn't* set up a way to prevent it, which was what I'd been suspecting.

And that led me to one very important question. Why hadn't *I* been hearing any of *their thoughts?*

"*It seems that you've somehow learned to turn our thoughts off unless we're attempting to communicate with you,*" Damon chimed in.

"*I didn't think that was possible,*" I thought back.

"*The one thing we've learned is that with you, Lena Falcone, anything is possible.*"

Harden and I joined the rest of the Alpha Brotherhood, who had already found seats towards the back of the classroom. I slid into an empty seat next to Alexis, who was sitting next to Sean.

At that moment, I heard the sound of Katerina's voice as she entered the room. "I simply can't believe you kept this a secret from me, Pattie."

Her mate, Patrick, glanced over at her. "I wanted it to be a surprise, Princess."

"It is absolutely the best surprise." She beamed at him.

"What's the best surprise?" I asked as they came to sit by us.

"Pattie surprised me by being here... as a student. He received an invitation to attend Shifter Academy this year!" She sounded completely thrilled.

I knew his invitation to Shifter Academy had something to do with their engagement. Patrick was about to become the next King of the Bears. He needed to be just as prepared as the rest of us when it came to ruling a Royal Kingdom.

Glancing around the room, I did a mental inventory of the other Royals in our class.

My ex-boyfriend Jake, the future King of the Coyotes, and my friend Morgan, the next Queen of the Snow Leopards, were sitting together at the front of the classroom. They were deep in conversation.

I used to hold a grudge against Morgan and Jake because they'd gotten together after he and I had broken up in the human world. I hadn't been sure who I'd hated more: my old best friend or my old boyfriend. But Morgan had managed to kind of win me over again. My feelings about her had changed after finding out about relationship with her own mate, the soon-to-be King of the Snow Leopards. It was tumultuous, to say the least. I was sad to hear her mate constantly cheated on her. She deserved better than that. She deserved happiness, and if being friends with benefits with Jake helped contribute to that, I fully supported it.

Anastasia Brink and the other Hellcats—Macy King and Penelope Sinclair—sat on the other side of the classroom. They weren't *technically* born Royals, and I wasn't sure if any of them would actually rule one of the cat shifter kingdoms, but I supposed that their high-quality bloodlines had allowed them to be placed into this class.

Plus, who knew what would happen if I didn't actually choose Rafael to be the next King of the Shifters? For all I knew, there was a chance he would end up making Anastasia Brink the next Queen of the Tigers. Or maybe she would win the Marriage Lottery. It wouldn't have surprised me if Queen Bria somehow rigged the lottery just so Anastasia could win.

The mere thought of Rafael and Anastasia ending up together left a bitter taste in my mouth. And the idea of not being with him made me really sad. That also wasn't to mention the sadness that tugged at my heart every time I thought about what would happen with the three mates I didn't choose.

I tried to shake the thought away, watching as other students from Royal bloodlines began to filter into the classroom.

Shan, Prince of the Panthers, entered the room. He wore his longish jet-black hair pulled back into a man bun. There was something about him that was so mysterious. He was always so quiet—*too* quiet for my liking. I had a feeling he had so many secrets.

The next student to come into the classroom was Hawk, the future King of the Birds. He was followed closely by Robin and Raven, who walked side by side. If I had to guess, one of the two girls was going to end up being the next Queen of the Birds. Robin reminded me of Zendaya, while Raven could have been Ariana Grande's shifter twin. I wondered which one of them Hawk would end up choosing in the end... and if they would stay friends after he made the choice. The three of them seemed inseparable. Someone's feelings were bound to get hurt in the end.

At that moment, Slither Draco, one of the Serpent princes, entered the room. His golden blonde hair was a lot shorter than it had been at boot camp. His eyes were lowered to the floor.

His sister Kaa, who was named after the Serpent from *The Jungle Book* Legend the family had descended from, followed after him. Her long, jet black hair fell over her shoulders in long, loose waves. Her golden eyes met mine from across the room, and I couldn't help but notice the solemn look behind them. They were both clearly still grieving the recent loss of their brother, Prince Rat, A.KA. Rattlesnake. He had been killed by a fire-breathing dragon at boot camp.

I realized something then. One of the Draco princes was missing.

"*Shouldn't Cobra be in this class, too?*" I asked my mates through mind-speak.

"*You didn't hear the news?*" Ezra's blue eyes moved over to mine from where he sat diagonally to me.

"*No?*"

"*Cobra was the one who was killed by the wolfsbane-laced dart during the last round of boot camp.*"

"*No one told me about that.*" I frowned. "*But that doesn't even make sense. I thought Serpents couldn't be killed with wolfsbane.*"

"*Who knows what those darts were actually laced with?*" Damon pointed out.

"*True.*" But a weird feeling took over. I wasn't sure what it was, but something about the whole situation just felt sort of off.

A lot of other students who I didn't even recognize continued to enter the room. It sort of surprised me to know there were so many Royals who I still hadn't been acquainted with. I wondered if they were first year students. It was the only thing that could explain why Ella Gray hadn't invited them to the boot camp, too.

I glanced up at the doorway just as a pair of eyes locked on mine.

My breath caught on my throat as his emerald green stare penetrated straight through me. There was an obvious look of recognition behind his eyes.

Rafael remembered me. That much was obvious from the way

he looked at me. I wasn't sure how or why it had happened, but some way, somehow, there had been a breakthrough in his memories.

"*Um, Lena,*" I heard Ezra say through mind-speak, but Rafael's hold on my eyes was so intense that his words just seemed to drone in my mind. It was almost as if Rafael had me under some sort of spell—one that had me focused on him and *only* him. Everyone and everything else in the entire classroom just seemed to fade away into the distance. I was completely captivated by him.

As he pulled his emerald green eyes away from mine, my heartbeat started to return to normal.

Then it hit me.

Rafael was sitting to the left of me. That could only mean one thing. The guy who had just entered the room *wasn't* Rafael.

It was Ricky.

Holy. *Freaking.* Crap.

Obviously, I had known the two of them were identical. But the reality of just *how* much they looked alike hit me full force.

Ricky's eyes flitted over to meet mine again as he headed across the room, and the same thing happened. Everyone and everything else in the room just seemed to become background noise.

This time, I somehow forced myself to look away. I wasn't sure why that kept happening, but I really didn't like whatever was causing it.

Was this just what happened when you were mated to someone's twin brother? I knew the theory was a crazy one, but nothing else really seemed plausible.

My thoughts were interrupted as Shere Khan entered the room, closing the door behind him. From his neatly trimmed dark hair to the black suit he wore, everything about him seemed so completely human-like. The only giveaway that he was even a shifter at all was his extremely muscular body. He was, by far, the most muscular shifter I had ever laid eyes on. And the only hint that he was a tiger shifter was the bright orange tie he had on.

"Good morning, class," his deep voice boomed. "As you already know by now, I am Shere Khan. You should all consider yourself lucky to be graced by my presence. I am a Legend, after all, and it is the reason I have been chosen to teach this class. You see, no one knows more about Ancient Royal History than yours truly." He smiled out at us, and his pointy, cat-like incisors gleamed under the bright lighting of the classroom. "I know things that even shifter historians don't know about the subject. I know all of the deep dark secrets."

At that moment, there was a knock at the door. Shifting my gaze across the room, I saw Ezra's brother, Eric, standing in the doorway.

Shere Khan glanced over at him, his emerald green eyes full of annoyance.

Moving towards the door, he unlocked it and twisted the door handle.

"You're late," he growled.

"I'm sorry," Eric replied. "It won't happen again."

"Oh, I can assure you that you're right. It *won't* happen again. Lateness will not be tolerated in this classroom. What is your name?"

"Eric Gray." There was a cool confidence to his tone that sort of surprised me. I would have been humiliated to be lectured in this way by Shere Khan. But Eric didn't seem to be too fazed by it.

"Eric Gray." The name rolled off of Shere Khan's tongue. "As in Ella Gray's son?"

Eric nodded. "Yeah. Unfortunately."

Shere Khan looked amused by his response. "Well, Eric Gray, you have been presented with an incredible opportunity here, the gravity of which you must not yet be fully aware of. I have been resurrected from the dead to teach you. You should appreciate just how lucky you are to have a Legend as your instructor." He turned his attention to the rest of us. "Every day I walk into this classroom—and any other classroom I will be teaching in, for that matter—I will be locking the door behind me. Starting next period, any student who shows up even *one minute* late will be locked out for the duration of the class period."

He glanced around the room. "The other Legends' time is equally as valuable as my own, so you should know that being late in any of your classes will hold similar consequences. If you receive five marks for lateness, you will be kicked out of my class *and* expelled from Shifter Academy—a decision that I can make as your new Headmaster." Glancing back over at Eric, he added, "Your lateness will be excused for today only. Please go take a seat."

As Eric walked across the classroom, his eyes met mine. I shot him a small smile. He returned it and then plopped down into a chair.

"You may have figured out the reason each of you have been chosen for this class. Each of you is extremely likely to rule one of the shifter kingdoms. Over the next few months, I'm going to teach you everything you need to know to be a successful ruler. I'm going to tell you the behind-the-scenes details of every argument, every battle, every bloodshed. You're going to learn about every betrayal, every rivalry. So, what I am about to tell you next should go without saying." His green eyes darted around the room before finally settling on mine, convincing me that his next message was primarily aimed at me. "You better pay attention."

EIGHT

As I left Shere Khan's classroom, my head was spinning. In just one class, we had already learned so much—things that I'd never read about in any textbook I'd encountered so far.

I had always wondered why the Royal House of Foxes, the first royal family to rule the shifter world, had fallen—and now I knew. During the ancient times, King Charles, the Fox King and first King of the Shifters, and his wife, Queen Isabella, were dethroned after they made a secret alliance with the Royal House of Coyotes. This was a mistake because the Foxes' biggest alliance, the Royal House of Wolves, were enemies with the Coyotes. When the Wolves learned about the secret alliance, they outed the Foxes as traitorous to the rest of the shifter world—and they quickly rose to power themselves.

This secret alliance was the entire reason the Foxes had earned a reputation as being sly and sneaky. It was a reputation that had even carried over to how foxes were portrayed in the human world.

Advanced Weaponry was my next class. I was disappointed that none of my mates—and neither of my roommates—were in the class with me. When I entered the gymnasium, I headed for the bleachers, where a lot of the other students were already sitting.

I had just taken a seat in the middle when I heard a familiar voice say, "Hey, Lena."

I glanced up to find Eric standing there. He sat down next to me.

"Hey, Eric."

"Long time no talk," he commented.

"Yeah, it has been a while." Even though I actually liked Eric, Ella Gray had warned me to stay away from her son because he was a "bad apple." Since then, I had avoided him as much as possible, mostly because I was already on her bad side. I didn't want to make things worse for myself. For that reason, I had completely avoided Eric during Ella Gray's sadistic bootcamp.

But I no longer needed to worry about any of that. Ella Gray was gone... for now, at least. She couldn't threaten me to keep away from her son when she was nowhere near Shifter Academy. What Ella Gray didn't know couldn't hurt me.

I glanced over at him. "How are you doing?"

"I'm alright, I guess." He shrugged. "How about you?"

"Good."

His blue eyes, which were a near perfect match for Ezra's, flitted over to meet mine. "Hey, can I talk to you about something?"

"Sure. About what?"

He glanced over his shoulder as if he was taking in all of the people who were sitting behind us. "I don't feel comfortable talking about it here. Can you meet me around seven?"

I considered it for a moment. That would have meant really pushing the limits on curfew, and Eric and I had already gotten into trouble once for being out past curfew (which was when Ella Gray had warned me to avoid Eric).

But the good news was that Ella wasn't here, and even though he seemed like he was tough, I knew Shere Khan wasn't going to expel me. He could threaten it all he wanted, but at the end of the day, he *couldn't* expel me. If there was anyone who needed to be here this semester, it was me.

"Yeah, I'll meet you on the quad at seven," I told him.

"Great." He looked like he wanted to say something more, but he remained silent.

We sat there for a few moments longer while I wondered what he wanted to talk to me about. Ricky headed in our direction, and for a moment, I thought he was going to sit with me. I wouldn't have even known it was him if I hadn't already gone over my mates' schedules with them. Rafael definitely wasn't in this class. But as my eyes locked on his from across the room, I felt drawn to him again; the room began to spin around us, and everything else just seemed to fade away again.

Forcing myself to pull my eyes away from his, I wondered why this kept happening.

I also wanted to know if it was one-sided or if he could feel it, too—this thing between us, whatever it was.

At that moment, the other door to the gymnasium flew open, and a huge gust of wind fell upon us.

Leo and Lycaon of Arcadia entered the room.

Leo had long, golden blonde hair that he wore in a ponytail and deeply tanned skin. He resembled Damon so much. As the Legend walked towards us, all I could seem to think about was how strong he looked. There was just this powerful energy that radiated all around him.

Lycaon of Acadia walked alongside him. His dark brown hair was cut short, and his striking blue eyes popped against his fair skin, even from across the room. He looked just like Ezra, but older and more powerful.

"Good morning, students," Leo said loudly. "As you may have already heard by now, the Legends have arisen from the dead. I am Leo, and this is Lycaon." He motioned to him. "Our job is to teach and prepare you for what's to come."

"We have a particular interest in preparing those of you who are Royals. We will be dividing you into two groups: Royals and non-Royals. It looks like we have four Royals in this classroom who will be receiving special training," Lycaon announced, glancing down at his clipboard. "Lena Falcone, Ricardo Khan, Ezra Gray, and Anastasia Brink, please come to the center of the gymnasium."

Rising to my feet, I walked to the middle of the gym with the other Royals. I was completely dreading being in a group with Anastasia. I also wasn't looking forward to being in a group with Ricky—and it wasn't just because he wanted to murder my mate so he could become the next King. I couldn't even look at him without feeling like the room was spinning. It couldn't have been healthy for me to have any close encounters with him.

"We're going to switch back and forth when it comes to your instruction," Leo informed the class. "The Royals will start with me, while the rest of you will begin this course with Lycaon. We'll switch it up in a few weeks. As different types of shifters, we both have different skill sets and things to offer you in our lessons." Then Leo turned to our group. There was a fierce look in his golden-brown eyes as they met mine. It intimidated me a little. "We're going to head outside to the football field for our first lesson. Follow me." He effortlessly scooped up a large black bag that looked like it must have weighed a ton.

The four of us followed Leo out the gymnasium door and up a stone staircase that took us to the field.

I avoided Anastasia and Ricky's gazes as we followed him.

I kept shooting nervous glances in Eric's direction, but he didn't look my way.

Once we reached the football field, Leo turned to us. "The reason we've separated you from the rest of the students is because being Royal means you are far more skilled and more talented than other shifters. Your abilities know no bounds. While this can give you the upper hand, it also puts you at an unfair advantage to train against your peers. Try as they might, they will never win and there's nothing anyone can do to change that." He glanced around at us. "We are going to start today off with sword fighting."

Leo opened the black bag he was carrying and pulled out four swords. As he laid them in a row on the ground, goose-bumps erupted all over my arms and legs. This was the first time I had ever seen a sword in real life.

Actually, that wasn't true. I had seen swords in museums in the human world, but I'd never actually held one before. If only I had known then that Leo, the legendary figure behind the zodiac sign, was going to be the one to teach me to use a sword someday. To say it was intimidating would have been an under-statement. I was scared shitless.

The last thing I wanted was to embarrass myself in front of him, and honestly? I was pretty sure I was going to because I didn't know the first thing about using a sword—or any other type of weapon, for that matter.

"Please step forward and grab a sword for yourself," Leo instructed.

I got in line behind Eric. He grabbed one of the swords from the ground. It had a shiny blue gemstone on the handle that glimmered in the daylight.

Once he had moved to the side, I leaned over and grabbed one for myself. It was surprisingly light. Ever since I had shifted over the weekend, I had noticed that a lot of things felt more effortless than they used to. It must have had to do with my newfound abilities.

Once we had all taken one of the swords, Leo said, "Eventually, you will all use your weapons against one another."

I noticed Anastasia's eyes shift in my direction. I wondered if she was looking forward to using her sword against me.

"But we won't be doing that today. Today, you are going to practice sword-fighting on Dark Spirits."

I had never heard that term before, but it didn't take a rocket scientist to figure out what they were. Dark Spirits sounded absolutely terrifying and not at all like something I wanted to practice using a sword on. They sounded like something I wanted to stay the hell away from.

"Unleash them," Leo said loudly, and at that moment, a short man wearing a tuxedo seemed to appear out of thin air.

"Yes, Sir." The man snapped his fingers then, producing a cloud of black smoke, followed by a thunder-like noise.

I watched as four, cloaked dark shadow figures—*four Dark Spirits*—appeared on the football field. As they began to head in our direction, Anastasia shot me a nervous glance. The fear in her eyes reflected my own feelings.

I tried to catch Eric's gaze, but his eyes were focused on the dark shadowy figures as they moved in our direction.

There was a Dark Spirit for each of us. I had never used a sword before, and somehow, I had to defend myself against one of those things.

One of them was already headed straight for me. It was moving *fast*, too.

I tightened my grip on the handle of my sword, unsure of how I was even supposed to use this thing. Shouldn't we have been given some pointers *before* the Dark Spirits started coming for us? There had to have been some sort of method or technique that would help us beat them. It seemed kind of cruel to unleash them on us without even giving us advice first.

I was just going to have to give myself my own advice: *Don't get stabbed, Lena.*

I tried to come up with a game plan. I decided to just pretend it was a baseball bat—a super sharp baseball bat that was going to slash this Dark Spirit for me.

I had never even *swung* a sword before, but I was going to need to figure it out now. I had no idea what these Dark Spirits were capable of.

As it came closer to me, I raised my sword into the air, holding it as high as I could. I figured the higher I held it, the more intimidating it had to be. At least, that was what I hoped. I knew it would have intimidated *me*.

But then the Dark Spirit lunged at me. It completely caught me off-guard when it pulled out a sword of its own and held it expertly. It had to have known how to use it better than I did.

My heart pounded against my chest as I began swinging my sword through the air. I needed to injure this Dark Spirit before it could injure me. But with every attempt I made, I ended up just narrowly missing its dark silhouette.

I swung my sword again and heard the sound of our weapons clanking against each other.

Fighting these things was such an intense feeling, one that was only comparable to what I'd felt at Ella Gray's bootcamp.

The truth was, I wasn't sure what would happen if I lost. All I knew was that losing wasn't an option. I had no choice but to win.

But how did you win against a Dark Spirit?

I wasn't sure, so I just continued to wave my sword through the air. As I came startling close to the spirit's neck, I pulled back.

Leo hadn't actually told us if we were supposed to *kill* the spirits or not. Actually, he hadn't told us if they could even *be* killed. But as the Dark Spirit came back with a vengeance, I didn't see any other alternative. I would worry about the consequences later—if there were any.

This isn't going to end well, a tiny voice in the back of my mind thought.

At that moment, the Dark Spirit's sword came so close that it almost landed on my shoulder. My heart pounded with the realization that it could have sliced through it.

Trying to dodge the sword, I ducked—and that was my biggest mistake.

I'd just learned it was a bad idea to take my eyes off my opponent—even *if* it was only for a second.

In one swift movement, the shadowy figure had me pinned to the ground. The end of its sword was hovering just above my chest, taunting me to make a move.

Panicked, and not caring that the other royals would hear me, I didn't even try to control the scream that escaped my throat. Or the many screams that followed.

I wasn't sure if there was going to be any surviving this. I was pretty sure I was a goner.

"Help!" I screamed out, squeezing my eyes shut.

"*Exite!*" Leo roared. Then he knelt down on the ground beside me and said, "Lena, calm down." He reached out and grabbed my arms, which were shaking uncontrollably. "The Dark Spirits aren't *real*. They cannot harm you."

"T-they're n-not real?" I managed to squeak out as I continued to tremble.

"No. They are nothing but an illusion. I just made it disappear."

Glancing around, I noticed that he was right. The Dark Spirit was gone. In fact, all of them were.

My heart was still pounding hard in my chest as I stared at

Leo, confused. Whatever the hell I had just dueled, it had *felt* real.

"But I heard its sword clanking against mine. I felt the air whooshing against my ear when it almost stabbed me," I insisted.

"Those were nice added effects, weren't they? It makes it feel real." There was a sense of pride in his voice. "The Dark Spirits you just encountered were holograms," he explained. "We didn't want you to know they weren't real so you would give it your best shot and we could test your natural sword-fighting abilities, but they're completely harmless." Leo's golden-brown eyes stared into mine. "But today's class made something very clear to me."

"W-what?" I whispered.

"We have our work cut out for us," Leo replied. "You're not yet ready for everything that lies ahead of you. You have a lot of hard work to do to prepare yourself."

I swallowed hard, knowing he was right. There was no denying it.

I *wasn't* ready to rule the shifter world yet.

CHAPTER
NINE

I was still feeling on edge from the Dark Spirits in Advanced Weaponry when I entered the classroom for Ancient Mating and Marriage Rituals. I hoped this class would be relaxing. I needed to calm down.

"This class seems bloody barbaric." I heard Katerina's voice before I saw her sitting at the center of the classroom. "Does no one think it's a good idea to start *new* traditions and rituals? Why must we forever live in the past, Pattie?"

"I don't know, Princess." Her mate shook his head, running a hand through his mess of strawberry blonde hair.

As I plopped down into a desk in front of her, Katerina's eyes flitted over to meet mine and a smile hit her pink, glossy lips. "Hello, love. How was Advanced Weaponry?"

"Ha," I muttered under my breath as I pulled my notepad out of my backpack. "It was a disaster."

"That bad, huh?" Patrick asked.

I nodded.

"Oh, boy. Pattie and I have it later on today." She looked nervous.

"Maybe you'll have better luck with it than I did." In fact, I was certain she would. I was pretty sure this was just a me thing. I was the only one in the class who had struggled in my fight against the Dark Spirit. When we'd left the football field, Eric kept asking me if I was okay. Even *Anastasia* looked like she was genuinely concerned—as concerned as she could be for someone who she disliked as much as me, anyway.

"I hope so. I'm nervous now," Katerina commented as other students began to filter into the room.

I was surprised to find that there were so many students at Shifter Academy who I didn't even *know*.

I noticed something strange. As each student began to enter the room, I somehow just *knew* what their shifter race was. It was a feeling I felt deep in my gut with every student who stepped into the room.

There was a boy who plopped down into a seat in the front of the classroom. He had short blonde hair, fair skin, and a semi-muscular figure. His appearance alone didn't give me any hints about his shifter race.

Werewolf, a tiny voice popped into the back of my mind.

I stared at the back of his head, wondering if there was a way for me to confirm my feeling was right about his shifter race. At that moment, he stretched—and his hand fell to his back. It was right there in plain sight, imprinted on his hand. *A werewolf tattoo.*

I was right about him.

Wondering if it had just been a lucky guess, I tested my intuition again when a girl entered the room.

Lion.

Instantly, I knew I was right—and it wasn't just her curly blonde mane of hair that confirmed my suspicions.

She had a lion tattoo on her ankle.

What was happening? How did I just *know* everyone's shifter race?

Ezra's voice filled my mind. *"I'm pretty sure this is one of your newfound shifter abilities, Lena."*

"Do all shifters get this ability?" I questioned.

"I've never heard of it before."

"Me, either," Harden agreed.

"I think this is what sets you apart," Damon chimed in. *"I think it's part of the prophecy. You can sense everyone's shifter race because you are the future Queen of the Shifters—and not just any Queen, but the greatest Queen there will ever be."*

I thought about what he was saying. It *did* make sense. Maybe this unique shifter ability was a part of all of that—a part of the big picture.

At that moment, I heard the sound of heels clacking against the marble floor, and I felt an overwhelming sense of energy.

Power. It felt like power, I realized, as I watched an Asian woman walk into the room. She had long, jet-black hair that fell over her shoulders in loose waves. She wore a vibrant red peplum dress that accentuated her petite frame. She seemed fierce, just like all the Legends.

"Good morning, class. I am Byakko. I would like to tell you a little about me. Many of you may have heard of me, thanks to the Chinese zodiac calendar. This may be confusing, perhaps, because I am Japanese—not Chinese. In ancient times, the Chinese Emperor chose twelve animals and mythological creatures to protect him. To select us, he held a race. It was open to anyone, regardless of their nationality. I was one of the winners. Today, I represent the tiger from the Chinese zodiac calendar—a fact that even humans don't know." She glanced around the classroom. "I won't be your only instructor for this course. Joining us today will be—"

"Bagheera. That would be me," a deep voice commented as a dark-skinned man entered the room. He was wearing black pants and a plain black t-shirt. Of any professor who I had ever encountered at Shifter Academy, his attire was the least professional.

His dark eyes fell on me. "I am a Legend. I haven't risen from the dead to teach a bunch of students in an outfit I don't feel comfortable in."

I shrank back in my seat, completely embarrassed that he'd heard my thoughts. Somehow, I needed to figure out a way to completely turn them off—*before* they ended up getting me in even more trouble.

"The reason we have been chosen to teach this class is because no one knows more about ancient mating and marriage than we do," Byakko continued. "You see, we are the only two Legends who have risen from the dead who were also mates."

"Who *are* also mates," Bagheera corrected her. Turning his attention to the class, he added, "You are mated to someone before *and* after death."

"Of course, darling." She smiled into his face for a long moment before turning her attention back to the class. "Your connection to your mate changes when—or should I say *if?* — you pass on. We aren't going to talk about that today, however. Today, we are going to discuss the bonding process."

The bonding process was code for sex.

It was the final step to placing your mark on your mate. So far, I had only completed the bonding process with Damon. It was something I still needed to do with my other three mates, something that *needed* to happen before the prophecy could be fulfilled.

I wasn't going to lie. It was incredibly nerve-wracking—especially since the last time I'd tried, it had resulted in Rafael losing all memories of me. To say that I was nervous to try it again with him, Ezra, or Harden would have been an understatement.

I was scared shitless.

"As many of you already know, the bonding process requires us to make love to our mate. This is the final step to seal the deal, if you will," Byakko explained. "It's one of the most romantic times during your journey together as mates. And once you have completed the bonding process, *everything* will change."

She glanced around the room as she continued. "Your connection as mates will intensify. What once felt like young, human love will suddenly begin to feel like something out of a Hollywood movie—or a fairytale, even."

"Your heart will begin to feel a sense of fullness, unlike anything you have ever known before," Bagheera added. "It will feel as if there is no room in your heart for anything or anyone besides your mate."

I frowned. There was no denying that Damon and I had a much more intense connection now than we had before we'd had sex. But I couldn't relate to this whole feeling of heart fullness. My heart didn't feel full of only Damon.

"That is because you are the exception, Lena." I heard Byakko say. When I glanced up at her, her dark brown eyes were piercing straight through mine.

I opened my mouth to respond to her, but she continued.

"*Shere Khan has informed us of your situation. All of this is different for you. You have one heart, but four objects of affection. You will never experience the full effects of being mated to someone the way other shifters will be. Over time, you will find that it is both a blessing and a curse.*"

I frowned. I could hear her talking to me, but her lips weren't moving. It was almost as if she had somehow figured out a way to get inside my mind.

"*Yes, Lena. The ability to mentally communicate with any other shifter in the world is one of my unique abilities. And don't worry.*"

Your mates cannot hear our interactions right now. I have manipulated your mind to prevent them from being able to eavesdrop on our conversation." She continued to stare at me from across the room. "There is something you must know before you make your decision — something that was once prophesied about you and your mates many years ago."

"What is it?" I asked as a feeling of dread took over. The last thing I wanted to know about was yet another prophecy about me.

"Your mate bonds with the other three will never be broken. All four of your mates will forever own a piece of your heart. Even if you choose only one of your mates in the end, your heart will always have room for the other three. This is a lot worse than it may sound."

"Worse how?"

"If you choose only one of them, seventy-five percent of your heart will feel forever broken for the other three. The pain, the devastation, the loss... It will never go away."

CHAPTER
TEN

The rest of the day passed by quickly. Even though I tried to pay attention in all of my other classes as much as I possibly could, I also couldn't seem to get out of my feelings about what Byakko had told me.

It was nice that she had given me a warning, but a part of me almost wished she hadn't told me. It only complicated things.

I had been hoping that once I made a choice, I would no longer have feelings for the rest of them. But knowing that there was going to be an empty space for each of them—one that would always make my heart feel broken—made this decision all the more overwhelming.

I would get to choose one of them in the end, but I'd spend the rest of my life missing the other three.

The truth was that I wished I didn't have to make the decision at all. I was dreading it even more. But prophecies were prophecies, and I couldn't do anything to ruin this one. The entire shifter world was relying on it—on *me*. No matter how I felt or how much it scared me to lose three of them, yet still feel their absence weighing heavy on my heart for the rest of my life, I couldn't fuck this one up.

～

When seven o'clock rolled around that night, I stood outside waiting on the quad.

"*I really don't like you being out there so close to curfew,*" Ezra's voice filled my mind.

"*Be careful, Lena. We don't want you to get in trouble,*" Damon said.

"*Let us know if you need us,*" Harden told me next.

Ugh.

This whole hearing each other's thoughts thing was getting pretty annoying. I had no privacy.

"*I'll be fine, but can all of you do me a favor and just butt out?*"

"*Lena, you know we only pay attention to your thoughts because we worry about you. We just want to make sure you're okay. It's not like we're trying to spy on you,*" Damon said gently.

"*I know.*" I knew he wasn't lying. But it still sucked to have zero privacy when it came to, well, any and everything. Like right now, when I was about to find out why Eric wanted to have this secret meeting with me. We hadn't discussed it, but what if he didn't want the Alpha Brotherhood knowing whatever he was about to tell me? Was I supposed to make him aware that by telling me, all four of my mates would find out?

"*Don't do that,*" Ezra said, his voice urgent in my head.

"*He can't even know you have four mates, Lena,*" Damon reminded me.

I knew he was right; I was supposed to keep the truth about

what I was a secret. Eric—and no one else, for that matter—could know.

Speak of the devil. At that moment, I spotted Eric walking towards me. He was wearing the Shifter Academy letterman's jacket, and his hands were shoved in his pockets as he headed in my direction.

"*Can you guys just butt out of my thoughts? Please?*" I asked my mates before I began to walk in Eric's direction. I really hoped my mates would give us some privacy, or at least *pretend* to.

As he got closer to me, he waved. "Hey, Lena."

"Hey." I waved back.

"Are you okay?" Eric asked as he approached me. "After what happened in Advanced Weaponry, I mean. I've been worried about you."

"Yeah. I just didn't realize the Dark Spirits weren't real," I explained. "I thought they could actually hurt me."

Now that I knew they couldn't, it was just so embarrassing to have to go back to that class again. How was I supposed to be the Queen of the Shifters when I was the scaredy-cat out of the bunch?

"I'm really glad you're okay." There was a look of sincerity in his blue eyes.

"Thanks. So, um, why did you want to meet me here tonight?" I asked.

"Do me a favor first." Eric handed me a little vial of an aqua-colored potion. "Then we'll talk."

Why did it seem like *everyone* was just handing potions over to me lately?

My eyebrows lifted. "What is this?"

"This potion will prevent your mate from hearing your thoughts for the next hour." His blue eyes met mine. "This is more for me than it is for you. My brother can't know what I'm about to tell you next."

I considered it for a second. On the one hand, it felt completely disloyal and almost traitorous to drink this potion. In a weird way, it almost felt as if I was choosing Eric over Ezra.

On the other hand, I would have given just about anything for even an hour of privacy from my mates. In the end, my curiosity over what Eric wanted to talk to me about helped settle the debate for me.

I brought the vial to my lips and tilted my head back. Downing the entire bottle of potion in one gulp, I glanced over at Eric. "How long will it take for this to kick in?"

"It should be working already."

"*Hey, can you guys hear me?*" I asked my mates.

Crickets.

Apparently, it really *had* worked... and I doubted my mates were happy that I'd taken it.

"I just checked. I don't think he can hear me," I informed Eric.

"Good. None of them can?"

I froze. How did *he* know the truth about what I was?

"I'm not sure what you mean—" I started to say, but Eric laughed.

"You don't have to hide the truth from me, Lena. I know you're the one the prophecy is about. I know that you're mated to my brother's friends. I want you to know that I'm not going to hurt you or the Alpha Brotherhood."

"What do you mean? Why would you hurt them?"

He stared at me for a moment. "You do realize that you're not the only one who has to be careful when it comes to this prophecy, right? If anyone wanted to squash this whole thing, all they'd have to do is hurt any one of you."

I had never really considered it before, but he was right. The prophecy wouldn't come to fruition if something happened to one of my mates before I chose one of them to marry, before I decided which shifter race would rule the world.

For the first time since all of this had begun, I felt this strong urge to protect my mates.

I was going to be their Queen; I had to protect all of my potential Kings.

"How did you know that I'm mated to all four of them?" I asked Eric.

"Well, it doesn't take a rocket scientist to be able to tell that you're in love with all four of them," he said pointedly. "But I also overheard Ella talking about it at bootcamp."

"Oh." I hoped no one else had overheard her talking about it. Clearly, the Legends knew the truth about me. But I wanted to keep it at just that.

As it was, with the Legends knowing, it felt like the news was going to spread like wildfire. It wasn't that I didn't trust them. There were just so many of them that could slip up and spill the beans by accident.

"I promise you that I haven't—and won't—tell anyone about it," Eric added. "I would never do anything to put any of your lives in danger. Ezra and I might not always see eye to eye and we aren't that close, but I would never want to see anything happen to him or his mate. Trust me."

The truth was, I actually *did* trust him with my secret. There was just something about him that I trusted so much. He had proven his loyalty to me the night we had gotten in trouble for staying out past curfew and he had been unwilling to let me take the fall for it alone. I wouldn't have taken the potion from him if I hadn't already trusted him.

"Thank you," I told him.

"Now, let's get down to business." Eric met my gaze. "The reason I didn't want Ezra listening in on our conversation is because I have a big favor to ask of you."

My eyebrows lifted. "What type of favor?"

"I need you to help me kill Ella."

A knot twisted in my stomach.

"You want me to help you kill your mom?" I just stared back at him with wide eyes.

He nodded. "Yeah. I know Ezra wouldn't actually approve of this. Even though Ella has done some really horrible shit, he still wouldn't want to see anything bad happen to her. He's too good. And it's not that I'm *bad*, but I know what needs to happen to Ella. It's for the best for *everyone*."

"I know what you mean." When it came down to it, Ezra was just too nice. He tried to see the good in everyone, even when no good existed. I knew he had recently begun to see what a monster his mom was, but I wasn't sure how he would feel knowing that his brother and mate were talking about murdering her.

"My brother and I are polar opposites. I have always seen our mother for the coldhearted, two-faced, lying monster she is. There's nothing I want more right now than to get rid of Ella, once and for all." There was a look of determination in Eric's blue eyes–it was a look that told me he was going to do this with or without me.

"How can we kill her when we don't even know where she is? *No one* knows where she is," I pointed out.

"I'm going to track her down. I'm going to ask Shere Khan for permission to leave Shifter Academy until I find her. I'm not going to be the next King of the Wolves, anyway. I don't need to be here that badly." His eyes met mine. "If anyone can figure out where my mother's hiding, it's me."

I knew that if there was anyone motivated enough to find her, it was probably him.

"Why do you want *me* to help?" I asked, purely out of curiosity. It just seemed like such a random request, since Eric and I barely even talk these days. There had to have been someone else he was closer to.

"Because of the prophecy." His blue eyes locked on mine with a look of seriousness behind them. "I think you might be the only shifter who's actually powerful enough to kill Ella."

CHAPTER
ELEVEN

By the time I reached the girls' dorms, it was already past curfew. I was about to enter the building when I heard something rustling in the bushes outside.

My heart pounded against my chest. Something wasn't right. Somehow, I just *knew* someone was waiting for me. I inhaled the birch, ginger, and apple scent that wafted towards me from the bushes. I recognized it immediately as a coyote shifter. It was just an instinctual feeling.

"Lena!" I heard a familiar voice whisper my name.

It took me a moment to realize who it was.

The coyote shifter himself.

"Jake? What are *you* doing here?" I hissed at him.

"I need to talk to you. Can you come with me?"

"Where would we even go? Where do you even live?" I wasn't entirely sure where Jake's dorm room was. I figured the coyote boys probably shared dorms with the werewolf and fox guys. Not that I even *wanted* to go back to his dorm room with him.

He ignored my question about his living arrangements.

"Well, I was thinking we could head to the beach... if you're willing." There was a hopeful look behind his gaze.

I considered it for a moment. I was already out past curfew. Could I get into more trouble than I was already in?

Yes, actually... I *could*. But the good news was that I still didn't think Shere Khan would do anything about it.

I wasn't sure if *Jake* was worth risking it all over, but I was already outside.

So, I nodded. "Yeah, I'm down for it."

"Great. We should probably do an invisibility spell to mask ourselves," he said quietly.

Oh, even better. This ex-boyfriend of mine had literally thought of everything.

"*Cloaken*," he spoke in a language I didn't think I'd ever heard of. Before I knew it, I was invisible. Transparent. Completely see-through.

I wasn't going to lie. It was sort of *nice* to be hidden like this. It made me sort of jealous of Harden, who had a gene that allowed him to go invisible—even though he hadn't been able to really master it yet. Still. He would figure it out someday, and that was pretty freaking cool for him.

As we headed for the beach, we passed the Alpha Brotherhood penthouse. I stared up at it. I hadn't gotten the chance to visit my mates in their home on-campus yet. I had a bedroom of my own there, where I knew I would spend a lot of time this year.

It was strange to think about everything that had changed in our lives since the first time I'd ever gone to the Alpha Brotherhood's penthouse. And now, the house was full of so many memories.

"Are you still next to me, Lena?" Jake asked from somewhere near me. "I can't see you."

"Yeah, I'm here," I replied with a nod.

"Okay, good."

We made it to the sandy stretch of beach. The moonlight reflected against the ocean, casting a pretty glow over everything. It reminded me of the party my mates had thrown on the beach. It felt so long ago now. So much had happened since that night.

"*Reveale*," Jake said, and just like that, the two of us were fully visible again.

"So, what is it you want to talk about?" I asked him.

"I thought you died at bootcamp," he admitted. "During the final round... I thought it was you at first. Knowing that I could have lost you..."

"Jake, I'm not yours to lose," I replied quietly.

If I'd known how awkward he was going to make this, I wouldn't have come.

"I know that. I know you don't belong to me. We're not mated. But at the end of the day, we have a history. We go back —so far back that I just can't keep secrets from you." His eyes flitted over to meet mine. "There's something I need to tell you, Lena."

My eyebrows rose. "What is it?"

"This guy came to my dorm room last night," he explained. "It was really late, and he knocked on the door. He asked questions about you." He paused for a moment. "I didn't want to answer him, but I couldn't avoid his questions, either. He had a gun."

My heart pounded in my chest. "What type of questions did he ask?"

"He wanted to know what your shifter race is."

"What did you tell him?"

"The truth. That I don't know what you are." His eyes met mine. "He had other questions, too. He wanted to know if you know the three bears."

A knot tightened in my stomach. "Who was this guy?"

"I don't know. He was wearing all black. He had on a black ski mask, so I couldn't see his face. He was taller than me, but not *that* tall, either." He shook his head. "I couldn't pick him out in a lineup even if I tried."

"Fuck." I wanted to know who this person was and why they cared to know so many personal details about me. "It doesn't even make any sense," I commented out loud. "Why would they go to *you* for the answers to these questions?"

"I have no idea," Jake replied, shaking his head. "The only thing I could think of is they somehow found out we used to date back in the human world."

"Maybe," I murmured.

"Lena, I just want you to know that I still care for you," Jake continued. "If you ever find yourself in any sort of situation and you need help, don't ever hesitate to call me."

"Thank you. I appreciate that."

He nodded at me. "That's all I wanted to talk to you about. We should probably head back to our dorm rooms now, before we get kicked out of school. But I felt that this was worth risking it." He paused and said, "*Cloaken.*"

As our bodies became invisible again, so many thoughts began to circle through my mind. There was mostly just one thought that stood out among all the rest.

This whole thing confirmed something for me. There was no doubt about it now; the Three Bears really *had* left that note for me.

I wondered if this guy who had visited Jake was one of them, or if it was someone else entirely.

I wasn't sure, but I knew I was going to have to be a little more careful around campus from now on.

I was fortunate that it was Jake who had been waiting in the bushes for me tonight. There was a chance that next time, I might not have been so lucky.

CHAPTER
TWELVE

The next day, I entered the Poisons and Potions classroom before any of the other students.

Kaa was already there, scribbling something on the chalkboard. She was a short woman with deeply tanned skin, and short, frosty blonde hair that she wore in a pixie cut.

She turned to me, her gold eyes narrowing in on me.

"Hello, Miss Falcone," she hissed.

There was no other way to put it—her voice *sounded* like a snake as she spoke. It made goosebumps creep their way down my spine.

"Hello," I replied with a small smile. It made me wonder how she even knew my name, but I figured it must have been some sort of shifter ability.

"May I have a word with you in private? My office is right across the hall."

"Oh. Um, sure." The truth was, I actually hated the idea of being alone behind a closed door with Kaa. She wasn't just any Serpent; she was the descendent of the current Serpent King, who had killed my parents. What if Kaa wanted to hurt *me*?

I tried to push the thought to the back of my mind. I had

to start overcoming my fears—even the super scary ones—if there was any chance of me becoming the badass Queen I was meant to be. I couldn't be weak anymore. I had to be strong.

Everyone was right: I *did* have a lot of work to do on myself.

"Okay, perfect." Kaa led me out of the classroom and across the hall. She flicked on the light and slid into a chair at her desk.

After I closed the door behind me, she motioned for me to take a seat across from her. "Please, sit so we can speak."

There had been a lot of emphasis on the letter 's' in that sentence. I half-expected to see a snake tongue dart out of her mouth. Trying to avoid gawking at her—and ignoring how hissy she had sounded—I nervously sat down.

"Miss Falcone, the reason I wanted to talk to you today is because of your shifter race. Your records state that your shifter race is 'To Be Determined'?"

"That's correct." I wasn't sure how to get that updated in my file. I assumed I would have to talk to Shere Khan about it, and after everything that had happened with Rafael, talking to him was at the absolute bottom of my to-do list.

"I am just so confused as to how that can possibly be when your shifter race is so obvious," Kaa said.

"It *is*?" I asked with wide eyes. The crazy part was that everyone who knew the truth about my shifter race hadn't been able to believe it, because I didn't look like a bear. What was Kaa seeing that everyone else wasn't?

"Yes, dear. It is quite obvious to me that you are a Serpent."

～

"Why would she think you're a Serpent?" Alexis asked as she munched on some Doritos in our dorm room that night.

"I don't know. She didn't say and I was too shocked to ask her," I admitted as I popped a Flamin' Hot Cheeto into my mouth. "It must have been whatever Queen Bria saw in me that made her think I was a Serpent."

"Queen Bria?" Katerina's light eyes flicked over to meet mine.

I nodded. "I overheard her telling King Roman that she thinks I'm a Serpent," I explained. "I was so offended at the time."

"I mean, obviously. Who wants to be called a Serpent?" Alexis said.

"I would be absolutely furious if anyone tried to draw that comparison for me," Katerina agreed. "On the other hand, the most significant Serpent Queen in history seems to think you're a Serpent. Is it possible that something about you is rather Serpent-y? Something that we're missing?"

I shrugged. "I don't know. Apparently I'm not *that* Serpent-y, considering I'm a bear."

"And you don't seem like a bear, either." Katerina frowned. "I don't know, love. You are quite the mystery." She paused for a moment. "I was thinking about something. Since you're a were-bear and the next Queen of the Shifters, why am I even taking these classes? *You're* going to be the next Queen—not me. I'm not going to end up ruling at all," she said with a sigh.

I hadn't really given that any thought before, but she was *right*. How could I be the next Queen of the Bears if *she* was supposed to be the next Queen of the Bears—and vice versa? There would only be room for one of us.

"I don't know. The prophecy says I'll be choosing the next race to rule the shifter world when I choose a King. That must mean that I'll reign in his kingdom."

"And that would mean I'd still be Queen of the Bears. I think."

"I think so, too, but I guess we'll have to figure out all of that when the time comes," I said finally.

She nodded. "We will. I am certain that if you're the next Queen of the Bears, you will make a bloody fabulous one."

But even as she spoke the words, there was a look in her eyes that made me wonder if she was sad about the possibility of not reigning. I couldn't imagine growing up thinking that you would, without a doubt, be the next Queen, only to learn that there was a very good possibility that no longer held true.

"Thanks. Whether it's me or you, I think the next Queen of the Bears is going to be an amazing one."

"Well, you can't get any worse than the current one," Katerina said with an eye roll. "I love my mum, but let's be realistic. She makes a horrible Queen."

"Why?" Alexis leaned in closer, eager to get some gossip.

Honestly, I was surprised Katerina was opening up about her mom. She never said much about either of her parents, especially since they started the war.

To be honest, I still didn't even know what the war was *about*. As far as I knew, *no one* knew. It was a mystery—one that the King and Queen of the Bears seemed to be keeping to themselves.

"My mother is very cold," Katerina explained. "She doesn't care about anyone in our kingdom. She's self-absorbed and entitled. To her, the other bears in our kingdom are like minions. They're ants that she'd rather see squashed. Half of the time, I'm not even sure that she cares about *me*, and I'm her only child."

"I'm sure she cares about you," Alexis said.

"I don't know. You've never seen the way my mother looks at me. At times, it's almost as if I'm not even her daughter. I know that probably seems dramatic. And maybe I'm *being* dramatic. We get along okay... sometimes. We've gotten along better since I've come here. Time apart has done us a lot of good, but we'll never be great." She paused. "To be honest, I think my mother is jealous."

"Jealous?" I asked.

Katerina nodded. "Yes. Jealous that I will one day be the next Queen. Or so we always thought." She turned to me. "Honestly, Lena, maybe it wouldn't be the worst thing if you *did* become Queen of the Bears. At least then my mother couldn't hate me for it."

I shot her a sympathetic glance. "I'm sure she won't *hate* you for it. I'm sure it will be an adjustment for her to step down after a hundred years of having that power, but I think all of the other Queens and Kings will feel the same way when the Royal Change of Hands takes place."

"Speaking of Kings, what's your dad like?" Alexis asked Katerina.

"Oh, my father is absolutely lovely. Don't let the news fool you. They always show pictures of him with the meanest mugs. Meanwhile, he's the gentlest bear you could ever meet."

Well, apparently, the media *did* have a way of swaying your opinions, because she wasn't kidding. The media made King George out to be a villain. He'd always seemed very monster-like.

Was it possible Katerina was biased? It *was* her father, after all. No one wanted to think bad of their own parents. Then again, she was pretty open about her parents being less than perfect.

"Did you ever find out what your parents started this war over?" Alexis asked.

I glanced over at her sharply. It seemed like such a rude,

intrusive question to ask, even though I knew she meant it innocently.

Katerina didn't appear to be fazed by her question. "No. I've asked them several times, but they refuse to tell me." She paused for a moment. "The only thing I *do* know is it has something to do with the Serpents."

"Really?" My eyebrows shot up. "I thought it was against the Birds."

"No. The first attack from the Werebear Army was in the Bird Kingdom. But the only reason is because King Goga—the King of the Serpents—happened to be visiting the Bird Kingdom at the time." She paused. "It's unfortunate, really, that the Bird Kingdom had to suffer the effects of the attack. It's also what led to this turning into a world war. They very quickly allied with the Serpents, which led to the rest of the shifter kingdoms getting involved. It was all very poorly planned by my parents, if you ask me. They could have avoided a shifter world war if they'd tried to get rid of King Goga some other way."

"And you have no idea why your parents wanted to get rid of King Goga?" Alexis questioned.

"No. They refuse to tell me. My father keeps saying it's for my own protection." She sighed. "I'm sure he means well... They *both* do. But I don't know why they think that keeping me in the dark about something of such significance can protect me."

"They must have their reasons," I murmured.

A strange feeling crept over me then. I knew it sounded absolutely paranoid and possibly a little self-absorbed, but I just couldn't help but feel like the war had something to do with me.

I thought about all of the puzzle pieces and how they just seemed to come together, somehow.

It was all but confirmed that King Goga had murdered my parents.

There was a possibility that he had also blackmailed Jake to stay away from me. I suspected it was because he knew Jake was the one shifter who knew the truth about what the Serpent King had done. But even if that wasn't the reason, King Goga had been so concerned about me for some reason. Not long after, the King and Queen of the Bears had attacked him.

I knew how crazy—and far-fetched—all of this probably sounded. Nothing about the two things directly correlated with one another. But for some reason, something deep within my gut told me that all of this, this entire war, all circled back around to me.

It was a feeling I just couldn't seem to shake, no matter how hard I tried. It was a feeling that kept me awake late into the night.

THIRTEEN

"Ruling a kingdom will be one of the most challenging things you will ever do over the course of your lifetime." Shere Khan stood at the front of the classroom as he spoke. "It's not easy for any shifter, but for those of you who are about to take the throne this year, it will be even *more* difficult. You are about to make this transition during a shifter world war, which is already one of the most trying of times."

Okay. I wasn't going to lie. So far, our *Ruling a Kingdom* class had only made me even more stressed out about everything I was going to be facing in the near future.

I could have been wrong, but I was pretty sure that was Shere Khan's intentions: to stress us the fuck out.

As if I wasn't already stressed enough after he'd wiped away all of Rafael's memories of me, I thought bitterly.

Shere Khan's emerald green eyes landed on mine then. I wasn't sure if he was able to hear my thoughts or not, but the look behind his gaze made me feel certain that he could.

"When you take the throne, it is important to make sure that you are both strong and brave. It would be in your best interests if the shifters in your kingdom fear you."

Prince Shan's hand shot up.

"Yes?" Shere Khan asked.

"Don't we want the shifters of our kingdom to trust us?"

"Most certainly."

"Then why would we want them to fear us?"

"For one to trust his or her leader, they must also trust said leader is capable of taking care of them. One of the best ways to instill this level of trust within the members of your kingdom is to make sure you are always—and I do mean *always*—able to protect them. To show no signs of weakness and always put on a brave face are some of the most important things any leader can do for the members of their kingdom." He paused for a moment. "It also shows your fellow Royals how strong you are. It shows them that an attack on your kingdom would be a mistake—one they should not make. This is more important now than ever before, given the current state of affairs in our realm."

Shere Khan stared out at us for a long moment. "There is something that I would like all of you to think about—and that is war. I am not talking about the war that is currently going on all around us. That is not in your hands... *yet*. The moment you all ascend your thrones, the war and how it evolves will be up to you. While you must do everything in your power to defend your own kingdoms, you must also not tip the balance and destroy the legacies of all the shifters who came before you. Now, I would like us to take part in a little exercise. I want you to take a moment and look around. Look every person in this classroom in the eyes."

I glanced around the room and watched as the other Royals looked around at each other and at me—from my mates to my roommates and their mates to the Hellcats to the other shifters in the room. All of my classmates looked just as confused as I felt about the purpose of this exercise.

A minute or so later, Shere Khan explained, "The purpose of this exercise is to remind you that while you are sitting in the same classroom as each other right now, most of you are going to go off into the real world. More than just that, most of you will reign. But what this means is that you are one another's presents and futures. When it comes time to attack another kingdom, when it comes time to form allies or enemies, what you will really be doing is attacking or allying with or against one another." He glanced around the room. "The grim reality is that while some of you are friends, not all of you will *remain* friends. Some of you are destined to be enemies."

∽

"I had simply never thought of this before," Katerina said once class was over. Her light eyes darted over at me and Alexis. "We're best friends. How could we become *enemies* over a silly throne?"

"We *won't* become enemies," Alexis said matter-of-factly. "I don't care what happens. We *do* have a say in it. I won't let anything come between our friendship."

"Me, either," I agreed.

"I bloody hope not." She took a deep breath. "Our classes are difficult this year in so many ways. I don't think I was mentally prepared for this."

"I don't think any of us could have been," Alexis agreed. "Especially for those of us who didn't even know when we first enrolled in Shifter Academy that we were going to become Royals."

"That's the truth," I muttered under my breath. Learning that I was a shifter had been hard enough, but to now know I was going to be *queen* of *all* the shifters was on a whole other level.

"I'll see you guys later," Katerina said with a sigh as she headed off in the direction of her next class.

"Yeah, see you," Alexis said as we all parted ways.

"Lena?" Damon's voice made me jump, just as I was about to enter my next classroom.

I whirled around.

He shot me a sympathetic look. "I really do make your heart race, huh?"

"When you sneak up on me like that," I replied as my heart rate returned to an even level.

"Can I talk to you?"

"Right now?" I asked with raised eyebrows. "Class is about to start. I can't be late."

I might not have minded being late with the right professor, I didn't want to be late to Kaa's class. She didn't seem like an easygoing instructor, even though it *did* seem like she liked me because she thought I was a snake shifter. If there was one professor whose class I didn't want to be late for, it was hers. I would have rather been late to Shere Khan's class—and that was saying a lot.

"It will only take a second." His golden-brown eyes locked on mine. I noticed the look of worry behind them.

"Okay." I walked away from the classroom with him. He led me down the hallway and outside onto the stone path. "What's going on?"

"I spent the entire night at the library last night."

He didn't need to explain why. I instantly knew. *He was trying to find a way to restore Rafael's memory.*

"What did you find?" I asked, feeling hopeful for the first time in a while.

"Well, that's the thing, Lena. I didn't find anything."

"Nothing *at all?*"

Damon shook his head. "No, and it gets worse than that."

A knot tightened in my stomach. So far, there was no way to fix Raf's missing memories of me. How much worse could it get then that?

"Tell me," I whispered, meeting his eyes.

"I asked the librarian for some help. She *was* able to locate the name of a book that probably contains the answer, but it was missing from the shelf. I checked *everywhere* in the library for it, and nobody even checked it out. It's just gone."

I swallowed hard, realizing what he was saying. "Someone stole it."

"Exactly."

"Why would someone steal it?"

"My guess? *Someone* doesn't want us to know how to get Rafael's memories back. They're doing everything they can to prevent it."

"Someone meaning Shere Khan," I muttered under my breath. Glancing over at Damon, I talked to him through mind-speak. *"Why would he try to hide this from me, even though he already gave me the potion?"*

"It's even more confirmation to me that he really didn't give us the antidote for Rafael's memory. Do you still have the potion?"

I nodded. I kept it in my bra at all times. I was too afraid of losing the vial or having it get stolen from our dorm room. My solution had been to keep it on me or near me 24/7.

"You should break it."

I shook my head. *"No. There has to be some way to confirm what's in the potion."* I was still clinging to the possibility of what the potion could do. I thought about it for a moment, and then it dawned on me. *"I know the perfect shifter to ask."*

After my Potions and Poisons class ended, I headed for the front of the classroom.

"Lena. I know you need my help." Kaa's eyes locked on mine.

"How did you know?"

"Intuition," she answered.

I should have known. It seemed like the majority of shifters —at least the powerful and Royal ones—seemed to have an incredibly good sense of intuition.

"Come to my office."

Kaa led the way across the hall.

I followed her into the tiny room, and she closed the door behind us.

"*Silencioso*," she whispered. Her gold eyes flicked over to meet mine. "I just put a silencing barrier between this room and the hallway so nobody can hear us. And by nobody, I mostly mean *him*."

"Shere Khan?" I asked.

She nodded. "Yes. The thing is, Shere Khan and I lived during the same time period. I might not know him better than anyone on this planet, but I do know him better than most shifters who are alive right now. And let me tell you something about Shere Khan, Lena." She leaned in closer to me. "He cannot be trusted. Even *if*, for some crazy reason, he makes you think you can trust him, just know that you cannot ever trust him. Not now, not ever, not under any circumstances."

"Why is he so untrustworthy?" I asked.

"The thing about Shere Khan is that he only cares about himself. He doesn't care who he hurts, as long as it suits his self-interests." She paused for a moment. "Have you heard anything about Shere Khan and me?"

"Well, I know that in the fairytale and the Disney version—"

"Forget about what you heard in the modern retellings," Kaa said, shaking her head. "I'm going to tell you the *real* story. Shere Khan was the King of the Tigers, the King of all the shifters in the land. I was the Queen of the Serpents. I was the heiress to the throne. I had a husband, the late King Conda— short for Anaconda." Her gold eyes locked on mine. "Shere Khan killed Conda."

"Why?" I asked.

"Conda was a kind man. It sounds weird for me to say this, but he wasn't like other Serpents. We are known to be sneaky, and I suppose that we *can* seem that way to outsiders. We might hide things or lie to other shifters, but it's often to protect our own kind. But Conda was not like that at all. He was an extremely caring man... very kind and compassionate. He cared about *all* shifters, not only the Serpents." She paused. "Conda was also a very smart man. He was able to see straight through Shere Khan and his intentions. We all started out as allies, but that changed over time. You see, King Conda found out that Shere Khan had plans to take over all the cat shifter kingdoms."

"Wait, he *did*?" I had never heard this before.

Kaa nodded. "Yes. He planned to become the only king there was for the lions, jaguars, cheetahs, and snow leopards. The way he planned to go about this was by killing off all of the Royal families in these kingdoms. Conda caught wind of his plans, and he let the King of the Cheetahs know. Shere Khan found out that Conda had betrayed him, so he had him murdered."

I processed everything she was saying. "I'm confused. If Shere Khan killed your husband, how are you here right now?

How are you teaching in the same academy as he is? How can you even look him in the eyes?"

"It's easier than you might think, Lena. When Leo and Shere Khan brought me back to life, I knew I had to come teach at Shifter Academy for the Serpents. I owe it to my kingdom, to my legacy, to my descendants, to pass on my knowledge and help them be as successful as possible. Especially after Ella Gray caused the death of not just one but *two* of my descendants." Anger flashed through her eyes at the thought. "But there's another reason I feel comfortable being here, even given the circumstances."

"What is it?" I asked.

"Shere Khan is afraid of me."

"He is?" For some reason, that surprised me, especially after the lecture he had just given our class on how we always needed to be brave.

"Yes, he is."

"Why?" To be honest, it was hard to imagine him being afraid of *anyone*—especially a woman as small in size as Kaa.

"Because, Lena. I'm the one who killed him."

FOURTEEN

"You killed *Shere Khan*?" I just stared back at her, completely shocked. I had always wondered who had ended his life. None of our history classes had covered that yet. It had always surprised me that he had died at all, considering he was known to be one of the most powerful—if not *the* most powerful—shifter to ever exist. To learn that the woman who stood before me was the one who had managed to end him completely shocked me.

"Yes. He had it coming to him, of course, after killing my husband." There was a slight defensiveness to her tone, as if she believed she had to justify why she had killed Shere Khan.

"I completely understand why you killed him. But what I'm surprised about is the fact that he allowed you to come back, given your history with him. Why *did* he bring you back?" I might have been wrong, but Shere Khan didn't exactly seem like the forgiving type. He struck me as more of a grudge holder.

"Leo and Shere Khan agreed that each kingdom deserved to have the most powerful shifter of their kind to teach them. Obviously, that left me. I believe I am mostly here because of Leo and the other Legends' influence on him." She paused for a moment. "Shere Khan has been cordial to me in our exchanges, but..."

"You don't trust him."

Her gold eyes flicked over to meet mine. "Precisely. And neither should you."

I wasn't sure why, but for some reason, I found myself trusting Kaa. I knew I shouldn't have allowed myself to trust a Serpent, but there was just something about her that seemed truly genuine. So, I found myself telling her what had happened.

"Shere Khan took over my mate Rafael's body. Then, for some reason, he *left* Rafael's body, except my mate didn't have any memories of me when they switched back. He still can't remember me. Shere Khan told me he wasn't the one who had done it, but he gave me this vial and said it could help restore Raf's memories." I pulled the vial out of my bra and handed it to her. "He just happened to have it on him, ready to hand it over to me. It was weird."

"I knew all of that," Kaa murmured. She shot me an amused look over my hiding place for the vial before holding it up to the light to examine it. "Your other mate was very wise not to trust it."

I didn't even question how she knew my other mate didn't trust the potion.

She continued to stare at the vial for a few long moments. Then she opened it up and sniffed it. She frowned and then glanced up at me. "I can tell you one thing. This isn't a memory serum."

"It's not?" My stomach sank. Any hope that I'd had about this potion was gone. We were officially back at square one.

On the bright side... at least I didn't have to carry it around in my bra anymore?

"No." She shook her head. "I can't determine exactly *what* it is, however."

"Do you think it's a poison?" I questioned.

"It's not a poison. That much I know for sure. Like I've mentioned in class, poisons tend to smell toxic or off-putting. Nothing about the liquid in this vial smells unusual, so it's probably a potion... assuming it's anything at all."

"Wait, you think it might be *nothing*?"

"It's always a possibility." She stared down at the vial for a moment longer, and then her eyes flicked up to meet mine. "Do you mind if I keep this for now, Lena? I want to run some tests on it to find out exactly what we're dealing with here. I'd like to know exactly what Shere Khan was trying to get one of our students to drink."

I nodded. "Of course." I hadn't even needed to consider it. Now that I knew it wasn't the key to restoring Rafael's memories, I had no use for it anymore. Maybe Kaa could figure out what it was. I wanted to know what Shere Khan's true intentions were.

So far, Kaa had already been right about one thing: Shere Khan clearly couldn't be trusted. Not only had he switched bodies with my mate and denied it, but he had given me a fake antidote on purpose.

The main question I had was *why?* What was the point in all of this? Was it some sort of power trip? Or was there some larger reason behind *everything?*

"I'll just put this in here for safekeeping," Kaa said, placing the vial in one of her desk drawers. Her gold eyes met mine. "I think there's something else we should discuss while you're here."

"Oh?" I eyed her curiously.

"I know you're wondering why I think you're a Serpent."

"Yes. I am curious. I just don't think there's anything

Serpent-like about me, but you're not the first one who's said this about me."

"There are a few things that make me think it," Kaa explained. "You're very olive skin-toned. Of course, anyone can have an olive skin tone, but it's very common among Serpents. Your body type is also very typical of a snake shifter. Most of us tend to be very thin, and a lot of us are on the shorter side." She paused. "You are cold-blooded."

"I *am*?" I just stared back at her, completely confused. How could I have been cold-blooded? What did that even *mean*?

Kaa nodded. "One of my Serpent abilities is that I'm able to feel someone's blood temperature from across the room. Yours, my dear, is cold."

I frowned. "But wouldn't I have somehow known before now if I was cold-blooded? My temperature was always normal whenever I took it back in the human world."

"Human thermometers aren't designed to work on cold-blooded human beings," she explained. "The thermometer just shows a regular reading."

"Oh. Hmm." I paused for a moment, allowing myself to process all of this. "But *why* am I cold-blooded if I'm not a Serpent?"

"Are you certain that you're not?" Kaa asked.

"I'm positive. I've shifted for the first time already."

"What type of shifter are you, if you don't mind me asking?"

I hesitated for a moment. Even though I had barely told anyone the truth about what I was, I just felt so comfortable with her.

"I'm a werebear," I answered.

"A *werebear*?" Kaa stared back at me. The look behind her eyes told me she was completely unconvinced. She shook her head. "You don't even look like a werebear."

"Well, I am one." I shrugged.

"Do you want my honest opinion, Lena? An opinion that I have formed mostly through intuition?"

I nodded.

"I'm pretty sure that this is what makes you the one the prophecy is about."

"You knew." Not that it surprised me. All of the Legends seemed to know.

"Yes." Kaa's gold eyes locked on mine. "And I'm pretty sure that your shifter race is far more complicated than you've realized yet. I think you have only *begun* to peel back the layers to your onion."

~

"I can't even wait! Baloo is the professor who I've been most looking forward to meeting," Katerina said on Thursday night as she, Patrick, and I headed for our Advanced Werebear Studies classroom.

"I'm looking forward to it, too," I admitted. I *was* excited, but it didn't have much to do with Baloo. Don't get me wrong; it was pretty cool to know we would be taught by the most legendary bear shifter to ever exist. But what I was mostly excited about was learning more about my shifter race.

It wasn't like I was completely in the dark about werebears. I knew a decent amount about our kind, mostly thanks to Katerina. But I knew I still had a lot left to learn.

I also wondered if Baloo might have some sort of explanation as to why I was cold-blooded. I had been wracking my brain since my meeting with Kaa, and I still hadn't been able to figure out a reasonable explanation.

The one thing I *wasn't* looking forward to when it came to Advanced Werebear Studies was the other students.

Katerina may have been one of my best friends, but honestly? She and Patrick were just about the only werebears I was cool with.

I knew it probably sounded ridiculous, but I was actually *afraid* of other werebears. I mean, I still had no idea who the "three bears" were or why they had ransacked our dorm room. I often found myself wondering what they could have possibly been looking for and, more importantly, if they had ended up finding whatever it was. Now I was about to enter a classroom that I imagined would be made up entirely of werebears, and I had no idea who I should and shouldn't have been suspicious of.

I tried to push the thought to the back of my mind as we reached the Werebear Tower.

Patrick and Katerina stepped inside the building. But for some reason, I just froze as a shiver crept down my spine.

"Are you okay, Lena?" Katerina asked, a look of worry in her eyes.

I wasn't sure what it was about this tower, but something about it *still* gave me bad vibes. There was just something so dark and eerie about this tower, which housed the werebear classes and dorm rooms. It almost felt sort of haunted.

"Yeah, I'm okay," I muttered, trying to shake away the strange feeling as I followed them through the door.

When we entered our classroom, Baloo was already standing at the front of the room. I couldn't help but feel sort of surprised by the way he looked.

He didn't appear to be any older than his late 30s. He had short black hair and a dark beard with some salt and pepper streaks throughout.

Like pretty much all werebears (besides me, obviously), he

was tall, with muscular shoulders and an otherwise slender frame. Honestly? I felt sort of deceived by the Disney version of Baloo; nothing about this guy told me he overindulged in the bare necessities.

"*He did just rise from the dead,*" Harden reminded me through my thoughts.

"*The lack of privacy around here,*" I responded, rolling my eyes. "*Aren't you supposed to be in your Advanced Cat Shifter Studies right now?*"

"*Touché. I'll butt out of your thoughts until later.*"

As Katerina, Patrick, and I took three empty seats towards the front of the classroom, I glanced around awkwardly. We were the last students to enter the room. It felt like they had all been waiting for us to arrive so he could start his lesson.

"Good evening, students. I am Baloo. I am sure that you have all probably heard of me by now. During my time, I was the King of the Bears. I have gone down in history to be one of the most famous bears to ever reign. Although that is exciting, in some ways, it's also mildly disappointing to think that no one has ever carried on my legacy to be greater than me. Hopefully, one of you will do so." He glanced around the classroom. "We have a lot of material to cover in this course, but I think it's important for us all to become better acquainted with one another first. So, for this class, we're going to try an exercise."

Katerina glanced over at me with an eye roll, and I knew we were thinking the same thing: *Another freaking exercise?*

"We're going to split off into groups of four. Just form a group with any four students, but make sure you don't already know them yet. We're going to take a few minutes to talk and *really* get to know each other."

Oh, great. This was the one class where I didn't *want* to be introduced to my peers. And yet here we were, being forced to do full-on group introductions.

"So, let's begin," Baloo instructed.

I shot Katerina an '*Are we really being forced to do this?*' glance. She looked just as upset about this exercise as I was. I knew she hated the idea of being forced to talk to other students who might judge her for the war her parents had started.

We started to fall into our groups.

"Hey," a tall girl with light brown hair and glasses said. "I'm Rory, short for Aurora."

"I'm Lena," I told her.

"I know." She leaned in closer to me and whispered, "*Everyone* knows who you are."

I knew she probably wasn't exactly wrong.

Another tall girl with short blonde hair and fair skin joined us. "Are you really a werebear, Lena? You're so short."

I suppressed my eye roll. I was so tired of hearing that.

"I don't know what my shifter race is yet," I lied.

"Well, you probably shouldn't be in this class then. Why *are* you?" She stared at me like I was somehow intruding on all of the bear shifter secrets we might learn about. If only she knew the truth—that I was probably going to be her Queen one day.

"It's possible that I could be a bear," I replied.

"Hmm." She stared at me, scrutinizing me, for a long moment. "I'm Candy."

"That seems like an odd name choice since you're not very sweet," Rory commented.

I held back my smile. It seemed like Rory was sticking up for me.

"Hey, ladies," a tall guy with light brown hair said as he approached us. "I'm Kevin."

"Lena," I said.

"I'm Candy."

"And I'm Rory."

"What type of bears are you guys? I'm a Kodiak bear," Kevin informed us.

"I'm a honey bear," Candi said. "That's how I got my name. Candy. Honey. Get it?"

Rory shot a glance in my direction and rolled her eyes.

I held back a laugh. I was glad I wasn't the only one who didn't like Candy.

"I'm a black bear," Rory said.

When Kevin's eyes landed on me, I shrugged. "There's a chance that I *could* be a black bear, but I don't really know my shifter race yet."

"Oh, wow. Late bloomer, huh?" he asked.

"Something like that," I muttered.

A few seconds later, Baloo blew a whistle. "Let's move onto new groups!"

I walked over to another girl who I'd never seen before.

"Hey, I'm Angela." The girl, who had dark skin and eyes, introduced herself. "And you are?"

"Lena," I replied.

"Lena Falcone?"

I nodded.

"I've heard of you. You're that girl who couldn't be sorted in the right shifter race during the Sorting Ceremony."

"Yeah. That would be me."

"So, you're a bear?" Angela asked.

"Of course she is," a voice said from behind me.

I glanced over my shoulder and found Cal, the guy who I'd met at the Bear Ball, standing behind me. "Hey, Lena. Do you remember me?"

"How could I forget?" I asked, hoping the bitterness wasn't obvious in my voice.

"What type of bear are you?" Cal asked.

"Yeah, Lena. Tell us what type of bear shifter you are." Dom, the other guy from the Bear Ball, approached me.

I froze.

I didn't like Dom—not even a little bit.

He was from the second most powerful line of bears. *If* something were to happen to Katerina, he would have been the next in line to be the next King the Bears. For that reason, he had asked me to help him get rid of Katerina.

Obviously, I had told him there was no way I would be willing to kill my best friend—or lead her to him to be killed.

I might have only been imagining it, but I couldn't help but think he looked irritated by me. He was probably listening in on my thoughts right now, considering that was one of his abilities.

"I'm not sure if I'm a bear at all. If I am, I might be a black bear. What type of bears are all of you?" Even though Dom had mentioned the powerful line of bears he came from, I realized he hadn't actually mentioned what type of bear he was.

"I'm a polar bear," Angela told us.

"I'm a grizzly bear," Dom replied. "*Prince* of the Grizzly Bears."

"And so am I," Cal added.

Hmm. Suddenly, all of this made a lot of sense.

Grizzly Bears weren't known to be the most loyal species of werebears. In fact, quite the contrary; they were known to be traitorous and deceitful.

A thought occurred to me then, one that I had never even considered before now.

The Bear Ball had taken place the weekend before the shifter world war had begun. The following Wednesday, right before we had been forced to leave campus, our dorm room had been ransacked.

Given the close proximity of the two events, I suddenly

began to wonder if Dom was behind our dorm room being ransacked.

I thought about the note they had left.

Come be our Goldie Locks. – The 3 Bears.

What if the reference to being their Goldie Locks somehow represented them wanting me to be the one who killed Katerina for them? I knew it might have sounded far-fetched, but a weird feeling had begun to form in the pit of my stomach.

Was it possible that Dom and Cal were two of the three bears?

At that moment, I noticed Dom glancing over in my direction. There was no doubt he had just listened in on my thoughts.

And if I wasn't right, then why wasn't he even trying to deny any of this?

FIFTEEN

"That class was not what I was expecting," Katerina commented once we were back in our dorm room that night. Alexis was spending the night in Sean's dorm room, so it was just the two of us tonight.

"Me either." I paused. "Listen, there's something I need to tell you."

"Oh? What is it, love?" Katerina plopped down on her bed and glanced over at me.

I hesitated. I wasn't sure how to tell her any of this—or why I'd sat on it for so long instead of telling her about it.

"Do you remember when I got the invitation to the Bear Ball?" I asked her.

"Yeah, of course I remember. I never understood why you got invited, and I should have gotten invited since I'm the Princess of the Bears." She still sounded bitter over the fact she had been excluded. "Anyway, what makes you ask?"

"Something happened that night. Something I completely forgot to tell you."

"Oh?" She looked curious.

"You know that guy Dom in our class tonight?" I asked her.

"Dominik Volkov. I simply can't stand him." She rolled her eyes. "No grizzly bear is great, but Dominik is the *worst* of the worst." She shook her head. "But what about him?"

"Dom was the entire reason I was invited to the Bear Ball," I explained. "He wanted to talk to me that night... and it had nothing to do with me. It had to do with *you*."

"Me?" She let out a little laugh. "What about *me* could have made Dominik invite you to the Bear Ball?"

"He asked me if I would help him kill you."

All of the color faded from her face. "I'm sorry. What?"

"Dom asked me to kill you or help lead you to him so that he could kill you or arrange to have you killed," I explained. "I completely forgot about it until class tonight."

"I'm a little confused, Lena. Why didn't you tell me about this at the time?" Her eyes met mine. "How could you possibly forget something like that?"

"Everything happened so fast. The Bear Ball came and went, and then we were forced to leave school—"

"We left campus on a Wednesday," Katerina recalled. "The Bear Ball took place over the weekend, didn't it?"

"Yeah. I just didn't know exactly how to tell you about it at the time, so I waited... and then I waited too long."

"Your failure to tell me could have gotten me killed, Lena." She looked incredibly disappointed by the fact that I had withheld this from her for so long. I didn't blame her. I felt like the worst friend ever.

"I'm sorry. It was a huge mistake on my part. I should have told you right away." I paused for a moment and then admitted, "I was probably too wrapped up in my mates to think straight at the time, if we're being honest. I really fucked up, though."

"It's alright, I suppose. I'm here... thankfully." She paused for a moment, seeming to process everything I'd just told her. "Let me guess. The reason Dominik wants to kill me is because he would be the next King to ascend the bear throne in the event of my death?"

I nodded. "Yeah, that's exactly what he said."

She let out a little laugh. "He's bloody delusional. If only he knew that he's been banned from ever ruling the bear throne."

"He *has*?"

"Well, not him, specifically. It isn't just my parents' rules that are preventing me from ever marrying a grizzly bear or a panda bear. Both of those kinds of bears are banned from ever ruling the throne," she explained. "The reason is because they're one of the shifter race species or subspecies that has been banned from ever being allowed to rule all of the shifter races—along with snow leopards, foxes, and serpents."

"Really? None of those races are allowed to ever rule the shifters?" This was news to me.

"Really."

"Why is that?" I asked her. I was sort of surprised that they had never taught us in any of our classes yet. Shouldn't this have been important information for us to know? For *me*, as the next Queen of the Shifters, to know?

"It all has to do with old agreements that were made with the bears and werewolves in the past," she explained. "The werewolves basically told the serpents, snow leopards, and foxes that they would only ally with them under the agreement that they would remain on the bottom of the hierarchy. *If*—and this is extremely unlikely to ever happen to begin with—the serpents or foxes should ever find a way to make it to the top of the hierarchy, they would need to agree to give up their spot to the werewolves to reign."

Katerina paused for a moment. "As for the bears, a similar agreement was made. Back in the day, King Alexander—that would be my five-times-great-grandfather—made an agreement that either the grizzly bears and panda bears could not fully reign if they wanted to remain a part of the Bear Kingdom at all. Our subspecies came very close to dividing into two separate kingdoms, but they ended up signing the agreement. Apparently, Dominik thinks he can change this Bear Kingdom law in the event of my death. He's gone completely mad. There's no way anyone would allow that to happen."

"Are there other bear princes and princesses besides him?" I asked.

"Besides him? Is that what he told you? That he's a prince?"

I nodded.

She let out a little chuckle. "He's not a prince. A prince needs to be crowned. Dominik did not receive that level of royal treatment. He is simply from a 'good' grizzly bear bloodline... if such a thing even exists. I don't believe there are good grizzly bears, but we know I'm biased." She rolled her eyes. "Regardless, there are other bear shifters from even better bloodlines, including ones who are *not* grizzly bears. We don't even know that I'm next in line to be the Queen of the Bears now," she reminded me. "But *if* I am, and assuming that something should ever happen to me, I believe that kid Kaden in our class would be the next in line to be King of the Bears. He's from a very powerful honey bear shifter line."

"Well, that's relieving, at least." Knowing that Dom was simply delusional and that he wouldn't actually ever be King made me feel better. He was the villainous type of shifter who didn't deserve to rule any kingdom.

"Relieving, yes, but I clearly need to watch out for him. You should, too, Lena." She shot a look in my direction. "You never know who can be trusted around here."

At that moment, the door to our dorm room flew open, and Alexis stepped inside. Tears were streaming down her face.

"Are you okay?" I asked her.

"No, I'm not." She sniffed. "I just had a vision, you guys—my first vision ever."

Katerina stood up and moved across the room. Sitting down on the bed next to her, she touched her shoulder gently. "What happened, love?"

"Sean's mom talked him out of marrying me," she explained, her tears streaming down her cheeks. "He agreed not to marry me. So, I left his dorm room. He doesn't even know about it yet, but I'm pre-angry at him... and so, so hurt."

"I'm confused. I thought Sean's mom really liked you. Why would she talk him out of marrying you?" I asked.

"Because I don't come from a Royal bloodline," Alexis replied with an eye roll.

"That's rubbish! If it's good enough for Prince William and Kate Middleton, it should be good enough in our world, too." Katerina paused. "Besides, the foxes will never rule the entire shifter world—no offense. What difference does it even make if Sean marries a Royal or not?"

"I know that, and *you* know that." Alexis agreed with a nod. "But apparently, Sean doesn't know that or we wouldn't be in this predicament. Well, in the future, that is. I know it hasn't actually happened yet."

"Maybe you could talk to him about it. Let him know what his mum is planning," Katerina suggested. "If he knows what her intentions are ahead of time, then maybe he'll make a different decision when and if the time comes."

"Maybe." Alexis didn't look too convinced.

"Is it possible that maybe your vision was wrong?" I asked. "You said it was your first vision, so maybe it won't actually turn out to be accurate, anyway."

"I don't know. It felt so... *real*."

"Well, maybe there's a part of the vision that you've yet to unlock yet. Maybe you simply haven't seen the part where Sean comes to his senses," Katerina said.

"I hope so, because I can't imagine what it would be like for your mate to marry someone else. Someone who isn't you." Alexis started crying again.

"That sounds bloody terrible," Katerina agreed.

It made me think about my own situation. Three of my mates were going to experience exactly that...

I couldn't even begin to imagine how they would feel to be the one who wasn't chosen. And it made me feel guilty as fuck to know that I would be the one causing them to feel that way. It wasn't fair to anyone involved. And even though deep down I knew it wasn't my fault, I couldn't help but feel like a monster.

CHAPTER
SIXTEEN

The weeks started to pass by quickly. Our instructors really started to pile on the homework, so it felt like the majority of my time was spent in my dorm room or at the library. I barely had time to spend time with my mates, and I hated it. I'd known this would be the most grueling year, but I hadn't expected I would be missing my mates so much. I'd thought I would see them as much as I'd seen them every other year.

One Friday night, I was just finishing up an assignment when my phone beeped with an incoming text message. I looked to see who it was.

Rafael.

My heart did a little flip. This was the first time he had texted me since Shere Khan had taken over his body.

With shaky hands, I opened the message.

Rafael: Hey, Lena. I was thinking of going for a swim at the Lagoon. Would you like to join me?

My heart pounded against my chest as hope spread through

JODY MORSE & JAYME MORSE

me. Was it possible that Raf's memories were back? I mean, why else would he have been texting me? He had to have finally remembered me.

So much hope washed over me as I texted him back.

Lena: I would love to join you. Meet you there in 10 minutes?

Rafael: Sounds good.

Grabbing my black bikini from my dresser, I headed for the bathroom. I tried not to get my hopes up *too* high, but honestly?

This was the best thing that had happened to me since the school year had started.

When I entered the Lagoon, I saw Rafael standing there waiting for me. His back was turned, and he was staring out at the rainforest that lay ahead of us.

It was loud today, between the birds chirping away at one another and the water trickling down from the tops of the trees. I wished it wasn't so foggy. I wanted to see all the brightly colored toucans and macaws. I forgot how relaxing the Lagoon was. But that wasn't why I was here; I had to stay focused.

I cleared my throat as I walked over to him.

He glanced over his shoulder at me, his emerald green eyes locking on mine.

"Hey, Lena." A smile tugged at his lips.

"Hey." I smiled back at him.

The silence hung in the air between us. There were so many

things I wanted to ask him, but I didn't want to overwhelm him. I was just going to let him take the lead.

He just continued to stare at me for a few moments. "Shall we go for a swim?"

"Yeah. Let's do it."

Reaching out, he grabbed my hand.

It caught me off-guard at first, but I laced my fingers in his. I couldn't control the smile that hit my lips.

More confirmation of his memories returning, I thought as he turned and began to lead me to the water.

As Raf let go of my hand and we entered the water, I took it all in. It looked even bluer than I remembered; it was like the clearest of oceans.

It felt completely magical to be there with him... my mate.

It felt like everything had finally fallen back into place.

"So," Rafael said, his eyes locking on mine. "You're probably wondering why I invited you to come swimming with me tonight."

"Well, I figured it was because your memories came back?" I glanced over at him.

"Unfortunately, my memories of you haven't returned yet."

A sinking feeling came over me. "Oh..."

"I'm sorry," he apologized.

"It's not your fault," I assured him.

"I know, but I feel like it is. This isn't how I want things to be." Rafael looked just as disappointed as I felt.

"I'm a little confused. If you still don't remember, then why did you text me? And, more importantly, *how* did you text me? How did you even know my number?"

"Well, I realized I had someone named Lena in my cell phone contacts. I don't know of anyone else named Lena, so I knew it had to have been your number." He paused. "As for *why*

I texted you… The rest of the Alpha Brotherhood told me about us, Lena."

"What, exactly, did they tell you?"

"Everything. I know about the prophecy. I know that you're the future Queen of the Shifters. They told me that we're mates —that we're *all* your mates. I wish I could remember you, but I just don't. My first memory of you is at the castle on National Felidae Day. The very first time I saw you."

"I see."

So much for everything falling into place…

I blinked back the tears that stabbed at my eyes. I knew that I probably shouldn't have gotten my hopes up about his memories being restored, but it had really seemed that way.

"But here's the thing, Lena." He reached out and grabbed my hand. "Just because I don't remember you or know you doesn't mean I don't *want* to. From the moment I first laid eyes on you, I knew there was something different about you. I just feel this… this *pull*… towards you. It really sucks that I don't remember you, but let me learn everything there is to know about you now. Give me the chance to get to know you."

Even though it made me sad to think that the memories we had already made together could be lost forever, I knew Rafael was right. There was really nothing we could do but move forward at this point.

"Okay," I finally agreed with a nod. "We'll just have to make new memories together."

"Exactly." Wrapping his arms around my waist, he pulled me onto his lap. His eyes didn't move from mine. "We've kissed before, haven't we?"

I nodded. "Yes. Many times."

"Well, for me this will be the first time," Raf whispered as he brought his lips to mine.

As our mouths met, I couldn't help but notice how different his kiss was this time.

His usual urgency was replaced with a slow sense of exploration. I got the sense that he was trying to learn every crevice of my mouth.

When we finally broke the kiss, his eyes locked on mine again. "Kissing you feels familiar."

"It does?"

He nodded. "It's almost like déjà vu. It feels like I've done this before, even though I don't exactly remember it."

"Hmm." I tried not to let my overwhelming sadness show, but it just made me so sad that he didn't remember our first kiss... or any of the hundreds of kisses we'd shared before now.

"Know what I'm thinking?" Rafael asked.

"What?"

"I'm thinking that I should just keep kissing you," he replied. "Maybe if I kiss you enough, it will somehow jog my memory."

As his lips came down on mine again, I just hoped he was right.

SEVENTEEN

"The connection a Royal shifter has with his or her mate is different from the bond other shifters experience with their mates," Byakko said as she stood in front of the classroom. "These differences are both emotional and physical."

She wrote both words on the chalkboard.

"Let's discuss the emotional differences first. Every shifter can sense his or her mate's feelings. They are able to communicate with one another through mind-speak. Many of them can sense when their mate is in danger or if something has happened to him or her. All of these feelings are heightened when it comes to Royal mates." Byakko glanced around the room. "Most Royal mates—males, especially—are generally able to feel their mate's emotions so strongly. And when they're in danger, their mate doesn't just helplessly feel it. They are often able to locate their mates. It's as if they have an internal compass that leads them in the right direction."

I breathed a slight sigh of relief. If I should ever end up in any sort of danger, hopefully at least *one* of my mates would be able to locate me. It was pretty reassuring that I would have four chances of being found. *If* Rafael's inner compass was still working, despite the memory loss.

"Now, onto some of the physical differences." She glanced around at the classroom. "One of these is sexual. There's no doubt that shifter sex, in general, tends to be a lot more intense than human sex. At least, that's what we all assume, based on what we've heard about human sex," she said with a little laugh. "No one in this classroom will ever experience this first-hand, since we are not human. So, while shifter sex is known to be intense..." She trailed off, as if trying to put her thoughts into words.

"Sex between Royal shifters is mind-blowing, by comparison," Bagheera said as he entered the classroom. He walked over to his mate and kissed her on the cheek. Then he turned to face us. "There is no reason or explanation for this. It simply *is*."

I thought about it for a moment. I had yet to have sex with all of my mates yet, but there was no doubt that sex with Damon was unlike anything I had ever experienced in my life. It was... well mind-blowing truly *was* a good definition for it. It was incomparable to anything I'd ever known.

But it wasn't like I had very much to compare it to. I'd never even had sex with a human before. The only guy who I'd ever slept with before Damon was Jake. And considering Jake was a Royal shifter, too, shouldn't it have been just as '*mind-blowing*'?

Byakko glanced over at me then, and I knew she had overheard my thoughts. It felt like she was directly answering me as she spoke. "Royal shifters, in general, tend to have stronger sexual connections than shifters do. But Royal shifters who are *mated* to one another have the deepest sexual connections of anyone in this entire world."

Oh. *Duh.* I hadn't even considered the whole mate aspect. Obviously, it was going to be a lot better with Damon than it had been with Jake.

I wondered what it would be like with the rest of my mates...

Even more than that, I wondered when I would find out. I hadn't even tried to complete the bonding process with Harden or Ezra since things had gotten so messed up the night I'd tried with Rafael.

Deep down, I was sort of afraid that if I tried to initiate sex with any of them, something else would go terribly wrong. I couldn't handle it if *another* one of my mates lost his memory. But I knew I needed to overcome my fear, since it was all a part of the prophecy. If I didn't complete the bonding process with Harden, Ezra, and eventually Rafael, the future of the entire shifter world was going to be disrupted.

And it wasn't like I didn't *want* to do this with my other mates. Because I did—I *so* did. I was just scared shitless of things changing in a bad way.

"There is another physical side effect that comes with the territory of being mated to a Royal that you should all be very aware of. This is an uncomfortable subject, but it's an important one," Byakko continued, snapping me out of my thoughts about my mates. I dreaded whatever she was going to say next, because so far, the whole class had been pretty uncomfortable.

As her brown eyes flicked over to meet mine, it again felt like she was speaking to me. "This one involves death."

Katerina shot a nervous glance in my direction as I felt a knot tighten in my stomach.

"Many of you have probably heard by now that it's possible to die from a broken heart if your mate dies. Well, this *is* true. The only situations where it has ever been documented, however, are between Royal mates."

Well, shit.

This wasn't good.

If any of my mates died, my own life might end. My risk of

dying was higher than *anyone's*, considering there were *four* of them and only *one* of me.

Not that I thought any of my mates were going to die. I hoped they wouldn't die. But considering we were in the middle of a war... Well, it was definitely a possibility.

The thing was, my death would have been *worse*. My death wouldn't just risk killing *one* mate. There was a possibility my death would cause all four of my mates to die. It seemed incredibly unfair.

"*Stop thinking so negatively, Lena,*" Ezra's voice filled my mind. "*You're going to be just fine. We're all going to be just fine.*"

I hoped he was right.

"Now, I want you all to keep in mind that this isn't *always* the case," Byakko continued. "There have been plenty of Royal shifters who survived after their mates passed. But others weren't so lucky." She paused for a moment and then added, "Bagheera and I were an example of this phenomenon. When he was murdered by Shere Khan, I died, too."

Two more legendary shifters who had been murdered by Shere Khan.

"And I wouldn't have wanted it any other way," she added. "See, that's the thing about being mated to anyone, Royal or not. Once your mate is gone, your heart can't simply can't stand the idea of life without them. As tragic as it is, Royals truly are the lucky ones."

I allowed her words to sink in, and I knew I agreed with them.

I would have rather died than have been without any of my mates—which led me to a very important question.

How the hell was I going to choose only one of them in the end?

That afternoon, I picked out a book at the library for some research I had to do for a project Shere Khan had assigned for Ancient Royal History when I saw her, sitting at a table.

Rachel.

I didn't even think twice about what I was doing. I headed over to her table and sat down beside her.

"Hey," I said.

As her eyes flicked over to meet mine, her lips formed a flat line. "Lena..."

"Rachel, listen. Please?" I asked.

She rolled her eyes and then nodded. "Fine."

"I'm sorry. The truth is, I just didn't know how to tell you about all of this. Everything was so overwhelming. I was still trying to get over my parents' deaths when Ezra, that guy from the carnival who kissed me, came to my window that night. He told me I was a shifter. He brought me to this place that I didn't even know existed. I learned that my parents had kept this huge secret from me, for whatever reason. I wanted to reach out, but honestly? I was in such a confusing place. And it's only gotten *more* confusing since then. But I really *do* miss you. Please forgive me?"

Rachel sighed. "I miss you, too, Lena. I'd rather move past this than not have you in my life at all."

A mix of excitement and relief washed over me. "I'm so glad. I have so much to catch you up on, but first I just need to know. What type of shifter are you? And how did I never know about it?"

"I'm a werewolf," she replied. "And, well, you never knew about it because I wasn't born this way." Her eyes met mine with a look of sadness. "I was bitten."

"*Really?*" It wasn't that shifters who were bitten didn't exist, but I hadn't met very many of them. There was one girl who I had classes with during my first year, but otherwise, everyone else at Shifter Academy had been born into this life—at least, as far as I knew.

"Yeah. It was the craziest thing. I was in a car accident," Rachel explained. "When I woke up, there was a letter from someone letting me know that they had bitten me to save my life. Apparently, I would have died if they didn't turn me into a werewolf. In the note, they told me I should get in touch with Shifter Academy immediately. I didn't believe it at first, so it took me a little while. Obviously, at first, I didn't even *believe* the letter could be true. I got it on April First, so I thought it was an April Fool's Joke or something. It just all sounded so far-fetched. But then I turned into a werewolf for the very first time, which was scary as hell, so I had no choice but to believe it. I knew I needed help. I didn't want to be the only werewolf I knew, so I got in touch with Shifter Academy, and well, here I am."

"Wow. I'm so glad that shifter bit you." I couldn't even imagine losing both my parents *and* one of my best friends, even if I hadn't talked to her in forever until now. And the scariest part of it was that I probably wouldn't have even found out about it for a while. "Did you ever figure out who saved your life?"

She shook her head. "No, the letter was completely anonymous." She paused. "I know this is going to sound crazy, but the whole thing gives me a weird feeling. The car accident was so... weird."

"Weird how?" I questioned.

"The reason I crashed the car is because I couldn't get my brakes to work." She met my gaze. "I think someone might have done something to them."

"What are you saying, exactly?"

"I think someone cut my brakes," Rachel replied.

I frowned. "Why would someone do that? *Who* would do something like that?"

"I don't know. Like I said, it sounds crazy, but... I just get this feeling that someone wanted me to die."

I thought about it for a moment. "I don't think someone wanted you to die. I think someone wanted you to become a shifter."

Her eyebrows lifted. "How do you figure?"

"I can't figure out why they wanted you to crash your car first, when they could have just turned you some other way, but... Think about it. You get into this car accident and almost die, and some werewolf just *happens* to be waiting on the sidelines at the scene of the accident just in time to save your life? I'm not sure if I completely buy that. I'm not saying it couldn't happen, but I'm just not sure if it did. It almost seems premeditated, and I can't help but wonder if it has to do with me."

"You?" Rachel stared at me blankly.

"You're one of my best friends. Is it possible that someone wanted to bring you to Shifter Academy for that reason?"

She raised her eyebrows. "What would be the point in that?"

"I haven't figured that part out yet." But somehow, I just *knew*, deep down, that I was right. Rachel was a shifter *because of me*. And I felt sort of guilty about that. Even though I loved my mates, I would never *choose* this life. Don't get me wrong. It came with a lot of perks. It was cool to be able to move so quickly and have amplified senses. And even though I complained about my mates hearing my thoughts and as annoying as it was at times, I loved that I had the ability to communicate with my mates without having to text them. It didn't just make life easier. It was comforting knowing they were always a thought away.

But there were also a lot of downsides to being a shifter, too.

Living in a realm that was currently in the middle of a war was one of them. I felt safe at Shifter Academy, but it almost felt like we were trapped here. It was the only place we had protection. If we were to go anywhere else, we could have been putting our lives at risk.

There was also a lot of pressure to become the best shifter you could be. Obviously, that pressure was heightened for Royals, but every shifter at the academy needed to worry about becoming the best shifters they could be.

There would be even *more* downsides for Rachel. She had to go to school in the shifter realm, even though her family was back in the human world. I didn't have anyone back there. Well, except for Aunt Lily, who I hadn't even spoken to since before I'd left the human realm.

I glanced over at Rachel then. "Do you know how my aunt's doing?"

"I actually bumped into her and her fiancé at the mall over the summer."

"She's *engaged*?" I was shocked, to say the least. My aunt's dating life had been a train wreck before I'd left.

"Yeah. His name is Josh. He's a college professor."

"Wow. Good for her." I was happy for her. It made me relieved that she had someone in her life, someone who was a constant. My parents and I were all my aunt had, and all of us had left her in one way or another. I was grateful she had Josh now.

"She thinks you're dead, you know." Rachel glanced over at me. "Just like everyone else."

I sighed. "I'm going to have to visit her at some point." As soon as I could... but who knew when *that* would be?

The truth was, I actually *wanted* to visit the human realm. It was just a matter of finding time. I knew that wasn't going to be easy this year with how intense my coursework was.

"I'll be going home to visit my family at least once a month, so maybe we can go together," Rachel suggested.

"That sounds great. I would love to visit your parents, too." And having Rachel visit Aunt Lily with me might have been a really good buffer. I wasn't sure how my aunt was going to take my reappearance.

"How are you going to explain your absence to everyone?" Rachel asked.

I shook my head. "I don't know what I'll tell your family. You can help me come up with something. As for Aunt Lily..." I thought about it. "She should already know I'm a shifter. She should be one, too."

A part of me sort of wanted to talk to her about it. I had this feeling that she had answers to some of my questions.

Maybe she knew something about why the King of the Serpents had wanted to kill my parents.

Maybe, together, we could crack this... and still avenge my parents' murders.

EIGHTEEN

When I got to my Potions and Poisons class on Friday morning, Professor Kaa was waiting for me. "Lena, can you please go wait in my office for me? I'll be there in just a minute."

"Sure, no problem." I walked back out of the classroom and headed across the hall.

As I entered her office, I was surprised to find that someone was already in there: Princess Kaa.

Her gold eyes flicked over to meet mine as I entered the room.

"Hello, Lena," she said politely.

"Hello," I replied awkwardly. I had actually never spoken to Kaa before, even though we had survived a whole entire boot-camp together and had classes with each other. "I'm sorry. I didn't realize you needed to talk to your..." I paused, unsure of their relation to one another. They had the same name and Princess Kaa had obviously descended from the Legend Kaa, but that didn't say much. I settled on saying, "To Kaa."

"No need to apologize, Lena. My grandmother invited me here to meet with the two of you."

"Oh."

I wondered what Professor Kaa could have possibly wanted us to discuss together. Princess Kaa wasn't even in this class with me.

"Yeah. I thought it was weird, too." Princess Kaa shrugged. Pausing for a moment, she added, "My grandmother seems to be very fond of you."

"She's a really nice woman," I replied.

"Actually, that's the thing." She lowered her voice. "Between you and me, my grandmother *isn't* the kindest or most welcoming woman. Some days, I'm not even sure if she likes me or our entire family, and we're her *descendants*. We're her own blood. So, it's actually a really big deal that she likes you so much." There was a hint of jealousy in her tone.

"Oh, wow. I didn't realize." I wasn't sure why that surprised me. I also couldn't help but wonder *why* Kaa liked me so much. I hadn't even done anything that extraordinary for her to take such a liking to me. At least, not in my opinion, anyway.

"Yeah. I wonder if this has something to do with the bears," Princess Kaa wondered out loud.

I glanced over at her sharply. "The bears?"

It seemed like an odd thing for her to say. Was it possible she somehow knew *I* was a werebear?

Then again, I supposed it wouldn't have been too far-fetched. Maybe Professor Kaa had told her descendants about my shifter race. Princess Kaa made it sound like they all saw each other regularly.

Princess Kaa opened her mouth to respond, just as Kaa came into the room and closed the door behind her.

"Hello, ladies." She smiled at us. "You are probably wondering why I brought the two of you together today."

That was an understatement. I was confused as hell.

"I *am* curious, Grandma," Princess Kaa admitted.

"Me, too," I agreed, deciding there was no sense in denying it.

"The reason we're all here today is because I thought the two of you could learn from one another—you, especially, Kaa. I know that you've led somewhat of a sheltered life when it comes to understanding other shifter races. It's time for you to break out of your comfort zone and become acquainted with someone from another shifter race," Kaa said. She turned to me. "And Lena, I know you are still fairly new to this world. Serpents are known to have a bad reputation, so I thought it might be a good idea for you to learn from one who you very well might have some things in common with."

I realized what Professor Kaa was doing.

She was trying to force a friendship between Princess Kaa and I. But the real question was *why?*

I wasn't buying the reasons she had given us. My intuition told me there was some ulterior motive behind all of this.

The truth was, I had mixed feelings about the whole thing. Even though Professor Kaa was right about learning from other shifters, I didn't *need* more friends. This year, I really didn't have time to make friends. With how heavy my course load was, I barely had time to see the friends I already had—not to mention my mates. I didn't want to waste time that I could have been spending with them by spending it with Princess Kaa instead. But that wasn't all.

I also knew there was no way Princess Kaa would mesh well with the friends I already had; Katerina, especially, wasn't her biggest fan. Somehow, I was going to have to keep this friendship on the DL—even *if* Professor Kaa was pretty much forcing it on us.

"Well, now that this is all settled," Professor Kaa said with a smile. I was pretty sure she was proud of herself for arranging this friendship. "Lena, can you please stay a little while longer? Kaa, you may go."

Princess Kaa nodded and turned to me. "I'll be in touch, Lena."

"Talk to you soon." I smiled at her.

Once she closed the door behind her, Kaa turned to me. "The silencing barrier is in place so she won't be able to hear us. I want you to know my true intentions here."

I was surprised that she was opening up to me but not to her however many times-great-granddaughter.

"Now that Cobra is gone, Princess Kaa is next in line to be the Queen of the Serpents," Kaa informed me.

"Oh. That's right." I hadn't even considered who was going to be the next heir to the Serpent throne now that not just one but *two* of the princes had been killed.

"I feel that it's very important for you and Princess Kaa to form an alliance with one another," Kaa told me. "Alliances begin with friendships."

I forced a smile. "Even though I know alliances are good to have, I'm not entirely sure why you think it's important for Princess Kaa and I to have one."

Kaa's gold eyes met mine. "My intuition tells me that this is very important for your future, Lena."

"Why?" I questioned.

"Just trust me on this. *Please.*" The begging look behind her eyes made it difficult for me to refuse.

"Fine. I'll be her friend," I agreed.

Kaa's eyes lit up with excitement. "Marvelous. Now, onto the other reason I asked you to meet with me this afternoon. I have the answer you have been waiting for. I know what's inside that vial. I got the report back from the toxicologist last night."

"The... toxicologist?" My eyebrows shot up. "I thought you

said it wasn't a poison."

"Toxicologists analyze both poisons *and* potions." She pulled the vial out of her desk drawer and set it on the table in front of me. "The contents of this vial are not a poison. They're also not a memory serum—not exactly, anyway."

I stared back at her blankly. "So, what *is* it?"

"This potion is for brain health. It contains a lot of essential vitamins and nutrients that may help restore one's memories," Kaa explained.

I noticed her choice of words. *May.*

"It can be an extremely powerful tool when it comes to memory restoration. It can restore *every* memory a shifter has ever had throughout their entire lifetime. That's the good news. The bad news, however..." She trailed off.

"What is it?" I asked.

"There is a very low likelihood that this potion will actually help restore his memories. It works in less than ten percent of the population. And it's the furthest thing from an instant fix. In cases where it *does* actually work, it can take anywhere from six months to three years to restore memories."

"So, it would be safe for me to give this serum to Rafael?" I asked her.

"Well. Yes. The potion is perfectly safe for him to consume," Kaa informed me with a nod. "But if I was you, I'm not entirely sure that I would waste my time. The odds of it actually working are obviously very low and it could take a very long time to see results. To be honest, I'm not entirely sure why Shere Khan thought it was even a good idea to give you this potion, knowing it's often not very effective."

"Yeah, I know." I nodded my agreement, even though I felt sort of the opposite way about this potion.

I couldn't believe Shere Khan had given me a potion and not

a poison. Even if the potion wasn't the most effective option, he actually *had* tried to help us restore Rafael's memories.

I wasn't going to lie. It made me hate Shere Khan less. A *whole lot* less.

"We should really return to the classroom now," Kaa said, glancing at the time on the wall. She shot a concerned glance in my direction. "*If* you choose to give your mate this potion, I would just be cautious. Understand that there are risks, which may be more harmful to you than they are to him."

I nodded. "I understand."

And I was telling the truth. I totally got everything she was saying. None of it was good. It worked in less than one out of ten shifters, and it took an incredibly long time for it to work its so-called magic. I understood all of that.

But at the same time, it actually gave me *hope*. There was a chance—even *if* it was less than a ten percent chance—that we might be able to bring Raf's memories back.

And that little bit of hope was all I really needed to feel okay about it.

"I don't know," Damon said as we sat on the rooftop of the Alpha Brotherhood's penthouse. "It's good to know that the potion won't hurt Rafael physically, but I agree with Kaa on this one. It could be hurtful to you. I just don't want you to get your hopes up knowing there's more than a ninety percent chance it won't even bring his memories back."

"I agree with Damon," Harden said with a nod.

"What about you?" I glanced over at Ezra, who was staying pretty silent.

"Well, I do agree with Damon and Harden." He paused, his blue eyes locking on mine. "But I also don't see the harm in giving it to him, either. What if there's a chance it *does* somehow work and restores his memories? What if Rafael is one of the less in ten who its effective for?"

"Even if it's effective, it will take at least six months," Damon said, shaking his head. "We don't have that long."

"We also have nothing to lose," Ezra pointed out. "It won't be a harmful potion."

"The alternative is that Rafael doesn't *ever* remember me. Can you imagine not having your own mate remember you?" I asked.

A softer look filled Damon's golden-brown eyes, but it quickly passed and was replaced by another look—one that I couldn't seem to identify.

"In six to three months, Rafael might not even *be* your mate, Lena," he said gently. "If you choose someone else to be King, it will end your bond with him. Wouldn't it be more painful for him to remember everything that's happened between you *after* the mate bond between you has already been undone?"

"What if Rafael remembers me *before* I make a decision?" I paused for a moment and then spoke my thoughts out loud. "What if it's actually meant to be him? What if we might not even get to find out if it was meant to be him unless his memory comes back?"

"I'm just trying to think of the most realistic scenario here, Lena." There was a sympathetic look behind his eyes. "Once you make a decision, three of us are going to have to get over you."

"So, you want to get over me?" I just stared back at him in total disbelief.

"I didn't say that, Lena. But the reality of this prophecy is that only one of us will get you in the end. Not four of us." He paused. "If not giving Rafael the potion helps make that process easier for him, then wouldn't it be worth it to not give it to him in the first place?"

"What if I actually choose Rafael in the end? You don't know who I'm going to pick, considering *I* don't even know who I'm going to pick at this point."

It almost felt, in a way, like Damon was trying to encourage me *not* to choose Rafael. I wondered if he was trying to increase his own chances of being chosen.

I glanced over at Harden and Ezra, who had both gone completely silent. I knew that thinking about the situation made them sad, but I was pretty sure they were probably surprised, too.

Damon and I never got this heated with one another. We had never actually fought before. But I was so, so angry at him.

How could he not want me to at least *try* to restore Rafael's memories of me?

There was obviously a very good chance that it might not work at all. But what if it *did?* It felt like I owed it to myself, and to Raf, to at least try.

Damon's golden-brown eyes fell on mine. "Do whatever you want, Lena. I've already given you my opinion."

Then, without saying another word, he walked across the rooftop and headed back inside the house, slamming the door behind him.

CHAPTER
NINETEEN

One Saturday morning in mid-December, I was in my dorm room studying for my midterm exams. I knew the hardest was going to be Advanced Weaponry. It wasn't a written exam, but a physical one instead.

We had to accurately demonstrate how to use three weapons in combat. I felt most comfortable with swords now that I knew how to use one, but I wasn't sure which other two to pick.

There were requirements for two of the weapons we had to choose. We had to pick one weapon that was laced with wolfsbane and dragon's blood. They were the deadliest weapons in existence, designed to kill almost all shifters. Of those, I was probably strongest with a bow and arrow or a club.

The other requirement was that we had to pick a firearm. That was the one that really got me. It wasn't that I completely sucked at shooting a gun, because I didn't. I was actually quite good at it. But guns made me nervous. Combine that nervousness with the overall nervousness of the exam, and well... eek.

Needless to say, I needed to figure out which firearm to pick, and I hadn't even narrowed it down to two or three yet.

Decisions, decisions.

There was a knock at the door then.

I rose to my feet, wondering who it could have been.

When I opened it, I was surprised to find Harden standing on the other side. I wasn't sure what it was, but he looked more attractive than usual.

"I cut my hair today," he explained, clearly listening in on my thoughts.

"Well, that must be it, then. It looks good." I smiled. "Anyway, what's up?"

It wasn't like him to come to my dorm room.

"Have you looked outside?" he asked.

I shook my head. Katerina kept our blackout curtains closed at all times.

"No, why?"

"I'll show you."

"Okay." Slipping into my jacket and winter boots, I followed him out into the hallway.

As we reached the glass door that led outside, I saw the snow falling. It had already begun to coat the sidewalks and grass.

"It's snowing." I smiled up at him.

Harden nodded. "Yeah. I knew there was no way you'd see it while you were couped in your dorm room, so I figured I'd drag you out here and show you."

"Thank you. I love snow. It's like glitter falling from the sky."

His violet eyes locked on mine. "You're so freaking cute, Lena. I can't stand it sometimes."

The intensity behind his gaze made my heart do cartwheels.

"I have a question for you." His eyes continued to linger on mine. "Where are you planning to spend Christmas Eve?"

"Oh, um. I don't know." Even though it was fast approaching, the truth was that I hadn't even considered it yet. Last year, we all spent the holiday together at the cabin. It had just been the four of us, hidden away from the rest of the world.

Things were different now. We no longer needed to hide from everyone... as much as I missed it just being the five of us, at times.

"So, Damon and I were talking about it. We were thinking about spending Christmas Eve in my kingdom and then Christmas Day in the Lion Kingdom. It will be good for Ezra to spend time with our families, considering everything that's gone on with his mom. Plus, you'll finally get to meet our families."

Even though it made me nervous, considering how much my other mates' moms disliked me, I knew that it was necessary.

I couldn't make a decision about who to marry, who to make my King and spend the rest of my life with, until I knew all of their families.

I wasn't sure if any of that even mattered, though. The fact that Ella Gray and Queen Bria both wanted me dead didn't change the fact that I was still madly in love with both of their sons. I wasn't sure how I was going to make a decision between the four of them, but I definitely wasn't about to not choose one of them just because of their moms.

Glancing up at Harden, I realized he was still waiting for an answer from me.

"I would love to come to your kingdom for Christmas Eve and to Damon's for Christmas Day. I can't wait to meet both of your families."

That was the truth. I really *did* want to meet their families.

"Okay." Harden paused. "There's something else, too. We

were thinking about spending New Year's Eve in the Tiger Kingdom."

I wrinkled my nose. "With Queen Bria."

"You don't have to come with us if you really don't want to. We just thought it would be fair for Rafael to get to spend a holiday with his family, too."

"I'll come. But we all need to be on high alert. Someone has to sleep with me that night to guard me from Queen Bria. She does want to kill me, after all. I'm not going to feel safe there."

"I would be more than happy to sleep with you." His violet eyes met mine again.

I wasn't sure what it was, but there was so much intensity behind his gaze—something I had never really seen in him before now.

So many emotions began to swirl through me.

Was I falling deeper in love with Harden?

Was he *falling deeper in love with* me?

I honestly wasn't sure what was going on between us, but it honestly felt like a turning point. There had been some sort of shift in our dynamic.

Before I even knew what was happening, his lips came crashing down on mine as we stood out there in the courtyard. We kissed for what felt like an eternity with the snow falling down all around us.

For a moment in time, everything felt right in the world.

CHAPTER
TWENTY

Our midterms came and went. I passed all of them with flying colors—including Advanced Weaponry, which was a huge relief. Leo kept telling me that the knowledge and skills I learned in that class were going to be the most valuable for me in the long-term.

I wasn't sure if that was true. I wanted to believe I would never have to actually attack someone, but I knew that was probably just wishful thinking.

I was pretty sure that, once I became Queen, I was going to be faced with a whole lot of enemies—enemies who I was bound to need to use violence against eventually. At least, I was trying to mentally prepare myself for that. Sometimes, I was pretty sure I was too peaceful at heart to be a part of this prophecy.

~'

I was packing to head to the Jaguar Kingdom. Katerina and Alexis had both already left for the holiday break.

As I zipped my bag, there was a knock at the door.

Figuring that it was probably one of my mates, I opened it.

Surprised that there was no one on the other side, I spotted the envelope on the ground.

LENA was written in bold letters.

I picked the envelope up and then closed the door.

I ripped it open and pulled out the piece of paper that was tucked inside. It had the Shifter Academy letterhead.

Lena,

Please come to my office immediately. There is something we must discuss.

Do not tell your mates you are about to meet with me. Thank you.

Sincerely,
Headmaster Shere Khan

Wondering why I wasn't allowed to let my mates know (and semi-hoping they had overheard my thoughts about it anyway), I slipped out into the hallway.

I went outside and then headed in the direction of the Headmaster's office.

It had been a long time since I had been to that office. I hadn't visited it since Ella Gray had been in charge.

When I reached the office, the door was already open.

Shere Khan was sitting at his desk, waiting for me.

His emerald green eyes locked on mine. "Please come in, Miss Falcone. And shut the door behind you."

I stepped into his office and closed the door.

"Have a seat." He motioned to the chair in front of his desk.

I sat down.

"What is this about?" I asked.

"There are several things I would like to discuss with you," Shere Khan began. "Please do not repeat any of these things to your mates. I know it may be difficult to keep secrets from them, but there are reasons I am requesting you to keep these matters private."

"They can hear my thoughts," I reminded him. "So, anything you tell me could easily get back to them."

"I have a silencing spell on this room right now, so what we say here will be said in a safe space," he explained.

"But I can't prevent myself from thinking about whatever we talk about."

Pulling a vial out, he placed it on the desk in front of me. "You should drink this. It will prevent your mates from being able to listen in on your thoughts for two weeks—long enough for you to stop thinking about the discussion we're about to have."

Hesitantly, I unscrewed the lid and brought the vial to my lips.

The potion tasted like mint, blueberries, and bad decisions. How would I even know if it did what Shere Khan told me it would do?

But a moment later, this weird feeling came over me. I wasn't sure how, but I just *knew* my mates couldn't listen in on my thoughts.

It was irritating to know I'd just lost the ability to mentally communicate with my mates for the next two weeks. What if I needed them? What if *they* needed me?

I was getting spoiled. I had only just gotten the ability within the past few months, and already, I couldn't imagine losing it.

"The first order of business we need to discuss is Ella Gray," he began. "Eric got in touch with me yesterday. He thinks he has a lead on Ella's whereabouts, but we're not sure yet. Once he does eventually find her, I plan to send you to her location. Myself and other Legends will join you. One of the most important things us Legends can accomplish during our time here is Ella Gray's death. It is her fault, after all, that we rose from the dead. We would like to see this through, and Eric isn't wrong. You must help us." Shere Khan's green eyes met mine. "You truly *are* the most powerful shifter in the entire world, Lena."

"I am?" I just stared at him, confused.

"Yes. I have just reviewed your midterm exams. Your scores are exceptionally good—*too* good. As it stands, you will graduate as the valedictorian of your class."

"I will?" I asked in disbelief.

Shere Khan nodded.

"*Wow.*" I wasn't sure how that had happened. I hadn't realized I did better on my midterms than everyone else. I thought I was just somewhere in the middle.

"But even though your midterm scores were incredible, there's still some room for improvement," Shere Khan continued. "This is why I feel it's pertinent for you to receive one-on-one tutoring every Saturday morning when you return from break." He paused for a moment and then added, "Miss Falcone, I will be your personal tutor."

A knot twisted in my stomach. "*You?*"

He stared at me evenly. "Is there someone else who you feel would be better suited to help prepare you to become Queen of the Shifters?"

"Well... No." And that was the honest truth. Shere Khan

really *was* the most powerful shifter who had ever existed. There was no denying that. If there was one shifter who I could learn from, it was probably him. But that didn't change the fact that there was bad blood between us.

"Then what, exactly, is the problem?" he asked.

I met his gaze. "Do you want me to be honest with you?"

"Well, I certainly do not want you to lie to me, Miss Falcone."

"I'm still bitter over the fact that you swapped bodies with my mate and caused him to lose every memory he had of me."

Shere Khan's eyebrows lifted. "You still believe that I traded bodies with the young Khan?"

I shrugged. "I'm positive that you did."

"Well, you are wrong, Miss Falcone." He shook his head. "I had no use for his body. In fact, allow me to show you where I really was that night."

He reached out and touched my hand. I watched as a memory played out inside my mind.

Shere Khan was sitting out on the rooftop patio at the palace.

He was staring out at the ocean as the stars twinkled above in the night sky.

There was the sound of a door sliding open. He glanced over at the balcony attached to Rafael's room.

A large black bear stepped out onto the balcony, staring at its own reflection in the glass door.

It was me.

The bear looked extremely worried. It glanced over its shoulder and then jumped off the balcony, clumsily landing in a heap on the sand below.

The bear began to run with an intense speed.

Moments later, a tiger stepped out onto the balcony.

It jumped—err, practically flew—off of it, landing gracefully on the ground. It raced past the bear and then began to run in the opposite direction.

Shere Khan watched the tiger as it ran down the beach before staring back up at the moon.

As his memory faded, he pulled his hand away from mine.

"Do you believe me now, Miss Falcone?"

I just stared at him, confused. There was no denying that his memory felt so... well, *real*. But things still didn't add up.

"*Sort* of," I admitted. "It doesn't make any sense. Whoever it was loved ice tea. *You* love iced tea."

"It is possible that someone may have caught wind of the fact that I love iced tea and tried to use that information to frame me," he suggested.

"Frame you?"

"It makes just as much sense as anything else," he replied with a shrug.

I considered it. It didn't seem completely out of the realm of possibility. But there was one other thing that didn't make sense.

"If *you* weren't the one who traded bodies with him, then why did you happen to have the potion you gave me?"

"Intuition, my dear. I had a feeling that *someone* was about to lose his or her memories. I wasn't sure who, but my intuition clearly didn't steer me wrong." His eyes met mine. "By the way, you never mentioned. Did the potion restore Rafael's memories back to their normal state?"

"I haven't given it to him yet."

"You were supposed to have given it to him months ago. What are you waiting for?" Shere Khan stared at me from behind wide eyes.

"I had it analyzed by a toxicologist," I explained, deciding to leave out the part about how Kaa had helped. "I was afraid that you gave me a poison or something that could have killed Rafael."

"Why do you think I would have wanted to kill my own descendant?" He sounded completely offended by the accusation.

"I don't know. I just didn't trust you," I admitted.

"Did you get the toxicology report back?" Shere Khan asked.

I nodded. "Yes. I know now that you didn't give me a poison."

"Have you given the young Khan the potion yet?"

I shook my head. "No."

"And why not?" he pressed.

"Because my other mates don't think I should give the potion to him," I replied quietly.

He leaned forward. "Are you going to live your life constantly listening to the opinions of others?"

"Well, no."

"You are about to become Queen, Lena. Even though your King's opinions will matter at times, it is up to *you* to do what you feel is right for your kingdom. Or in this case, for Rafael and yourself."

I couldn't even argue with him, because he was right. There was no denying that.

But it was complicated. At times, Damon felt like the Alpha of the Brotherhood to me. I didn't want to tip the balance and make him angry, even though this really had nothing to do with him... or Harden or Ezra, for that matter.

"That's all up to you, I suppose. Either your mate can potentially remember you, or he won't. Feed him the potion or don't. The choice is yours. But let's move on to the last matter we need to discuss," Shere Khan continued. "We must discuss your shifter race."

"I'm a werebear," I told him.

"I am aware of this," he replied with a nod. "I have known your shifter race ever since the memory I just showed you. I knew it was you jumping off of Rafael's balcony that night." He paused. "That being said, I am afraid that you might not actually be *just* a werebear."

My eyebrows shot up. "What do you mean?"

"I have spoken to Kaa," he explained. "She seems rather convinced that you could be part Serpent."

I suppressed an eye roll. "Well, she's wrong."

"She says you are cold-blooded."

"So, what if I am?"

"It is a very strong indicator that you very well could be a Serpent."

"Well, I have never shifted into a snake, so I think we can probably rule that out."

Shere Khan stared at me for a moment. "You do know what it would mean *if* you did shift into a snake, right?"

I nodded. "That I wouldn't be allowed to be the Queen of the Shifters."

"That is correct. Therefore, if Kaa is right... *if* you do change into a Serpent... then you must keep it under wraps. If someone found out the truth, it would interfere with the entire prophecy, and we simply cannot let that happen."

"Why?" I asked him. "If I'm a Serpent, then maybe it just means I'm not meant to be Queen of the Shifters."

"You *are* meant to be the next Queen. If you weren't, you wouldn't have four mates—four Alphas from four Royal bloodlines."

I knew he was right. There was no denying the truth in that.

"I'm a little confused about something, actually. In the prophecy, it states that I will be mated to one Alpha from each of the four shifter races. But there are more than four shifter races."

"The werewolves, lions, tigers, and jaguars are the four original shifter races," Shere Khan explained.

I frowned. "I thought the foxes were the first shifter race to rule this world."

"They were the first to reign," he replied with a nod. "But they weren't born into existence until *after* the four original races were already well documented."

Well, that made sense.

"We're getting off topic now." Shere Khan's emerald green eyes locked on mine. "This is more important than you may realize right now. If you are part Serpent, Lena, and Kaa highly suspects you are, no one can ever know except for the three of us—not even your mates. I know you probably tell them everything, but this is a secret that you must guard at all costs... at least until after your coronation."

"You're right," I agreed with a nod. "*If* I am a serpent, my mates can never find out the truth. But the good news is that we won't ever need to worry about that, because despite what Kaa may think, I'm really *not* a Serpent."

I was confident about that. But judging from the look behind Shere Khan's eyes, he wasn't even the slightest bit convinced.

No, I was pretty sure he agreed with Kaa. He believed I was a Serpent.

CHAPTER
TWENTY-ONE

The Jaguar Kingdom was absolutely breathtaking.

The palace sat on a hill overlooking the ocean. The Spanish-style architecture was stunning. There were four towers that stood taller than the rest of the brown-stone walls that lined the palace.

The emerald green grass surrounding the palace almost seemed to sparkle beneath the sun. It was dotted with red, yellow, orange and purple flowers, and seemed to span for miles on end before descending to white sands that surrounded the sparkling blue waters. Palm trees created a border between the beach and the ocean.

"I can't believe this is where you grew up," I told Harden as we climbed the stairs that wrapped around the hill, leading to the main palace. "It's beautiful."

His violet eyes, which looked lighter in the sunlight, flitted over to meet mine. "It's nowhere near as beautiful as you, Lena."

I tried not to swoon *too* hard at his comment. I just wasn't used to him making them, but they had become fairly regular since our kiss in the snow that day.

169

It felt like I was unlocking parts of him that I hadn't even known existed, and honestly? I really liked this side of him.

"I can't wait for you to meet my parents," Harden told me. "And more importantly, *they* can't wait to meet *you*. They love the idea of you."

"I can't wait to meet them, either." I forced a smile, even though the truth was that I was extremely nervous about meeting them.

Then again, what was the worst that could happen? His mom would want to murder me, too? If so, maybe she, Bria Khan, and Ella Gray could start a We Want to Kill Lena Club.

"I'm nervous," I admitted. Even though I felt bad about it, I needed him to know how nerve-wracking this whole experience was for me.

"Lena, it's understandable that you'd be nervous," Harden said gently. "But my whole family knows all about you."

I glanced over at him with wide eyes. "What, exactly, does your family know about me?"

"That you're my mate," he said quietly.

"Wait, what? I thought you guys all agreed *not* to tell your families I was your mate," I said with a frown.

"Ah, that's what Rafael and Damon talked about at one point. I'm not sure if that's changed for Damon or not. We haven't discussed it lately. But I never actually agreed to those terms. I'm way too close to my family to keep secrets like that from them," Harden explained as we reached the top of the staircase.

"But how do I explain to them that you're not my *only* mate?" I asked.

"They know *everything*, Lena," Harden assured me.

"Wait. They know about *the prophecy*?" I asked.

"Yeah, they do." He nodded as he reached for the door handle and glanced over at me.

I could feel anger running through my veins. "We agreed not to tell anyone about the prophecy. The less shifters who know, the better. Remember?"

How could he expose our secret like this? Do my other mates know he did?

"You have nothing to worry about when it comes to my family, Lena. They're not going to tell anyone. They would never do anything to hurt me. If something should ever happen to you, that would mean hurting me."

"What do they think about the prophecy?" I questioned. What I was really asking was pretty obvious. What did they think of *me* being stuck at the center of it?

"They don't think anything bad. I promise." His violet eyes met mine. "Relax. They're going to love you as much as I do. Are you ready to go in now?"

I took a deep breath and then nodded.

Harden opened the door, and I glanced inside the palace.

It was absolutely beautiful... and huge. The white marble floors seemed to span forever. There were beautiful carvings in the walls and artwork that had an Aztec feel to them.

There were two grand staircases, both covered in red carpet. In between them was a large Christmas tree. It had to have been *at least* fifteen feet tall, if not taller. It was decorated primarily in red and gold ornaments.

As I glanced around the palace, I realized those were the colors *all* of the décor was done in.

"Those are the colors the Jaguar Knights wore traditionally," Harden explained quietly. "The palace is decorated in memory of them."

"Makes sense."

"Come on, let's go find my mom." He grabbed my hand.

We had just rounded the corner when a voice said from behind us, "Harden, you're home!"

I glanced over my shoulder to find a girl standing behind us. She had short black hair that she wore straight. She was younger than I was; I was willing to guess that she was probably about fourteen years old.

She had similar features to Harden; they had the same rounded nose, and their foreheads were nearly identical. The main difference between them was their eyes. Whereas his eyes were that unique shade of violet, her eyes were a light gray color that popped against her caramel skin tone.

"Hannah!" Harden stepped away from me and ran over to his sister, scooping her up in a big hug.

"Hey, Lena." Hannah smiled at me warmly over his shoulder.

"Hey. It's nice to meet you," I replied, smiling back at her. She seemed genuinely friendly.

At that moment, I heard the sound of heels clicking against the red marble floor.

"Hello, Harden."

I glanced over my shoulder to find Harden's mom standing in the doorway.

She looked just like an older version of Hannah with long, curly black hair.

"Hello, Mom," Harden replied. "I want you to meet my mate, Lena. Lena, this is my mom, Queen Maya."

"Hello, Your Majesty." I curtsied.

"There's no need for that, Lena." She smiled at me. "I've heard so much about you."

"Only good things, I hope," I replied with a laugh.

"All good things, my dear." Queen Maya scanned me up and down. "You're just as beautiful as Harden described."

There was a warmness to her tone and behind her eyes. It felt like a *genuine* warmness, one that I hadn't recognized in any of my other mates' moms.

"Thank you." I smiled at her.

"Why don't you come have some tea with me and tell me more about yourself?" Queen Maya asked, leading me into a large sitting room. "Harden, go fetch your father and your brother."

"Okay, Mom." His violet eyes met mine and then his voice filled my mind. *"Are you okay with me leaving you here alone with her?"*

Remembering the potion Shere Khan had given me to prevent my mates from hearing my thoughts, I nodded and mouthed, "Yes."

"Okay." Harden's eyes held mine for a moment longer before he turned and left the room. Hannah followed after him.

Once they were gone, a maid walked into the room carrying a tray of tea.

As she began to pour the tea into two cups, Queen Maya turned to me. "So, tell me more about yourself, Lena."

"Oh, umm..." I trailed off, unsure what to say. It was sort of awkward knowing that Queen Maya knew I was mated to not just Harden but the entire Alpha Brotherhood.

"What's your favorite subject you're studying in school?" she asked.

"I really enjoy Ancient Royal History," I admitted.

"I've always been a huge fan of shifter history in general. It's quite interesting." She took a sip of her tea. "Harden tells me that you're a bear shifter."

I nodded. "Yes."

It surprised me to know he had shared *so* much with his family.

"You know, many of the Royal Elders don't believe their children should date outside of their own kind."

A knot tightened in my stomach. Was she about to tell me *she* believed that?

"You know what I say to that?" Queen Maya asked.

"What?"

"To hell with Royal bloodlines and shifter races. Marriages and ruling kingdoms together should never have been about races at all. It should be about *love*. We should all be encouraging our children to be with their mates, even if that means marrying outside of their own shifter race. Without love, you don't have a good foundation to rule a kingdom, and that's how Kings and Queens end up both weak and miserable."

I breathed a sigh of relief. At least *one* of my mates' moms was willing to accept the possibility of us ending up together, even though I wasn't a jaguar or even a cat shifter.

"I must admit, however, that Harden was right. From a physical standpoint, it *is* surprising that you are a werebear," Queen Maya continued. "I'm not sure how else to put this, so please excuse my candor, but you are micro-sized."

A smile hit my lips at how polite she was trying to be over it.

"I get that a lot," I told her.

"I can see why." She laughed. "What Harden didn't mention is what type of bear you are."

"I'm a black bear."

"That makes sense," she replied with a nod.

I lifted my eyebrows. "It does?"

"Yes. Black bears are the most even-tempered and mellow of all the types of bear shifters," Queen Maya explained. "The grizzlies, on the other hand..." She let out a little laugh. "You should always watch out for the grizzlies. I've never met a friendly grizzly bear."

I thought of Dom and his desire to kill Katerina so he could become King.

"Anyway, I'm looking forward to the rest of the Alpha

Brotherhood arriving later on tonight," she said, changing the subject. "I can't think of a better way to spend Christmas."

"Me, either," I replied with a smile.

"You know, I have known all of these boys for so long—pretty much their entire lives. They're like second sons to me." Her eyes met mine. "Have you given any thought to which of the four you'll end up choosing in the end?"

I nearly choked on my tea. That was the absolute last thing I had been expecting her to ask me.

It should have been completely awkward for me to answer, considering she was Harden's mom. And yet, for reasons I didn't even fully understand, I actually felt really comfortable talking to her about it. It was a *huge* difference from talking to Queen Bria or Ella Gray.

"Of course I have given thought to it. I've given *a lot* of thought to it. But I still don't know what choice I'm going to make in the end," I admitted. "I care about all four of them so much. We've become so close over the past two years, and every single one of them has great qualities that I don't want to live without." I paused for a moment and then added, "This is the hardest decision I've ever had to make in my life, to be honest."

"I can only imagine," Queen Maya replied. "You're not just making a decision for you. You're making a decision for *all of us*."

"Exactly," I agreed with a nod.

She set her tea cup down. "If I'm being honest, Lena, the truth is that I just don't know if Harden is... well... *fit*... to be the next King of the Shifters."

Her words surprised me. "You don't?"

"Don't get me wrong. Harden is a very strong shifter. He is, no doubt, the strongest jaguar shifter there is," she explained. "But there is a reason the jaguars don't come first, second or even third on the hierarchy. The lions, werewolves, and tigers are simply more powerful than we are."

"I'm sorry. Are you trying to discourage me from choosing Harden?" I asked, a little confused by her motives. Even though she seemed like a nice woman, I was beginning to wonder if she really *didn't* want me to be with her son just as much as Ella Gray or Bria Khan didn't want me to be with either of theirs.

Had she just put on a front to make herself *seem* accepting of the two of us, even though she really wasn't?

Lowering her voice, Queen Maya explained, "It's not that I'm trying to discourage you from choosing Harden, Lena. I think you should follow your heart. If you believe he is the mate who will make you happiest—and the one who *you* personally feel is the most fit to be King—then, by all means, choose him. All I'm saying is that, in my personal opinion, it would be in the best interest of the entire shifter world for you to choose one of the others."

"I appreciate your honesty." I understood where she was coming from, and I believed that her advice was well meaning. But I also could only imagine what Harden's reaction would have been if he somehow found out that his mom was *sort of* trying to talk me out of choosing him.

I felt kind of relieved about the thought-blocking potion Shere Khan had given me now. The last thing I would have wanted was for my thoughts to be the bearer of bad news.

At that moment, I heard the sound of a man clearing his throat from behind us.

Glancing over my shoulder, I saw Harden standing in the doorway next to a man with darker skin than his own. His features were sharper, but the resemblance was still uncanny. I couldn't believe how much Harden looked like *both* of his parents.

"Hello, Lena," his dad said, moving forward and extending a hand. "I'm King Santiago, your future father-in-law."

Um.

"Lena never said she's for sure choosing Harden, dear," Queen Maya intercepted. "She has a choice between the entire Alpha Brotherhood, remember?"

"Yes, of course I remember. There's no way I could have ever forgotten this important detail about our son's mate." King Santiago seemed annoyed that his wife had even suggested that he could have forgotten. "But if Lena knows what's in the best interest of the entire shifter world as we know it, she'll choose Harden here to be King."

"Dad, let's not put any extra pressure on Lena than she already has," Harden said with a frown.

"Nonsense, son. Your brother Henry has been the biggest disappointment of my life. He was meant to be King, and at the surface, he would have made an incredible one. He is both strong and powerful. His downfall is that he never could seem to put his kingdom or his family first. He won't even be joining us for this holiday."

"Where is he?" Harden asked with raised eyebrows.

"Juvenile detention... *again.* Talk about an embarrassment to the Jaguar Kingdom. But we can redeem ourselves and the entire shifter world will regain respect for us again when *you* become the next King of the Shifters." King Santiago looked extremely proud by the idea.

Both Harden *and* Queen Maya shot nervous glances in my direction.

It was obvious that Harden's dad had his heart set on his son becoming the next King of the Shifters and on the jaguars becoming the top shifter race of the hierarchy. I was sort of nervous that if I didn't choose Harden, his dad was going to be more than just upset. I was pretty sure he was going to be pissed at his son.

No freaking pressure.

∾

I was relieved when the rest of the Alpha Brotherhood joined us in the Jaguar Kingdom later that evening. It made me feel on edge to be away from them, especially when the thought-blocking potion prevented me from communicating with them.

The Swift family held a large Christmas Eve festival for the entire Jaguar Kingdom on the beach. Normally, the festival was open to anyone, but there were obviously restrictions this year due to the war.

There were rides, games, and food and beverage stands set up all over the beach. There was a flying reindeer carousel, a Christmas train that went all the way around the island, and a stand that served hot chocolate and fresh baked chocolate chip cookies.

My favorite part about it all? The magically-induced snow. It was the perfect Christmas touch my heart needed.

"Lena, do you want to ride the Ferris wheel with me?" Harden asked.

"Sure."

He reached out his hand to me.

Weaving my fingers through his, we headed to the Ferris wheel together. It was a lot taller than any other Ferris wheel I'd ever been on in my life.

We climbed into one of the gingerbread man-themed carts.

Moments later, the ride began to slowly make its ascent into the sky.

"Lena, I just want to apologize for my dad's behavior earlier," Harden told me. "He can be really intense sometimes."

"Don't be silly. There's no need to apologize." I waved my hand at him.

"I know. I just feel bad. I don't want you to feel pressured to choose me just because my dad was sort of being a dick about it."

"He was *completely* being a dick about it," I corrected. "And I might feel *slightly* pressured," I admitted. "But I've decided not to factor *any* of your parents into my decision. I need to choose what's right for the entire shifter world."

"Okay." He paused for a moment and then added, "My mom really likes you."

"I really like her."

"And I really like you." Harden's eyes lingered on mine. "I'm not sure if I tell you that enough."

"I really like you, too," I whispered.

His lips came down on mine then, this time harder and with more passion than usual. I wasn't entirely sure what had gotten into Harden lately, but honestly? I really liked this newfound side of him.

We broke our kiss, and I glanced up at the night sky that hung above us.

How in the world was I ever going to pick one of these guys? I wondered to myself. I liked all of them way too much to decide.

At that moment, I noticed the way the clouds seemed to form letters.

I watched in complete astonishment as an L was formed, followed by an E, N, and A.

All of the clouds in the sky seemed to come together then to form a message.

Lena,

Meet with Gretta ASAP.

"Harden, do you *see* that?" I asked him, wondering if only I could see the message or if it was visible to everyone else, too.

He glanced over at me. "See what?"

I pointed to the sky. "The words in the clouds."

Harden shook his head. "No, I don't see anything."

When I glanced back at the sky, I realized the clouds had returned to their usual state.

The message was gone.

TWENTY-TWO

"There was a message for me written in the clouds," I told my mates as we all sat around the fireplace in Harden's personal living room that night.

"What did the message say?" Ezra asked, a concerned look in his blue eyes.

"That I have to go see Gretta as soon as possible. Gretta is that psychic from the human realm," I reminded them.

Damon frowned. "That's really strange. I wonder who would put that message in the sky for you... and why. What information does Gretta have for you?"

"I'm not sure," I admitted.

"Whatever information Gretta has, it must be important," Rafael commented.

"Yeah, it must be," I agreed with a nod. "All I do know is that I need to actually listen to the message. So, I'm going to be returning to the human realm the day after tomorrow."

I knew the message had said ASAP, but there was no way I was about to miss Christmas in the Lion Kingdom just to find out what Gretta had to say. I couldn't help but feel like if it was *that* important, then she would have figured out *some* way to relay it to me.

It crossed my mind that maybe Gretta was the one who had written the message in the sky for me, but I wasn't sure if she was that powerful. Sure, she had been able to see things about my future, but did she have whatever magical abilities it took to write in the sky with clouds? It seemed a little far-fetched.

Then again, in this world, I had learned that nothing was too far-fetched anymore.

"Do you want us to go with you, Lena?" Ezra asked me.

I shook my head. "No. The message specifically said that *I* had to go see Gretta. It didn't tell me to bring you guys."

"Maybe they just left that part out," Harden suggested.

"I don't think so. I just have a feeling about this. I'm supposed to go alone." I paused. "I don't even know where to *find* Gretta."

"Well, that will be easy enough. We'll use Moon Magic tomorrow night to do a Locator Spell," Ezra said.

"Oh. Good idea."

"I don't know, Lena. I really don't like the idea of you traveling through the portals by yourself right now. I haven't even been able to hear your thoughts lately," Damon said.

"Oh. Yeah. I may have taken a potion that was supposed to block you guys from being able to hear my thoughts."

"Why would you do that?" Ezra asked with raised eyebrows.

I wasn't sure what explanation to give them. I couldn't just tell them the truth: that Shere Khan wanted me to take it so they wouldn't know what we talked about. If they knew that, then they would for sure want to know what we talked about.

I shrugged. "I just wanted to experiment with it to see if it works. Apparently, it does. It's supposed to block your access to my thoughts for two weeks," I informed them.

"Of all times to take a potion like that," Damon said, shaking his head.

"What do you mean?"

"It's just that there's a shifter world war going on, and you are very important." Damon's golden-brown eyes locked on mine. "Since you can't even communicate with us through mind-speak, I would feel a lot better if you would let at least one of us accompany you to the human realm."

"I agree, Princess," Rafael said with a nod.

I glanced over at him, surprised by his choice of words. It was the first time Rafael had called me 'princess' since he had lost all of his memories of me.

Was it possible some of his memories were somehow starting to come back naturally? How else would he have known to call me 'princess' the same way he always had in the past?

"I just have a gut feeling that I'm supposed to go alone."

"We don't have to go into Gretta's house or her office or wherever she does her readings from," Ezra said. "We can wait outside."

I sighed. "Fine. I guess that can be arranged."

"Good. It's decided then." Damon looked happy.

I suppressed an eye roll. It felt like something else in my life he was trying to control, just like not wanting to give Rafael the memory-enhancing potion...

I tried to push the thought to the side. Damon was as stubborn as they came.

The problem? So was I.

We were going to have to just agree to disagree from now on.

"So, we should probably head to bed. We have a long day ahead of us tomorrow." Harden yawned as he stretched.

"Yeah. That's probably a good idea," Ezra agreed, rising to his feet. His blue eyes met mine. "Goodnight, Lena."

"Goodnight, Princess," Rafael said as he stood up, too.

There it was again. I didn't even try to suppress the smile that hit my lips.

"Goodnight, Lena." Damon's golden-brown eyes lingered on mine for a moment longer than usual.

I was pretty sure he was wondering what all of them were wondering: *Whose bed was I sleeping in tonight?*

I had decided that since we were in the Jaguar Kingdom, it was only fair to spend the night with Harden.

Plus, the truth was that I really *wanted* to spend the night with him. With our dynamic shifting so much, I felt... *different.* The connection I felt to him was deeper now. I wanted to explore it further.

Judging from the way Damon was staring at me, I wondered if the thought-blocking potion Shere Khan gave me had already worn off. I might have been wrong, but I could have sworn that he seemed... well, jealous.

"Goodnight, guys," I told them all.

Once they left the room, Harden glanced over at me. "So, uh, you ready to head to bed?" He paused for a moment and then added, "To *my* bed?"

I nodded. "Yes, I am."

A smile hit his lips as we headed up the spiral staircase that led to his bedroom.

He flicked on the light, allowing me to see his room for the first time.

"Wow, your room is amazing." All four of the room's glass walls were actually fish tanks. Colorful fish of various sizes were swimming around inside of them. It was as if his room was an aquarium.

"I love marine life," he explained. "It feels so tranquil."

My eyes widened. "I didn't know this about you."

"There's a lot that you don't know about me, Lena," Harden replied quietly.

"You are quite the mystery," I agreed with a nod. Somehow, I was going to have to dig deeper and learn more about him. It was crazy for me to think we had once lived together for nearly a year, and there were *still* things I didn't know about him. I wanted to unlock every aspect of him.

He climbed into bed and I laid down next to him, resting my head on his chest. He covered us with the ocean-themed blue comforter before wrapping his arms around me, pulling me into his tight embrace. It felt so good to finally be in his arms.

I followed his gaze to the clock on his nightstand. It was midnight.

"Merry Christmas, Lena."

"Merry Christmas," I replied.

Reaching over to his nightstand, he opened the drawer and pulled out a rectangular box wrapped in metallic gold paper with a red bow. "I wanted to give you your gift now, while we're alone together."

"You got me a gift?" The truth was I hadn't thought to get any of my mates a gift. School had been so crazy, and we hadn't exchanged gifts last year since we had been hiding out in the cabin together.

Harden nodded.

I shot an apologetic glance in his direction. "I didn't get you anything. I'm sorry."

"Don't be sorry, Lena. I don't care that you didn't get me anything. Christmas is about what you give, not what you receive." He pointed his chin at the gift. "Open it."

Even though I still felt bad about it, I neatly unwrapped the gold paper and pulled out the black velvet gift box.

It looked like a jewelry box.

I glanced over at him with wide eyes. "Did you get me jewelry?"

"Go on, Lena," Harden urged me with a laugh. "Just open it."

I pulled the box open and saw the gold charm bracelet that stared back at me.

There was a black bear charm made from black and brown crystals at the center of the bracelet. Next to it, there was a gold lion charm, an orange and black tiger charm, a gray wolf charm, and a black and gold jaguar charm, with purple crystals for eyes.

"It's all of us," I murmured.

He nodded. "It's so you can have us with you at all times." He paused and then added, "The crystals came from the Jaguar Kingdom, so no matter what happens, you'll always have a part of my kingdom with you, too."

"Harden, this is beautiful. Thank you."

"You're welcome. I'm glad you like it."

"I more than just like it. I love it. No one has ever given me such a meaningful gift before." And I meant that. I was pretty sure no one had ever put this much thought into any gift they had ever given me—not even my parents back when they were alive.

It was my second Christmas without my parents, and even though it never got easier, I was glad to spend the holidays with my mates. It wouldn't have been a whole lot lonelier without them.

"There's something else I want to give you tonight," Harden told me then.

"*Something else?*" My eyes widened. "You've already given me more than enough. In fact, I don't think I can accept another gift from you."

"This is different, Lena. I wouldn't even call it a gift. It's just something I've been hanging onto for a very long time, because I wanted it to be special. I've wanted to say this for a long time, but now just feels like the right time." His violet eyes met mine. "I love you, Lena. I'm in love with you. Today, tomorrow, for the rest of my life, I love you."

Butterflies swarmed through me.

It was the first time Harden had ever told me he loved me. Even though I knew he did, those words had been left unspoken until that very moment.

It was the best "gift" he could have given me—even better than the charm bracelet.

"I'm in love with you, too, Harden."

"I know, Lena," he whispered. His lips crushed against mine as he pressed his body against mine.

I wrapped my arms around his neck, deepening the kiss.

As his lips broke away from mine, he planted a trail of kisses down my neck.

My skin tingled every time he moved his warm mouth against my skin.

Frantically, he pulled my shirt off. Reaching behind my back, he unhooked my bra and tossed it to the side.

His eyes scanned the length of my body, drinking in every inch of me for the first time.

"*Here?*" I whispered, feeling a little awkward about his family *and* the rest of my mates being in the palace, too.

"The walls are soundproof, don't worry." Then he brought his lips down on mine again as his hand fell between my legs.

As he stroked my clit, my entire body trembled. I realized how badly I'd been craving him. So much tension had built up between us over the past two years.

It didn't take long to feel myself coming undone against his fingers. I moaned against his mouth.

Once I came down from my high, I undid his belt and then his zipper.

As his own pants dropped to the floor, I found myself staring at his rock-hard dick.

When I glanced up at his face again, his violet stare pierced through me. "Are you sure you want to do this, Lena?"

I nodded. I didn't just want to; I needed to.

I needed *him*.

Harden kissed me again, pinning my wrists to the mattress. He hovered above me and then pushed himself into me in one swift movement.

I gasped as he entered me.

He moved in me, slowly at first, hitting all of my nerve endings as he built up to a steadier pace.

Before I knew it, we were both breathing raggedly as we exploded together.

As we rode out our orgasms together, his violet gaze locked on mine.

I could feel it then, an even bigger shift in our dynamic. His aroma, a combination of vanilla, brown sugar, and spice, became intoxicating.

The bonding process was complete. We were officially mates.

TWENTY-THREE

I woke up the next morning, tangled up in Harden's arms. I watched him as he snored peacefully next to me.

My heart felt different today. Fuller than it had the day before.

In that moment, everything felt perfect. I could have laid there with him forever, but it was Christmas. We were supposed to have breakfast with Harden's family before heading to Damon's kingdom. That meant meeting the Crowne family.

A nervousness came over me.

At that moment, Harden's eyes flew open and he pulled me closer to him.

"Are you okay, Lena?" His voice was full of concern.

"Yeah, why?"

"I could feel your anxiety."

"I'm sorry. I didn't know you'd feel it."

But *of course* he could feel it. I should have known. We were mated more now than ever before.

"I can feel everything." He stroked my hair. "Do you want to talk about it?"

I hesitated. I felt bad about telling him the truth, that my mind wasn't on us anymore. It somehow felt like it should have been, after everything that had happened between us last night. But there had never been secrets between me and my mates, and I didn't want to start now.

"I'm just nervous about meeting Damon's mom," I admitted. "And all of his sisters. There are *a lot* of sisters."

There were five sisters, to be exact. That meant there were five sisters who could potentially hate me.

"Don't be nervous, Lena. It's all going to be okay," Harden replied, rubbing my bare shoulder reassuringly. "Queen Kiara would be crazy not to love you."

I tried to push the thought to the back of my mind, even though I knew my uneasiness about this wasn't going to die down until I met them.

"We should probably get up," I said with a sigh.

"Not yet." Harden pulled me closer to him.

He kissed me and then made love to me again, this time like he wanted it to last for an eternity. There was an urgency unlike anything I'd ever felt from him before, a passion that lasted late into the morning.

Deep down, we both knew this couldn't last for an eternity.

Once it was over, all I could seem to think about was the fact that he was number two. I still had to complete the bonding process two more times.

It made so many emotions come over me.

Desire for the mates who I hadn't made love to yet, the mates who I still needed to complete the bonding process with.

Love, for all four of them.

Guilt. I knew I shouldn't have felt guilty, but I *did*. It made me feel bad that I still wanted Rafael and Ezra, even though Damon and Harden both were enough for me. *Sort of.*

I knew that each of them was enough for me as individuals. I could have been happy with each and every single one of them. And yet, my heart craved and desired all four of them in ways that were entirely out of my control.

Most of all, I was able to recognize how complicated this whole arrangement truly was.

~

After our Christmas brunch with the Swift family, we took a portal from a secret passageway in the palace to the Lion Kingdom.

We landed on the beach that surrounded the castle.

The island sort of reminded me of the Tiger Kingdom. The main difference was that where the Tiger Kingdom had been made up of rainforest, the Lion Kingdom was full of high grass. It was supposed to resemble an African savanna, for obvious reasons. There were trees that lined the beach, which made me feel like I had time warped into *The Lion King*.

The water in the Lion Kingdom looked even bluer here than it did in the other kingdoms. It was the color of blue topaz.

The gold-colored stone that made up the castle had a glittery look against the bright morning sun.

In the palace courtyard, there was a swimming pool surrounded by palm trees.

It was just as stunning as all of the other kingdoms I had visited so far.

I glanced over at Damon, who was walking next to me. He had been weird with me all morning, and I was pretty sure it was because he knew what had happened between Harden and me. All of my mates could probably smell Harden's scent on me now, but I was pretty sure Damon could probably feel it more deeply than the others since we were already officially mated.

Damon was my first official mate. I was pretty sure he was bitter that he was no longer my *only* mate. Even though we had all known this was going to happen eventually, that didn't mean that it hurt anyone any less.

"Your kingdom is gorgeous," I told Damon then.

"It's alright. It's home." He shrugged and then his golden-brown eyes slid over to meet mine. "It could be *your* home soon, too."

I hadn't really given it a lot of thought, but he was right. No matter who I chose in the end, we would end up ruling together in their kingdom.

Could I picture myself living in the Lion Kingdom? Abso-freakin-lutely. I would have loved to spend even a few hours lounging around that pool. But I knew that, when it came down to it, I would have loved to call *any* of my mates' kingdoms home. The Jaguar Kingdom had the most beautiful landscape, while the Tiger Kingdom just felt like a place of tranquility and solace.

Well, aside from Bria and Roman plotting to kill me, that is.

I realized there was one kingdom I wasn't even taking into consideration. I still needed to visit the Wolf Kingdom in order to be able to draw a fair comparison between all of the kingdoms.

Not that the comparison even mattered. I knew that who I would choose in the end had nothing to do with their kingdom or how much I wanted to live in it.

It was all about who I wanted to weather the storm with. And I knew there were going to be many rainy days ahead, so I needed to choose the guy who would be the most built to weather it with me.

The only problem?

I couldn't imagine coming out of the storm without even *one* of my mates.

TWENTY-FOUR

T he moment I set foot inside the palace, the breath caught in the back of my throat.

It was, by far, the most beautiful royal palace I had been inside so far.

All of the décor was done in shades of gold and bronze, and there were gemstones everywhere: in the artwork, on the walls, and woven into the architecture.

The grand staircase was my favorite part. It was gold and adorned in red rubies that were arranged to look like red roses. The gemstones just seemed to gleam beneath the light of the gold chandelier that hung from the high ceiling. It felt like something straight out of a fairytale.

"Lena, I want you to meet my family. They're waiting for us outside in the garden." He glanced over at the others. "Can we have some privacy for this?"

"No problem," Rafael agreed.

"Yeah, of course," Ezra replied with a nod.

"Sure." Harden looked hesitant. I knew it was probably because the two of us being apart was so difficult right now. Even though I wasn't going very far, our souls were so newly connected to one another that it was weird to think about not being in the same room as one another. I knew, because my heart felt the same way.

But I forced myself to follow Damon out of the room. He led me down a long hallway that took us to the palace exit.

The nervous knot in my stomach began to tighten.

Damon seemed to pick up on the anxiety I felt. Grabbing my hand, he gave it a tiny squeeze.

"It's going to be okay, Lena." His gold eyes found mine. "Take a deep breath."

I did what he said, but it only *slightly* calmed my nerves.

Deep down, I couldn't help but wonder one thing. *How the hell was I going to rule the entire shifter world when meeting the Queen of the Shifters and her daughters made me this nervous?*

"Ready?" Damon asked a moment later.

I nodded.

He pushed the door open, and we stepped outside.

The garden was beautiful. It was filled with beautiful red rose bushes that looked like the ruby roses on the grand staircase.

As we entered deeper into the garden, I saw all six of them standing there: the Crowne women.

They were standing in a line, as if they were each waiting to meet me.

Damon led me to the first girl who stood in the line. The girl, who stood about my height, had chin-length, platinum blonde hair. She had the same gold skin tone as Damon, but her eyes were a shade of gray.

"Lena, I'd like you to meet Kylene," he introduced us.

"Hey, Lena." She grinned at me. There was something so authentic about her smile.

"Hey." I smiled back at her. "It's nice to meet you."

"It's nice to meet you, too." I could tell that she was really shy.

We moved to the next of his sisters who stood in line. She had long, straight dark brown hair. She was tall and thin, and she had fair skin.

"Lena, I would like you to meet my sister Catherine."

"Hey, Lena. It's so nice to finally meet you. You can call me Cait, by the way."

"It's nice to meet you, too, Cait."

Moving past her, we approached the next sister who stood in line. She had deeply tanned, golden skin, and a shade of golden blonde hair that she wore in long, loose waves. When her eyes locked on mine, I noticed they were the same exact shade of golden-brown as Damon's.

"This is my sister Elsa," Damon told me. "Elsa, this is Lena."

"I know who she is, you dummy." Elsa rolled her eyes at her brother and then threw her arms around me in a loose hug. "It's so good to meet you, Lena. We're going to be sisters."

Um. I guess Damon was nothing like Harden. He apparently hadn't told them about the prophecy and the fact that I was mated to three other guys who I could potentially choose from.

I darted my eyes over at him, but he looked completely unfazed by her words.

"It's so good to meet you, too," I told Elsa, deciding that now wasn't the time to correct her.

"Hey, Lena!" the next girl who stood in line said, hugging me, too. She had long auburn hair that fell over her tiny shoulders in loose waves. She had the same golden-brown eyes as Damon. "I'm Megan, and it's so good to meet you."

"It's so good to meet you, too," I replied with a smile.

The next sister who stood in line looked similar to Kylene. She had the same shade of platinum blonde hair, but she wore hers long and curly. She had big, gray-blue eyes, the same sun-kissed skin, and her makeup was flawless. She looked like she had stepped straight out of a Hollywood movie or something.

"Hey there, Lena. I'm Dolly." She shot me a smile, showing off her super white teeth. "Call me crazy, but I have this really strong feeling that we're going to be besties."

I wasn't sure why, but I could feel the same thing she did. I knew it was my shifter intuition, but a feeling deep within my gut told me that Dolly and I *were* going to be BFFs at some point in the future. I didn't think I was going to not get along with any of Damon's sisters, but I was pretty sure that Dolly and I were going to have a special bond, for some reason.

"Well, not to prevent this friendship from taking off right now, but there's still someone else Lena needs to meet right now," Damon told Dolly.

She nodded and smiled at me. "We'll catch up later on, Lena."

"Okay." I was actually looking forward to it.

I wasn't going to lie. This whole meeting Damon's family thing was going a lot better than I had expected it to go... *so far,* anyway.

As we rounded a corner, deeper into the garden, I saw the woman standing there.

She had thick, wavy light brown hair and hazel eyes that popped against her sun-kissed skin. It was in her facial features where I saw it the most. She had the same chin, the same forehead, the same broad-tipped nose, and the same downturned eyes as Damon.

There was no doubt she was his mom.

"Mom, I want you to meet my mate Lena," Damon told her. "Lena, this is my mom, Queen Kiara."

When Queen Kiara's eyes met mine, it felt like there was a genuine kindness behind her gaze.

"Hello, Lena. You're even lovelier than Damon made you out

to be." She smiled at me. "I have been looking forward to meeting you for so long now." She glanced over at Damon. "Would you mind giving us some privacy? I would like to have a one-on-one conversation with your mate."

He nodded. "Yeah. Of course."

"Merry Christmas, by the way," she told us both.

"Merry Christmas," we said in sync.

Leaning in closer to me, Damon kissed me on the lips. "I'll be waiting for you with my sisters."

"Okay." I smiled at him, trying not to let him know how nervous I was. Even though his mom seemed nice so far, I was afraid about what she was going to say to me in private. Was it possible that she was going to tell me to stay the hell away from him?

Once Damon walked away from us, Queen Kiara turned to me. "Let's move further into the garden, shall we? I don't want my son to eavesdrop, and there is a noise-blocking spell in between the peony bushes."

"Okay," I agreed, even though the idea of Damon being unable to eavesdrop made me uncomfortable. If his mom was about to be rude, I *wanted* him to overhear it.

She led me through a maze of rose bushes and azaleas. Finally, we entered a section of the garden that was lined with peony bushes in various shades of light pinks and white. There was a bench at the center of them.

Sitting down on the bench, she patted the seat next to her.

Nervously, I sat down.

"There's no need for you to be nervous, Lena," Queen Kiara said, as if reading my mind. "I don't bite."

I let out a nervous laugh.

"I've heard about how horribly things have gone with Queen Ella and Queen Bria," she continued. "I just want you to know that I am nothing like them. I don't believe that it's up to us to decide who our children should be with. My son seems to be incredibly taken with you. I have never heard him talk about any female the way he talks about you. You hold that boy's entire heart."

Which also meant I had the potential to completely shatter it if I didn't choose him in the end. The thought made me feel sick to my stomach.

"Unlike the other mothers, I don't think it's necessary to preserve our bloodlines. It's a barbaric way to think during a time like this. Do you want my honest opinion?" Her gold eyes locked on mine.

"Sure." I nodded.

"Damon has told me about the prophecy, Lena. I think the entire reason you're destined to end the shifter world war is because you're meant to marry one of the Alpha Brotherhood," Queen Kiara told me. "We are in the middle of a shifter world war, which is ultimately a war between the shifter races. What better way to unify all of the shifter kingdoms than to marry someone from a different race? Imagine what the rest of the world's opinion would be if the Prince of the Lions marries a Werebear?"

Or if I married the Prince of the Werewolves, the Prince of the Jaguars, or the Prince of the Tigers. Either way, no matter who I ended up choosing in the end, her logic made sense.

"The Lions and the Werebears would be forced to form an alliance with one another," she went on. "That means that each of those kingdoms' allies would also have to come together. Considering the lions and the bears are currently at opposite ends of this war, it could bring everyone together. The only ones who would remain outcasts are the Serpents. I'm not sure if anyone will *ever* become allies with the Serpents, but that's the way it's always been. I'm pretty sure that they prefer to be alone, if we're being completely honest."

"Interesting. All of this does make a lot of sense," I admitted. "Maybe the marriage really *is* the key to unification."

"I do believe so," Queen Kiara told me with a nod. "I know that this may be a little bit bold of me, especially after we've only just met. But I have just been waiting for so long to tell you this." Her eyes met mine. "I want you to know that you have my blessing to marry Damon, Lena. I have already discussed this with my husband, who you'll meet tonight. We are both ready and willing to welcome you into our kingdom with open arms. Knowing how in love Damon is with you has only made us already fall in love with you."

"Thank you. Hearing you say all of this really means a lot to me," I told her honestly. It was a great feeling to know that at least *one* of my mates' moms was willing to accept me.

"There's no need to thank me, Lena. I only speak the truth." Queen Kiara paused for a moment and then told me, "You know, regardless of whether you choose Damon in the end or not, I want you to know that I'm here for you. It's not always easy being the Queen of the Shifters, and that role is only going to be more challenging for someone who wasn't raised in the shifter world. If you ever need help, at any point in time, please just let me know."

"Thank you. I appreciate that more than you know," I told her.

Most of all, I appreciated the fact that she wasn't assuming I *would* choose Damon. She was acknowledging that there was a possibility we wouldn't end up together.

When it came down to it, the last one who I would have wanted extra pressure from was his mom, the Queen of the Shifters.

"Well, let's rejoin the others." She rose to her feet. "The Christmas festivities don't begin tonight, which gives you plenty of time to become more acquainted with the girls. Don't let them overwhelm you, by the way. They're all very anxious to get to know you better. They all want to be bridesmaids, even though I keep reminding them that a Royal bridal party of that size isn't traditional."

"Do they... *know*?" I asked her as I followed after her. "About the prophecy, I mean?"

"Dolly and Elsa are the only ones who know. Damon is closest to the two of them."

"Okay. Noted."

I had mixed feelings about all of this. Deep down, I knew that the less shifters who knew the truth about the prophecy, the better.

But I also couldn't help but feel like if Damon's sisters didn't learn the truth about me—and *soon*—they were going to be in for a world of disappointment if I didn't end up choosing him in the end.

Later that evening, we all crowded around a banquet table alongside the pool.

The Lion Kingdom did Christmas so much differently from the Jaguar Kingdom. While there was a tall Christmas tree outside, there was no magically-induced snow. And I was perfectly okay with that. It was nice to see how each of my mates' families celebrated the holiday.

"Your father will be joining us any minute now," Queen Kiara told Damon as she sat down across from us.

"Where is Dad, anyway?" Damon asked as he piled some fruit salad onto his plate.

"Your father went to the Cheetah Kingdom, where he met with King Rufus," she replied.

"On *Christmas*?" Damon looked really shocked by this news.

She nodded. "Yes. King Rufus received word that the Coyotes are planning to try to lift the magical shield protecting our island," she explained. "They wanted to discuss some strategies on what to do if this should happen."

"That doesn't seem good," Damon said.

"Well, there's no need for you to worry. The Coyotes are the least of our worries. They lack the technology needed to remove our magical barrier. Even more than that, they also lack the strength and power to seriously harm our kingdom." She met his gaze. "There truly is nothing to worry about. Your father was simply following basic protocol, even though he's not worried about this, either."

"Okay." Damon didn't sound even the least bit convinced.

"*My father has never missed Christmas*," he told me through mind-speak.

I grabbed his hand and shot a sympathetic look in his direction. I wished I could respond to him through mind-speak. I couldn't wait until the potion Shere Khan gave me wore off.

"Anyway, let's talk about your midterm exams. How did you all do?" Queen Kiara asked.

"We passed," Rafael said with a shrug.

"With flying colors," Ezra added. "Lena did particularly well."

"Congratulations, Lena." His mom shot a glance in my direction.

"I'm so excited to go to Shifter Academy next year," Dolly commented as she took a bite of her salad.

"Freshman year is a lot of fun," I told her.

"We're all going to Shifter Academy already," Elsa explained. "We're just doing it online."

"Given the state of the war, I didn't feel comfortable sending all of them this year," Queen Kiara explained, glancing across the table at me. "It was hard enough to let Damon go this year, but I knew it couldn't be avoided. He has to be prepared for the Royal Change of Hands. But the girls won't be reigning, so it just wasn't as important for them to get an on-campus education this year. Next year, things should calm down."

I wondered if she thought the war would end because of the prophecy. But it didn't actually state that the war would end as soon as I became Queen. There actually wasn't a timeline. And if I listened to the advice Shere Khan had given me when we'd first met, then maybe I shouldn't end the war right away—not until I was sure the world was ready for it to end.

"But next year at Shifter Academy won't be as good as this year, since we won't get to have the Legends in real life," Cait complained.

Megan glanced over at the rest of us. "The Legends are the ones who are teaching our online classes, but their lectures are pre-recorded, so we don't even get to interact with them in real time."

I understood why they wished they were attending Shifter Academy on-campus this year. Being taught by the Legends really was a once in a lifetime opportunity.

At that moment, I heard the sound of someone clearing their throat.

Glancing up, I found a guy standing at the end of the table. With his muscular frame, sun-kissed skin, and dirty blonde hair, I instantly knew who he was.

Damon's dad.

"Dad, you're home." Damon rose to his feet and gave his dad a tight hug. He turned to me. "I want to introduce you to my mate, Lena Falcone. Lena, this is my dad, King Ari."

The King's golden-brown eyes locked on mine as he walked over to me. He shocked me when he kneeled down in front of me and kissed my hand. "Welcome to our kingdom, Lena. I have so been looking forward to meeting you." His eyes met mine. "I am surprised by how much you resemble your mom."

His words completely caught me off-guard. "Y-you knew my mom?"

"Yes, I know your mom very well." His eyes met mine. "It's all in your smile. You and your mom both have that smile that can light up a whole room."

I swallowed hard, blinking away the tears. He kept talking about her in present tense, almost as if she was still alive. I knew that this happened sometimes; we couldn't always grasp the fact that someone who we once knew is no longer with us. But knowing that didn't make it any easier.

I could tell that Damon noticed his dad's choice in wording had upset me, because he jumped in then. "Dad, why don't we take a walk? I want to hear more about your meeting with the King of the Cheetahs."

"Sure, son." King Ari rose to his feet then. "Please excuse me, Lena. I would love to get to know you better later."

I nodded. "Of course."

The truth was, I really wanted to hear more about what he knew about my mom. I didn't know much at all about her life as a shifter. I wanted to know *everything*, and it seemed like King Ari may have been an important key to that.

TWENTY-FIVE

After the Christmas festivities came to an end with the Crowne family for the night, Damon turned to me and the rest of my mates. "Do you guys wanna go to our secret spot?"

"I'm down," Rafael said with a nod, rising to his feet.

"Me, too," Harden and Ezra both said in unison.

"Where's your secret spot?" I asked with raised eyebrows.

"You'll see. Come on." He led us away from the pool and out onto the beach. We began to make our way down the island.

Once we were a good distance away from the palace, each of my mates began to cut through the tall savanna grass.

We headed towards the trees off in the distance.

Once we reached one of the trees, my mates began to climb a ladder.

I glanced to the top of the tree, taking the wooden structure in.

"It's a treehouse," I realized out loud.

"Yeah. We built this place when we were kids," Damon explained as he climbed the ladder. "It was our hideaway from my parents and sisters."

As I began to climb the ladder, I lost my balance.

I thought I was going to fall backwards, but my ass fell straight into Rafael's hands.

His emerald green eyes locked on mine. "Lucky catch, but I'm not sure which one of us is luckier, Princess."

I was pretty sure Raf was falling hard for me now—just as hard as he had been before he'd lost his memories of me. It was in the way he looked at me, as if I was the only thing in the world.

It made the butterflies swarm around inside my stomach.

Once we had both made it inside, Ezra flicked the light on.

"This is amazing," I said as I glanced around the treehouse. It was, by far, the most bougie treehouse I had ever been in.

The entire treehouse was constructed from high-quality wood that just seemed to shine. There were two sets of bunk beds, one on each side of the large room.

There were lots of windows, including sliding glass doors that opened up to a balcony-style porch overlooking the beach that lay ahead of us.

Seeing their treehouse made me realize for the first time that their childhood was kind of... well, *normal*. Human-like, even. They had just been normal teens hiding out in their tree-house, away from Damon's family and the rest of the Lion Kingdom.

"We want to give you your Christmas gifts, Lena," Ezra said then.

"I already gave her mine," Harden said proudly.

I touched the bracelet I wore around my wrist, making sure it was still there.

"I didn't get gifts for any of you. I'm sorry," I apologized to them. "It didn't even cross my mind that we would be exchanging this year."

"Don't worry about it, Lena. We all wanted to get you gifts to show you how much you mean to us. We don't care that you didn't get us anything in return," Damon said.

"Okay." I sighed, feeling bad again. Maybe next Christmas, I would get them big gifts to make up for not getting them anything this year.

A thought crossed my mind then—a thought that I didn't even really want to consider.

Next Christmas, I would be celebrating with only one *of them as my mate.*

The thought made me feel sad. I tried to push it to the back of my mind and just focus on the here and now.

"So, I'll go first." Ezra handed me a small box wrapped in shiny red paper.

I tore the wrapping paper open and pulled out a small gray velvet box. I was surprised to find a gold compass inside.

It was beautiful. The shiny gold etched star was encrusted with what I was fairly certain were authentic diamonds and an amethyst at the center.

"You got me a compass?" My eyes flicked over to meet his gaze.

"It's not just any compass, Lena. It's one of the most accurate compasses in the entire world. It once belonged to Bagheera. It took a lot of begging on my end to get him to agree to sell it to me." He shrugged. "I know it may not seem like much right now, but I think it might come in handy once you're Queen."

"I love it, Ezra. Thank you." Even if I never had any use for it, I still appreciated the amount of thought he'd put into the gift.

"You're welcome."

"My turn," Rafael said then, pulling a slightly larger box out of his own pocket. It was wrapped in silver paper.

As I tore into the paper, I tried to guess what was inside, but I had no idea what it could have been. It felt sort of heavy, and I was pretty sure it was... vibrating?

I pulled out a red box. When I opened it, I was surprised to find a gold chain that held four heart-shaped stones, each a shade of pink marble in color.

"This isn't just any necklace, Lena. Each of those stones is one of our heartbeats. If you look at the back of the stone, it has our initials on it so you can know which one belongs to who," Rafael explained. "If something should ever happen to one of us and you can no longer hear our heartbeats, all you need to do is listen to the stones."

I reached out and touched the stones, realizing they were pulsating. So, *that's* where the vibrating had come from.

Instantly, I knew which of the stones belonged to which one of my mates. My suspicions were confirmed when I flipped each stone over to read the initials inscribed on the back.

I knew my mates well enough to know whose heartbeat sounded like what. It shocked me, because I hadn't even been able to feel my mates' heartbeats for *that* long.

"This is a beautiful gift, Raf. Thank you," I said, glancing over at him.

"I'm glad you like it."

Damon's golden-brown eyes caught mine then. "You can open my gift later, Lena... in private."

"Okay," I agreed with a nod. I was planning to spend the night with him since we were in his kingdom, anyway, so it worked out pretty perfectly.

"This has been the best Christmas," Ezra commented then.

"The best Christmas of my life, hands down." Harden winked at me.

A blush rose to my cheeks. The fact that we were officially

mated to one another, just in time for Christmas, *was* pretty amazing.

"I've had a great time with all of you," Rafael added.

"Me, too," Damon said. "It should be interesting to see what next Christmas is like."

The tone of his voice told me he was thinking the same exact thing I was. It was our second Christmas together, but next year, everything would change.

The Royal Change of Hands Ceremony was going to take place in May, just five months from now. After that, everything would be different.

In May, I would have to make my decision, once and for all.

I glanced around at my mates, drinking them all in. I loved them all so much—each and every single one of them. The idea of not having even one of them in my future made my heart hurt.

But it was more than just that. They were all *so* close. They truly were like brothers. Would their friendship with one another stand the test of time—or would I be the one to ruin it?

Who was I going to end up choosing in the end?

The thing was, I didn't *want* to decide. I wasn't even sure if I *could* make a decision... not now or ever. I was pretty sure I would feel no differently about it in five months from now.

Even though I sort of felt like I needed more time, I knew time didn't matter. No amount of time would be enough for me to decide which of these four amazing guys I wanted to spend eternity with... and which four of them I wanted to spend the rest of my life *without.*

Glancing up at the night sky through the treehouse window, I saw it again, written there for me in the clouds.

Lena, come see Glenda tomorrow morning.

It hit me then, the reason this message kept appearing in

the sky. I had been thinking about which of my mates I was going to choose the first time I saw the message, too.

This was what I was supposed to talk to her about.

Glenda must have had the answer for me.

CHAPTER
TWENTY-SIX

Later that night, Damon and I laid outside on the treehouse porch. We had a large fluffy blanket and pillows. Somehow, he had even managed to get cookies, chocolates, and champagne here ahead of time.

The rest of my mates had gone back to the castle for the night, but this had been the perfect way for us to get some much-needed privacy with one another.

I hadn't felt very close to Damon ever since we had fought about Rafael's memory. I didn't want to talk about that tonight —not on Christmas. I just wanted to enjoy his company.

Damon's golden-brown eyes met mine. "The view here is gorgeous."

"Yeah, the ocean is really beautiful," I agreed. I wasn't about to tell him that I had a really hard time paying attention to the ocean when *he* was right here next to me. I had a hard time peeling my eyes away from him.

"I wasn't talking about the ocean, Lena. I was talking about *you*." His eyes continued to linger on mine. "You're the most beautiful person I have ever known, both inside and out."

"Thank you." Something about the way he looked at me made something stir inside of me. It was just this...*feeling.*

The chemistry between us was out of this world. All he had to do was look at me, and the heat from his gaze spread through my body like wildfire.

I could tell he felt it, too. He leaned in closer to me then, and his mouth came crashing down on mine.

He moved so that he was hovering above me, and I wrapped my legs around his waist.

Running my fingers through his hair, I deepened the kiss.

I could feel his hardness pressing against me as I grinded my hips against his. His eyes locked on mine, and I could feel the carnal desire behind his gaze.

He wanted me just as badly as I wanted him.

Damon pulled my dress off over my head. He unhooked my bra and drug my panties down over my legs, tossing them to the side.

My heart raced with the anticipation of what was about to come next.

Bringing his lips down on my nipples, he kissed each of them. Then with one swift motion, he pushed himself inside of me, eliciting a gasp from me.

He moved in me slowly at first before building up to a steady pace. It didn't take long before I could feel it building up within me.

As the waves crashed against the shore below us, we crashed into each other until we came undone together.

"Are you ready to open your gift now?" Damon asked me after we made love several more times.

I wrapped the blanket around my still naked body and nodded. "As ready as I'll ever be."

He walked back into the treehouse. I stared at his bare ass as he walked, trying not to drool. That ass, and the gorgeous guy it belonged to, was *mine*.

For now, a voice at the back of my mind whispered.

When he returned, he placed a gold wrapped box into my hands.

It was fairly large and heavy. I eyed him curiously, wondering what was inside.

Sliding my finger underneath the paper, I undid the tape and pulled out a shiny gold box.

I met his gaze. "You got me a… gold box?"

"Your gift is inside the box," he replied with a laugh. "Open it."

Finding the lid, I carefully pulled it open and glanced inside.

A gold crown, adorned in amethysts and peridots stared back at me.

"It's your first crown," Damon explained. "My mom plans to give you her first crown, too, once you go through the coronation. But I wanted to get you one that had never been worn so that it would be entirely yours. It's custom made."

"This is incredible," I whispered. Pulling the crown out of the box, I looked at it closer. It was so beautiful. "Thank you."

"Try it on," Damon said.

Hesitantly, I pulled the crown on. My hair probably looked super sexed up beneath it.

"You look gorgeous, Lena. A beautiful crown for a beautiful Queen." His golden brown eyes lingered on mine. "I just hope that, in the end, you'll be *my* Queen."

~

The next morning, I was surprised to find that Damon was gone. He had texted me.

Damon: I have to go back to the palace, but I don't want to wake you. Meet me there when you wake up. I love you.

I pulled my clothes back on, knowing I needed to drag my ass back to the palace as soon as possible.

The message in the clouds last night had been crystal clear. I had to go visit Glenda this morning. It was already 10:30 a.m. I needed to get back to the human realm, and fast. What if there was a time limit on the answers I was so desperately in need of?

TWENTY-SEVEN

I t was strange to think there had ever been a time I hadn't believed in magic—a time when I'd thought monsters weren't real and that the supernatural existed only in TV shows and movies.

If only I had known then that magic would one day consume every aspect of my life. And that my future—and the future of the entire shifter world as we knew it—completely rested in the hands of a psychic and her ability to see into the future.

But I would worry about talking to her later. Right now, I had to locate my mates... but I couldn't seem to find them.

As I headed out into the grassy courtyard, I nearly stumbled over the lion body that lay before me.

His golden body looked so strong, yet so... *lifeless.*

His blonde mane was splayed out all around him. It didn't look like he was breathing; I didn't see his chest moving up and down.

Crouching down on my knees on the ground next to him, I felt for a pulse.

Nothing.

A lump formed in the back of my throat, making it difficult to swallow or even breathe. Tears sprang to my eyes.

This wasn't supposed to happen.

"Damon!" I managed to scream. "He's dead! Damon is dead!"

Moments later, Rafael and Ezra both helped me to my feet.

"Lena. Lena, it's okay. It's okay," Raf whispered, nuzzling his chin against my neck. "Damon's okay."

"But he's dead," I insisted, pointing at the body on the ground. It was still there. I wasn't dreaming or imagining this. He *was* dead.

"Damon's not dead, Lena," Ezra said gently. "That's not his body."

I blinked. I had seen my mate's lion form enough times to be able to recognize it. But then I looked a little closer.

This lion looked a little more weathered than Damon did. Older.

I realized what that meant. If it wasn't Damon's body, it must have been...

"It's my father," Damon's voice said from behind me.

Fuck.

There were so many things I had wanted to ask King Ari, questions about my mother that I would now never know the answers to.

I could feel Damon's sadness come over me. It consumed every ounce of my being.

When I glanced over at him, I watched as a single tear slid down his cheek.

"Who could have done this?" he asked. "We have to find the killer. I must avenge my father's death."

"What is all this ruckus about?" I heard Queen Kiara ask from behind us.

As she moved closer to us, her eyes fell on the King's lion body lying in a lifeless pile in the grass.

"My husband!" She cried out, collapsing to her knees and sobbing into his mane. She sounded completely broken.

My own heart broke for her. I could feel Damon's breaking, too.

Moving closer to him, I wrapped my arms around him, pulling him close. I thought he was going to fight my embrace at first. But instead, he just stood there, visibly shaken and giving in to my hug.

~

As the coroner came to remove King Ari's body to perform an autopsy on it, Damon turned to me. "You were supposed to go see Gretta this morning, Lena."

"It doesn't matter. I can go see her some other time."

He met my gaze. "But the message told you to go this morning."

"I want to be here for you," I insisted.

"I would feel a lot better if you left our kingdom, Lena," Damon said quietly. "If there's some sort of murderer or something, I would rather you be far away from here. The human realm is probably the best place for you to be right now—at least until this investigation is underway."

"Are you sure?" I asked him with wide eyes.

"I'm positive. Please. Go." His golden-brown eyes met mine. "Take one of the others with you."

"I'll go," Ezra volunteered.

Damon nodded. "Yes, please take her." He glanced over at

me. "I'll let you know through mind-speak if the coast is clear of any potential attackers. If it is, you can return here later on."

"Okay," I agreed with a nod. "Remember that I can hear your thoughts, but I can't respond to them because of Shere Khan's potion."

"Right, of course. Thankfully, we're able to communicate with each other because of you," Damon noted. He leaned in closer to me and gave me one more hug before walking over to the officers investigating the case.

Turning to Ezra, I said, "I don't know how we even get to Gretta."

"I do. She lives in Cherry Valley. We just need to make it back to the human realm, and then we can find her. Come on."

Ezra took my hand as he led me to the portal on the beach.

As we jumped into the hole in the sand, a mix of emotions washed over me.

It was sort of nice to be going back to the human realm for the first time in two years, even though I hated leaving Damon behind when he had just lost his dad. I knew we would meet again, but in the meantime, my heart was going to ache for him.

But I couldn't *not* go, either. I needed answers, and Gretta apparently had them for me.

~

To say I was nervous as hell as I watched Gretta stare into her purple, shimmery crystal ball would have been an understatement. I was scared shitless about what she was going to tell me. She was always spot on with her predictions.

An uncomfortable silence lingered in the air for the longest time.

Finally, I cleared my throat nervously. "Should I ask you a question?"

"That won't be necessary, Lena. We both know the reason you came." Her amber eyes flicked up to meet mine, and her wine-colored lips curved into a knowing smile.

Reaching across the table, Gretta handed me a black, velvet drawstring bag. "I need you to put this on before we begin."

Taking the bag from her, I opened it and pulled out a silver chain. It held a crescent-moon shaped pendant, adorned with sparkly crystals.

I shot a confused glance in Gretta's direction. "You got me a... necklace?"

"It is more than a necklace. This pendant is spelled to prevent your mates from listening in on your thoughts," she explained. "It will give you privacy."

"That won't be necessary. I've already taken a potion to prevent that from happening."

"This will be a long-term solution."

"But I don't keep secrets from my mates," I insisted.

"Maybe you should. Don't you want to be able to always think about them without them knowing?" Her amber eyes met mine challengingly.

"I guess," I murmured, pulling the necklace around my neck.

As soon as I did the clasp, I could just feel, deep in my gut, that my connection with them was even further lost. The necklace worked.

"You need to keep this pendant on."

I didn't *want* to keep it on. "For how long?"

"You shouldn't take it off until *after* you become Queen. If you remove it too early, the consequences could be devastating."

"What would the consequences be?" I asked.

She stared into the crystal ball, which was glowing red now.

"All I see is death." Her amber eyes locked on mine. "So much death."

I swallowed hard. Even though I hated the idea of not being able to communicate with my mates through our thoughts, I knew I couldn't argue with Gretta, either. So far, everything she had ever told me had been on point. I didn't want to find out if she was right about this, too. It wasn't worth the risk.

"Now, let's talk about why you are here." Gretta stared across the table at me. "I see a crossroads between four."

I didn't even need to ask what she was referring to. I already knew.

My mates.

I nodded.

"It is almost time for you to make a decision, but you are afraid you'll make the wrong one."

"Yeah." I swallowed hard. "What *is* the right one?"

She lowered her eyes to the crystal ball again. "With one of them, you feel a sense of completeness. Wholeness. With him, there is everything: chemistry, passion, friendship, security, confidence, and power. Especially power. He makes you feel safer than the rest of them."

Damon.

"The problem is you can both be stubborn at times. You always want it to be your way or no way, and as the natural born King of the Shifters, the lion is used to always getting his way. This will lead to a constant battle between you... a power struggle. And unfortunately, neither of you is very good at compromise."

I nodded, knowing she was right.

"His dad passed away this morning," she added.

"Who killed him?" I asked her. Maybe she could help point the investigation in the right direction, at least.

She stared into the crystal ball, focusing deeply. After a moment, her eyes met mine. "All I can see is that it was one of his allies."

I swallowed hard. Why would one of his allies have killed him?

"Now, let's not get off track from the original question—the reason you came. The crossroads." She paused. "With another one of the potential Kings, there is a very strong bond. An unbreakable bond. It is a sweet love. A tender love. I see that you sometimes feel you owe him more loyalty than you do the rest. This is because of a kiss. An *important* kiss." She closed her eyes. "He was the first kiss. The one who started it all."

Ezra. He was the first of my mates I had ever kissed.

"I see a strong friendship. Happiness. Gentleness and kindness. But choosing him would not be without problems." She met my gaze. "Unlike the lion, the wolf gives in *too* easily. You need someone who will challenge you more, or you will grow very bored in time." She paused for a moment. "The wolf's mother will also pose a challenge."

Well, that was on point. Nothing good could ever come from Ella Gray, but I already knew that.

"It is the jaguar who is the most difficult for me to read." Gretta focused on the crystal ball. "He is very closed off. And smart. Tech-savvy. He's certainly very devoted to you. There is respect there. He loves you and will do anything in his power to protect you, but..." She trailed off.

"What is it?" I asked, shifting in my seat nervously.

"I feel an overwhelming sense of disconnect."

"Disconnect?" That didn't seem right...

Gretta closed her eyes. A moment later, she opened them. "I don't think the jaguar completes you. He may never."

"You don't think Harden is the one?" I whispered.

Just the thought that Harden—or *any* of them—might not have been "the one" completely broke my heart. And that right there was the problem. I didn't want to picture my life without even one of them.

"The bond you have with him is the weakest of the four. He is the mate who you don't know well enough. He is a bit of a mystery even to you. It's as if he is a puzzle with missing pieces."

Well, she wasn't wrong there. Of all of my mates, Harden was the one who kept to himself the most. It had been challenging to get him to open up to me. I hadn't even known his bedroom was an aquarium until two days ago.

"If you are able to locate the pieces you are missing and crack the surface of who he is, then anything is possible. But who really knows what the completed puzzle may look like?" She paused for a moment. "As for the tiger..." Gretta closed her eyes, clearly deep in thought.

I held my breath, nervous to hear what she was about to say next.

"I see a passion unlike anything you have ever known before. A deep emotional and physical connection. There is a heat between you... a fire that cannot, and will never be, extinguished." She met my gaze. "The problem you face with the tiger is one that you're already aware of. A dark force has been working against you for some time now—a force that wants to destroy your bond. This evil force will stop at nothing to come between the two of you."

"Is the dark force whoever wiped away his memories?" I asked.

She nodded. "Yes."

A shiver crept down my spine. This was exactly what I'd been afraid of. "Who is this dark force?"

Now that I knew it wasn't Shere Khan, I didn't know *who* it might have been.

She stared into the crystal ball for a few long moments before finally shaking her head. "That part is unclear. They are good at covering their tracks, because of their dark magic. But I can tell you one thing." Her eyes met mine. "The only one who can stop this dark force is *you*."

"*Me?*" I let out a little laugh. "I'm not powerful enough."

"Ah, but that is where you are wrong, Lena. You're forgetting who you are. Remember the prophecy."

I suppressed an eye roll. "To hell with the prophecy."

The truth was that I was so over this stupid prophecy. It had wreaked so much havoc on my life that I was beginning to wish there *wasn't* a prophecy—not one that I was at the center of, anyway.

Gretta shot a sharp glance in my direction. "It's more than just a prophecy, Lena. It's a curse."

My eyebrows lifted. "A curse?"

"Have you never wondered why this prophecy came to be in the first place? Have you really *never* wondered why you're at the center of it all?" she questioned. "Why were *you*, of all the shifters in the land, chosen to be the next Queen of the Shifters—the one who would eventually unite all of the shifter races?"

"It's crossed my mind more times than I can count," I admitted. But I had never considered the possibility that it was actually a *curse*. Now that I knew it was, it seemed so... dark. So eerie. Why would someone curse me?

On the other hand, it made perfect sense. It *felt* like a curse.

"You must figure out the origins of this curse. It will give you answers to some of the questions you have wondered about."

"Well, don't *you* know the origins of the curse?" I pressed.

"I'm afraid I cannot see the answer." Meeting my eyes, she forced a smile. "Unfortunately, there are some things that even a psychic cannot see."

"How can I find out the answer?" I asked.

She stared back into the crystal ball. "I see a coyote and a crown. A Coyote King. He holds the answers."

Great. Jake's grandfather was the King of the Coyotes. The last thing I wanted was to deal with my ex-boyfriend's family.

"Now, we must discuss the bears," Gretta continued. "They are still your greatest enemies."

"Who are the bears I need to worry about?" I asked her.

"You haven't met them yet."

Well, that wasn't the answer I had been expecting. It ruled out Dominik and Cal.

"I don't understand." I shook my head in confusion. "How could anyone be my enemy if they've never even met me?"

"They have been your enemies since you were conceived," she replied. "It is because of the prophecy."

So, these bears were my enemies because I was going to be the next Queen of the Shifters. Talk about some shitty luck.

"The first time I met you, you said the cats will protect me from the bears. I assume that by 'cats', you were referring to my mates."

She nodded. "That is correct."

"What about Ezra?"

Her facial expression became unreadable to me. "When it comes to the wolf, it is *you* who will need to protect *him*."

"From who?" I asked, even though I had a feeling I already knew.

"His mother," she replied, confirming it.

"Wait. You didn't actually tell me which of the four I'm supposed to choose," I said. "Which one do you see me ending this war with? Who will make the most powerful King?"

Gretta's answer had revolved around who would make me happier. But when it came down to it, my happiness didn't matter. The only thing that mattered was ending the war and saving the shifter world. Everything about all of this was so much bigger than me and my mates. And when it came down to it, regardless of what Gretta believed, I was pretty sure that all *four* of them could make me happy in their own way. Each one of them was a worthy contender.

"You already know the answer, Lena." Her eyes met mine. "You already know which of your mates is your destiny."

"If I knew the answer, I wouldn't have asked you."

"That is what you would like to believe, but deep down, you know. There is only one answer that comes to mind when you think of who you'll choose. But that answer scares you. You're afraid of what it will mean for you—for the entire shifter world. But you must follow your heart."

"But if I follow my heart..." I trailed off.

"Everything will change," Gretta replied matter-of-factly.

"Yes," I whispered.

"It won't come easy. You must fight for what you want. But you should know that it will be worth every ounce of fight."

"How do you know?"

"Because change," she said, "is good."

I really hoped she was right, but honestly? I wasn't sure if the shifter world would be able to handle a change of this magnitude.

CHAPTER

TWENTY-EIGHT

"Is everything okay?" Ezra asked as I rejoined him outside Gretta's house.

"Yeah, everything's fine." As fine as it could possibly get, anyway.

"Did you get the answers you needed?"

"I don't know. Sort of." I paused, thinking about the answer that was bothering me the most. The curse. I needed to know more about this curse, and there was only one way to find out the answers. "What do you think about going to the Coyote Kingdom with me?"

"I don't know. The coyotes aren't exactly allies to the werewolves," he reminded me.

The Coyotes and Werewolves had only ever had a fragile alliance, at best. Their relationship with one another had only gotten worse since the war.

"If the coyotes found out an uninvited werewolf is in their kingdom..." Ezra trailed off.

"I will make sure they don't do anything to hurt you."

He didn't look convinced.

"I *promise*. I know the King of the Coyotes. He's my ex-boyfriend's grandfather," I reminded him. "Even though Jake and I are no longer together, there's no bad blood between me and his grandfather."

At least, none that I was aware of. Back in the human world, Tom had been like a second grandfather to me.

Ezra sighed. "Why do you want to go there?"

"Gretta told me Jake's grandfather has an answer for me about something I really need to know."

"Okay." His blue eyes met mine. "I'll go with you."

"Are you sure?" I asked.

"Well, I'm not letting you go there alone. It's far too risky."

"How will we even get through their portal?" I asked. "They have a magical shield on their kingdom, don't they?"

"Actually, they don't. That's one of the reasons why this *is* so dangerous," Ezra explained. "The coyotes lack the magical abilities or the finances to keep a magical shield up at all times."

"Oh. Okay."

I wasn't sure how to feel about that, honestly. Even though it was a good thing because it meant that we got to enter the Coyote Kingdom without being stopped by a magical barrier, it also meant that it was more dangerous. I hadn't been anywhere that didn't have a magical barrier in place since the whole war had begun.

But it looked like I didn't have a choice. I had to get to the bottom of this curse so that I could understand why this prophecy was in place, once and for all.

The Coyote Kingdom looked like a warzone. The cobblestone streets were empty... desolate.

In the distance, I could see that some of the streets were blood-stained. It made my stomach churn.

It made me feel really depressed to see how bad things had gotten here. And it also put me on edge.

"I think our best bet is to take the underground tunnel that leads to the castle," Ezra whispered as we stood in an empty street.

"How do you know there's an underground tunnel?" I asked with raised eyebrows.

"My mom brought me here once when I was a kid," he explained. "The tunnel entrance is right through here."

He lifted up a tree that I would have thought was a *real* tree, but it turned out to just be a cover for a large drainage grate in the ground.

Lifting the grate, Ezra leapt down into the hole and then glanced up at me. "Jump, Lena."

I didn't even think twice as I hopped down into the hole after him.

As I landed on the cement ground, I glanced around. The tunnel was dark and sounded like it was wet and dripping. It reminded me of an underground sewage tunnel like the ones in the movies.

"*Lumen*," Ezra said, and a torch-like light appeared in his hand.

Somewhere behind us, I could hear the sound of voices. We definitely weren't alone down here, even though it sounded like whoever was down here with us was a good distance away.

"Let's move quickly towards the castle. It's that way." He pointed ahead of us.

I grabbed his hand, and together, we ran in the direction of the castle.

The faster we moved, the quicker it sounded like the other shifters down here were catching up to us.

Finally, light streamed into the tunnel, and I realized that we were reaching the end.

Ezra came to a stop and pulled a ladder down from the ceiling.

He began to climb it and opened the trap door. He climbed inside.

I began to climb the ladder, too.

I was just about halfway up the ladder when I heard the sound of a low growl from behind me.

Glancing over my shoulder, I saw the coyote that stood there, snarling at me.

I quickened my speed, beginning to climb the ladder steps two at a time.

Once I was inside with Ezra, he pulled the ladder up and closed the trap door behind us, locking it.

"That was a close call," I whispered.

"Eh. Sort of. The coyotes are weak," he reminded me. "We could have taken that one down in a heartbeat."

I knew he was right, but *still*. Maybe it would have deserved to win in this case, considering we were the ones who were intruding on their kingdom.

Not that we meant any harm. All I wanted was answers and then we would leave.

"Well, now that we're in, we should probably go locate King Thomas," he commented.

Sometimes, I was still unable to believe that Jake's Grandpa Tom, who I had known pretty much my entire life, was the King of the Coyotes. It didn't matter how much time passed; this information was still so surreal to me.

As Ezra and I rounded a corner, I heard the sound of an alarm going off.

"Intruders have entered the castle! Intruders have entered the castle!" a robotic voice alerted.

Shit.

My heart began to pound against my chest. We were about to get caught.

I glanced over at Ezra. "I thought you said they didn't have technology around here!"

None of the other kingdoms I had ever been to alerted the Royals when intruders entered the building. At least, as far as I knew, they didn't. Maybe there hadn't been any intruders when I was visiting.

"It's okay, Lena. Relax. I can *feel* your anxiety." He grabbed my hand tightly as we continued our way down the castle hallway.

Even though the alarm was still going off in the background, I glanced around the castle, taking it all in.

Everything about the place felt so much older than the other kingdoms. It was as if they hadn't been able to afford to renovate the place or even maintain its original beauty... assuming that it had *ever* been beautiful.

"There they are!" I heard a security guard shout from behind us.

"Shit, shit, shit," I muttered under my breath. I was about to speed up, but Ezra slowed down.

"Let's just tell them the reason we're here. Maybe they can help," he suggested through mind-speak.

Or maybe they would kick us out and I would *never* be able to get the answer I needed, I thought to myself.

Just as the security guard had about caught up with us, I heard someone call out my name from behind me.

"Lena! What are *you* doing here?"

I turned to find Jake standing behind me, looking completely surprised to see me.

"Jake, I'm so glad you're here." I breathed a huge sigh of

relief. "I need to see your grandfather. It's really important. Can you help?"

"Yeah, of course." Jake turned to the guards. "These are my friends, not intruders. You can leave them alone."

One of the guards looked me up and down for a moment. He looked extremely suspicious of me. I was pretty sure if it was up to him, he wouldn't have backed down.

The other guard nodded. "Our apologies, Prince Jacob."

"It's fine, but don't let it happen again with these two," Jake ordered.

I was surprised to hear him act so bossy towards the guards. It was a side of him that I'd never really seen before.

It was proof that we were practically strangers. I didn't know the guy who stood before me at all these days.

Not that it mattered. All I needed was for him to take me to his grandfather. The rest was history.

"My grandfather is in his office. It's right down this hall-way," Jake explained, leading us down one of the castle wings.

Once we reached the door, Jake said, "I'm going to just go inside and talk to him for a second."

"Okay," I replied with a nod.

As he went inside the office and closed the door behind him, I waited nervously in the hallway.

I heard the sound of their muffled voices on the other side of the door, but I couldn't make out anything they were saying.

What if his grandfather didn't want to see me? I doubted that would be the case, but it had been over two years since I'd seen him. A lot could change in that time... especially given that we were in a war.

"It's going to be okay, Lena." Ezra reached out and touched my shoulder reassuringly.

I grabbed his hand again. I was relieved that he had agreed to come here with me. I couldn't imagine what it would have been like to come to the Coyote Kingdom alone. I probably would have still been trying to find a way into the castle.

Finally, the door reopened and Jake came back into the hallway. "My grandfather said he'll see you now, Lena."

"Okay. Thanks."

Ezra glanced over at me. "I'll wait out here for you."

"Actually, why don't we go play some pool, Ez?" Jake asked. "We'll give them some privacy."

"Thank you," I told him.

"No need to thank me. We'll be down that hall"—Jake pointed his chin— "when you're done."

"Okay," I said with a nod. Taking a deep breath, I walked into the office.

I found Jake's grandfather sitting at a large oak desk. He glanced up at me as I entered the room.

"Hi, Lena. It's been a while, hasn't it?" Tom asked.

"About two years, I think."

"I'm pretty sure the last time we saw one another was at the funeral. I'm still terribly sorry for your loss. I think about your parents often."

"Thank you," I replied quietly.

Closing his laptop, he leaned forward. "So, Jake said you want to talk to me. I'm pretty sure that I can probably guess what this is about."

My eyebrows rose. "You *can*?"

He nodded, his dark brown eyes meeting mine. "This must have something to do with the curse."

"Yes. I need to know more about the curse." I hesitated for a moment. "How do *you* know about the curse?"

"I was very close to your parents, Lena. They told me everything there was to know about it. Well, *almost* everything."

"Wait. My parents knew about the curse?" I asked, surprised by this news.

"Yes, of course. They knew all about the curse and the prophecy."

"I don't understand. If they knew about it, how come they never told me about it?"

It was bad enough that my parents had kept me in the dark about the fact that I was a shifter at all. But I had always just assumed that they didn't know about the prophecy. Why hadn't they bothered to prepare me for all of this? It would have been nice to know that someone had put a curse on me, a curse that would pretty much destroy any chance at me ever having anything that even remotely resembled a semi-normal life.

"Your parents put a lot of thought into how much they should or shouldn't tell you," Tom replied. "Even though they wanted you to be ready, they also wanted to do everything they could to protect you." He met my gaze. "There's something you must know about your parents, Lena. It's a good thing you're already sitting down, because this is going to change your life as you know it."

"What is it?" I asked.

"I know this is going to come as a huge shock to you, and there's no easy way for me to say it. But your parents, the ones who passed away, weren't your biological parents."

"W-what?" I whispered.

Tom nodded. "Yes. I am sorry to be the one to tell you this, but your biological mother wanted to protect you... because of the curse. She wanted you to live an ordinary life—a human life. The mother you've known your entire life was a very good friend of your biological mother, so your parents agreed to adopt you and raise you as a human in order to protect you."

"I don't understand," I replied, shaking my head. I tried to process everything he was saying, but it wasn't easy.

How was it possible that my parents, the mother and father who had raised me, weren't my biological parents?

How could they have kept this secret from me, too?

"And that's not all," Tom continued. "Your biological parents were Royals, Lena."

"They *were?*"

"Yes." He nodded.

"Who are my biological parents, then?" I questioned.

"I'm afraid that I don't actually know the answer to that question. But I do know the details. Your biological mother was having an extramarital affair with a King from one of the other shifter races when she fell pregnant with you. When her own husband, the King of her race, found out that she was pregnant with another man's child, he had a witch place a curse on the baby—*on you.*"

"What was the curse?" I asked.

Tom's eyes met mine. "It stated that you would be able to shift into multiple shifter races, so you would constantly be at war with yourself. This would complicate your life forever."

I frowned. "But I'm *not* more than one shifter race. I'm a werebear. That's all."

"It's quite possible that you simply haven't shifted into another shifter race yet, Lena. Give it time." He paused for a moment. "When your biological mother found out about the curse her husband had placed on you, she paid a visit to a witch. The witch placed a spell on you—a spell that said you would be the most powerful shifter of all time. She said you wouldn't be at war with yourself, but instead you'd be the one to end a war between all of the shifter races. The spell that she put on you led to what we now know as the prophecy."

I allowed everything he was saying to sink in. The truth was that it actually made *so* much sense. All of this time, I had thought I was destined to become the next Queen of the Shifters without even descending from a Royal bloodline. But why would fate have chosen a random shifter to be Queen? It wouldn't have even made sense.

A realization hit me then.

I was born to do this. I was born to be Queen.

~

When Ezra and I reached the portal to leave the Coyote Kingdom, I was still trying to wrap my head around everything I had just learned.

"*Is it safe for us to come back now, Damon?*" Ezra's thoughts entered my mind.

There seemed to be some hesitation on Damon's end. Finally, he responded, "*We haven't gotten a chance to do a search of the entire island yet. You'd be better off going somewhere else for now, just until we can make sure the coast is clear.*"

Frustrated that I couldn't respond to Damon through my thoughts, I glanced over at Ezra. "Can you tell him that Gretta said it was one of his dad's allies who murdered him?"

Ezra repeated what I'd just said through mind-speak.

"*Which one of his allies?*" Damon questioned.

"She didn't know," I told Ezra to convey the message.

"*Damnit.*" Damon's frustrations were obvious in his tone. "*Where do you think you guys will go for the time being?*"

"*We're going back to my kingdom,*" Ezra informed him.

My eyebrows lifted. "But your mom..."

His blue eyes met mine. "No one can find her, meaning she isn't in our kingdom."

Well, he had a good point.

"I want you to meet the rest of my family, Lena. You've

gotten to meet all of the other guys' families and see their king-doms. It's my turn."

"Okay," I agreed with a nod. Just because Ella Gray had been a really sad excuse for a werewolf, it didn't mean the rest of his family was just as bad. Ezra had *a lot* of siblings, and I hadn't met any of them yet besides Eric.

As we traveled through the portal, I hoped that our visit to the Werewolf Kingdom would go okay, but honestly?

I had no idea *what* to expect.

CHAPTER
TWENTY-NINE

The Werewolf Kingdom was nothing like the other kingdoms I had visited so far. The only similarity was that there was an ocean with a sandy coast. But beyond the shore, all you could see for miles was forest. There was also a snow-covered mountain in the distance.

It made sense why the werewolves had a piney, earthy scent to them. They smelled like their home, their land.

One of the things I instantly noticed about this kingdom was the temperature. It was *much* colder than the other kingdoms. I was wearing a sleeveless dress, and I found myself shivering.

Ezra noticed right away that I was freezing. "I'll get you a jacket as soon as we get inside the palace," he told me. "Why are you so cold, though?"

It wasn't very common for shifters—especially werebears—to get cold very easily, since we had unnaturally high body temperatures. And then there was me, the cold-blooded one.

Of course, there was no way I could tell Ezra about that without letting him in on the fact that Kaa and Shere Khan both strongly believed that I might have been a Serpent. And even though I wanted to believe they were wrong, that there was nothing Serpent-like about me, I also couldn't ignore everything Tom had told me about myself.

There was a chance that I had multiple shifter races.

"I'm not sure why I'm so cold," I lied to Ezra, glancing over at him. "It must just be the extreme temperature change."

"Maybe," he replied, even though he looked far from convinced.

As he led me over a drawstring bridge that led to the palace, he glanced over at me. "So, I should probably prepare you for my dad."

I narrowed my eyes at him. "Prepare me *how*?"

"My dad is just very... gruff."

"Oh." That was sort of hard to imagine, considering Ezra was the exact opposite of gruff. If anything, he might have benefited a little from some gruffness, but he was entirely sweet.

"He also *hates* my mother with a passion," Ezra added.

"Well, I don't think there are many shifters in this world who don't hate your mother because of the bootcamp," I said quietly. The news had aired Ella Gray's approval ratings, and they had continuously declined ever since her deranged bootcamp.

"It's not just because of the bootcamp, Lena. My father has always hated my mother."

"He must have been able to see her true colors," I said.

"Guess so." Ezra kicked up some dirt as we got closer to the castle. "I wonder why I was never able to see her true colors."

"When we love someone, we just want to see the good in them," I told him. "You even more so than others. There's nothing wrong with that, Ez. It's something I love about you— one of the *many* things I love about you."

Glancing down into my eyes, his blue irises pierced straight through mine. He tilted his head and brought his lips down on mine.

We stood there for a long moment, kissing in front of the castle.

I felt the rain start pouring down all around us then.

It might have been crazy to think, but I couldn't help but wonder if our kiss had somehow brought it on.

Were our kisses *magic*?

I wasn't sure why, but for some reason, it had always felt that way with him.

~

Ten minutes later, I was wearing one of Ezra's light blue plaid jackets and sitting in a lounge room with all of his siblings.

Ethan, Eddie, Elijah, and Emmett were all a lot younger than us. They were all just one year apart, with their ages ranging from eleven to fourteen years old. All four of them looked so much like Ezra and Eric; it was uncanny how strong the Gray genes ran on the male side.

His sisters—Emmalyn, Elouise, and Erica—were younger, too. Emmalyn, a quiet girl with blonde hair and freckles, was fifteen. Elouise, a brunette with a major princess complex, was twelve; she was Eddie's twin sister. And Erica, who had black hair and was extremely chatty, was sixteen.

"So, what's Shifter Academy like, Lena?" Erica was asking me. "I'm going to be going there next year on campus. I can't wait."

"It's a nice school. The professors are great." I decided not to mention that they were better this year than they would be next. "You'll be going to school with the Crowne girls."

She wrinkled her nose. "I don't like the lions."

"You don't?" It sort of surprised me to hear her say that, considering Damon was one of Ezra's best friends.

"Heck no. The girls are *so* much drama. They think that just because they have really nice hair, their shit doesn't stink. Newsflash: there are other good features besides hair. Like eyes, for example."

Every single of the Grays had incredibly beautiful blue eyes. They ranged from a light grayish blue to turquoise blue in color, but all of their eyes made you look twice.

"Hey, Ezra, have you heard from Eric lately?" Emmett asked, changing the subject.

We all glanced over in Ezra's direction.

"No, I haven't heard from him since the first couple of weeks of school." He shook his head sadly. "All I know is he's off looking for Mom."

"Yeah, I know," Emmett replied. "Do you think he's actually going to find her?"

"I don't know, Em. He's been looking for a pretty long time now, and it seems like he hasn't turned up anything yet," Ezra replied.

"Well, I hope he does. Mom deserves to go to prison for the rest of her life for what she did to those students," Emmett said.

"Your mother deserves more than just life in prison," a male voice said.

I glanced up to see a man who looked just like an older version of Ezra enter the room.

"Off with her head," he added with a sinister smile.

Ezra looked mildly uncomfortable by what his dad had just said. "Hey, Dad."

"Welcome home, son." His eyes fell on me, sitting next to Ezra. "Is this that mate of yours?"

"Yes. Dad, I want you to meet Lena Falcone. Lena, this is my dad, King Axel."

"It's nice to meet you," I told him politely.

"You, too. And I mean that from the bottom of my heart, Lena," King Axel said, shaking my hand. "Honestly, you're already one of my favorite people."

"I am?" I asked with raised eyebrows. I knew it was normal for a parent to be happy for their child to find true love, but his reaction to me seemed a little... well, *extreme*.

Was it possible that he liked me—or *claimed* to like me—so much because of the prophecy? Maybe he was excited by the possibility of Ezra becoming the next King of the Shifters, and he figured that he'd better suck up to me so that I might choose him in the end.

"Absolutely. My wife Ella hated you. She wanted to kill you so much that the Legends had to be summoned from the dead. That's how strong my wife's hatred for you was." He spoke the words as if I didn't already know that all of this had happened. "The thing is, I hate Ella. My wife is one of the worst shifters you will ever meet. So, knowing how much she hated you makes me realize one thing about you, which is that you must be incredible."

Ezra hadn't been kidding about his dad's hatred of his mom, that was for sure.

On the upside, it seemed like Axel and I were going to get along just fine.

Damon told us we should spend the night in the Werewolf Kingdom. So that night, Ezra led me to a tower at the far end of the castle.

"My bedroom is a little drafty, so I hope you won't be too cold," he informed me.

"Well, hopefully your body heat will be enough to keep me warm."

A blush rose to his cheeks. "Actually, Lena, I was thinking that maybe we should sleep in separate beds."

"I'm sorry. What?" I asked, hoping that the disappointment wasn't written all over my face.

I had actually figured that tonight would be the perfect time to, uh, complete the Bonding Process, since I was spending the night alone with him.

"Don't get me wrong. I love to sleep with you. It's just that it might make me want to do... things with you." His blue eyes met mine. "It would be really hard not to give into temptation."

"Well, why do you want to fight it?" I questioned as he opened the door to his room. I tried not to sound defensive, but I was sort of offended that he didn't want to be with me in that way.

"Remember what I told you, Lena. I want you to save me for last." His blue eyes met mine. "I got to be your first kiss, and I want to be the last one you complete the Mate Bonding Process with."

"You're really going to hold me to that?"

Ezra nodded.

I was surprised that he had so much self-restraint. I wished I could say the same.

"I know that you've done it with Damon and Harden already. You need to be with Rafael next before you get to me." His eyes met mine, and there was a look of urgency within them. "What are you waiting for, Lena? Why haven't you done it with Rafael yet?"

I thought about it for a moment. The real reason I hadn't gone there with Raf yet was because he'd lost his memories of me. Of course, I wasn't helping that process out by not giving him the potion. But... still. Even *if* I gave him the potion, there was still no guarantee he would actually remember everything in the end. And we *did* seem to get along really well as we made new memories. So, what *was* I waiting for?

Deep down, I knew a lot of my hesitancy still had to do with everything getting messed up the last time I had tried to make it happen. I knew it was unlikely that anything that bad would happen again, but still. I was so afraid of wrecking something.

Of course, I couldn't tell any of that to Ezra, not without telling him I had planned to have sex with Rafael the night he had switched bodies with whoever.

So, instead, I just said, "I guess I've just been waiting for the right time."

That was *sort of* the truth.

"Sometimes, there really is no right time," Ezra replied. "Sometimes, it's now or never."

"Yet, you want to make *me* wait," I pointed out.

"That's different."

"I don't see how," I replied.

"I'm a little more sentimental than the others," he replied. "These sorts of things matter more to me. Actually, I was thinking... Why don't we take this one step further?"

"What do you mean?" I asked.

"Well... *if* you choose me, why don't we wait until our wedding night?" His eyes met mine. "That would make it even more special."

"I don't know, Ezra," I replied with a sigh as he tossed some pillows and blankets onto the ground. "You're going to sleep on the floor tonight?"

"Well, you're certainly not sleeping on the floor. It has to be me."

I tried to avoid arguing with him, even though I wanted to. I didn't like the fact that he could just control these urges. It made me think that his urges must not have been a match for mine, because I had really been looking forward to doing this tonight.

But no. He didn't want to just wait. He wanted to wait until our potential wedding night.

No freaking pressure.

THIRTY

The next morning, Ezra and I headed back to the Lion Kingdom. I wasn't sure why it shocked me to see crime scene evidence tape blocking off the majority of the palace grounds. It felt like a human crime scene.

We found Damon in the study with his mom.

They both glanced up at us as we entered the room.

"Hello, Lena," Queen Kiara said.

"I'm so sorry for your loss," I told her.

"Thank you. The funeral will be held tomorrow afternoon," she informed us. "It will be a private ceremony, but we want both of you to attend."

"I'll be there," I replied with a nod.

Glancing over at Damon, I couldn't help but notice that he seemed... hardened. Emotionless, even.

I was sort of worried for him. I knew firsthand how much the death of a parent could change you, especially when murder was involved. But I was afraid that Damon's dad's murder was going to make him cold and angry.

"Well, I should really go work on some of the arrangements," Queen Kiara said. "Would you mind helping me, Ezra?"

I realized she was trying to give me and Damon some privacy.

"Yeah, sure," Ezra replied, following her out of the room.

Closing the door after them, I turned to Damon. "Are you okay?"

"It's all a part of life, isn't it? Grieving the loss of a parent."

"It's not meant to be a part of *our* lives. Our parents are supposed to be immortal." I hesitated for a moment before adding, "And it's not a natural part of life to lose a parent to murder."

"I just keep trying to figure out who all of his allies are. Well, who his allies were *supposed to be*, since the ally who killed him was clearly a fraud." He sighed. "So much has changed since the war first began. It's hard to know who he was getting along with, and who he wasn't." He paused for a moment. "I do find it highly suspicious that he had just gone to that meeting with the King of the Cheetahs. My mind keeps coming back to him as our prime suspect."

"What motives would he have even had to kill your dad, though?" I questioned.

"Maybe he thought it would help weaken the lions so that the cheetahs could climb in the hierarchy."

I frowned. "Even *if* killing your dad somehow made the lions weaker, it's not like the cheetahs would make it to the top of the hierarchy." I paused, shaking my head. "I could be wrong, but I just have this feeling that the King of the Cheetahs is too obvious. I think it's someone who you wouldn't even suspect."

Damon sighed and sat down. He handed me a tablet where he had written out a list of allies and enemies with notes about potential motives and other details next to them.

"You think it could be Queen Bria and King Roman?" I was surprised to see their names on the list.

"They want to kill you, Lena. If they could want to kill *you*, the most beautiful person I have ever known, then I wouldn't put it past them to kill my father."

I knew he wasn't wrong. I didn't trust them even a little bit.

"Plus, they'd be closer to the top of the hierarchy if something happened to my mother, too."

Well, that made sense.

"Are you going to tell Rafael that his parents made the list?" I asked.

He shook his head. "No. I have notes on there for all of the other guys' parents, but none of them can know I suspect their parents. Except for Ezra, I guess. At this point, it's not at all unreasonable to suspect Ella Gray."

"Yeah, who *wouldn't* suspect Ella Gray?" I sighed, glancing over at him. "You know you don't have to solve this overnight, right? Maybe try letting the police do their jobs with the investigation and see what they come up with first."

"I know you're right, Lena. I know I'm going to drive myself crazy if I don't give it a break, but that's not who I am." His eyes met mine. "I am the type to take charge. If you want something done right, you've got to do it yourself. So, I will continue to do this investigation myself." He paused for a moment. "I know it's not going to be solved overnight—not even close. I actually had a vision. You know I'm not one for visions. I've only ever had maybe three in my lifetime. Well, in this particular vision, it was towards the end of the school year, right before the Royal Change of Hands ceremony, and the murder wasn't even close to being solved."

"So, we're in it for the long haul when it comes to figuring this out," I said with a sigh.

His golden brown eyes met mine. "*We're?*"

"Damon, you're my mate. I love you. Of course it's a *we* thing... an *us* thing. I'm going to do everything in my power to help you solve this."

"Thank you, Lena. I appreciate that so much more than you'll ever know." He paused for a moment before adding, "I don't want to get used to your help, though. I know there's always a chance that you might eventually stop your investigation. You know... like if you choose one of the others."

"I will never stop helping you," I told him.

I wished I could tell him everything.

I wished I could tell him all about the decision I was planning to make, about who I was choosing. But I didn't want any of my mates to know what I had decided on yet, so I was going to keep it to myself.

It was, undoubtedly, the hardest secret I would ever keep from them. But little did I know then, it wouldn't be the biggest.

CHAPTER

THIRTY-ONE

At the stroke of midnight, fireworks shot off over the beach in the Tiger Kingdom. It was the biggest fireworks display I had ever seen in my life.

"Happy New Year!" Ezra and Harden shouted in sync.

"Happy New Year!" I smiled at them.

"Happy New Year, Princess." Rafael's emerald green eyes glimmered in the moonlight, popping against the orange polo t-shirt he had on, as he brought his lips down on mine.

The thing about having four mates was I wasn't sure who to kiss when it was midnight. I was planning not to kiss *any* of them. I was glad Raf had taken the guesswork out of it for me.

When we broke away from one another, I glanced over my shoulder, realizing for the first time that Damon wasn't near us.

It had been amazing that we'd even been able to convince him to leave the Lion Kingdom for the holiday. He'd wanted to stay at the palace to protect his mom and sisters. It had taken a lot of convincing from Queen Kiara, who told him how important it was for him to return to Shifter Academy on Monday

253

morning; as much as he may have wanted to stay to protect his family, it simply wasn't a realistic solution.

But ever since we had arrived in the Tiger Kingdom, Damon had seemed like he was having a miserable time.

Glancing around, I spotted him standing on the beach below.

To my surprise, he was talking to Shere Khan.

Huh. *That* was strange.

I wasn't sure what they were talking about. But from where I stood, it looked like the conversation was getting heated.

"I'll be back, you guys," I told the rest of my mates.

"Okay," Ezra replied with a nod.

Climbing down the steps that led off the rooftop, I knew I needed to get to Damon. It wasn't that I thought he needed rescuing. No, he was perfectly capable of looking out for himself... *physically*, that is.

But right now, Damon was in such a fragile emotional state that I knew I had to watch out for him. It made me channel a lot of chess game energy.

A Queen always protects her King.

I was just about to cut across the stretch of sand that led to where they were standing when someone tapped me on the shoulder.

Turning around, I found a pair of emerald green eyes piercing straight through mine.

I might have been tricked into thinking it was Rafael if it weren't for the orange shirt he had on.

It was Ricky.

"Hey, Lena."

"Hey." I shifted in my sandals uncomfortably.

"It's nice to see you in my kingdom. You've been here before, right?"

"Yeah, I was here during National Felidae Day," I replied.

"Isn't that strange? We never ran into each other that day, even though we were both here."

"A little strange, I guess," I replied with a shrug.

His eyes met mine. "Funny, isn't it? We've never actually spoken to each other until right now, even though we have a class together."

"Yeah."

"You've been to my kingdom *twice*. We have class together. You're always hanging out with my brother. And yet, never once have you initiated a conversation with me." Ricky laughed. "It's almost starting to feel like you've been avoiding me. What I can't seem to figure out is *why*."

"The opportunity or need to have a conversation with one another simply hasn't come up," I replied.

"Are you sure that's it? Or is there a reason why I'm not good enough to talk to the infamous Lena Falcone?"

"Infamous?" I just stared back at him with wide eyes.

"Ah, yes. You *are* the girl who was unable to be sorted as a freshman, are you not?"

"That would be me." What I wasn't sure of was why he was bringing it up. I wasn't sure why he was bringing *any* of this up.

"We should kiss," Ricky said.

"I think I'll pass on that," I replied.

"But how will we ever know if we're mates if we don't kiss?"

"I can tell you, without a doubt, that we're not mates," I replied matter-of-factly.

"How can you be so sure?" His eyes met mine. "You have beautiful chocolate-colored hair and honey-colored eyes, by the way."

I realized what he was getting at then—the entire reason he

255

wanted to kiss me, the reason he wanted to see if he could potentially be my mate.

He knew about the prophecy.

I wasn't sure how he had figured it out, but somehow, he had.

He wanted to kiss me to see if I was his mate because he wanted to become the next King of the Shifters. He saw me as a possible way to become King, a way to become more powerful than Rafael.

That wasn't exactly how the prophecy worked, but he must have either misunderstood it or he hoped he could change the details of it. Either way, he was wrong.

And there was no way in hell I was going to kiss him.

"Thanks, but I'm pretty sure we're not mates," I told him. "The reason I know that is because I already have a mate."

I decided not to confirm his suspicions about me and the prophecy.

"I see." Ricky looked like he wanted to say something more, but he didn't.

"Now, if you'll excuse me."

As I walked past Ricky, I could feel him staring at my back as I walked away.

Talk about an awkward and uncomfortable first conversation with him. If anything, it had just confirmed what I already knew.

I really didn't like Ricky. I didn't trust him, either.

When I reached where Damon was standing on the beach, I found that he was standing alone now, staring out at the ocean. Shere Khan was gone.

"Hey," I said as I approached him.

His golden-brown eyes slid over to meet mine. "Hey, Lena."

"Happy New Year."

"Happy New Year." His gaze shifted to the ocean again. "I'm not sure if it's going to be a happy one or not."

"It's normal to feel that way after the loss of a parent," I said quietly.

He shook his head. "It's not just that."

"Then what is it?" I pressed.

"This is the year that everything will change." His eyes settled on mine again. "Our lives as we know it are about to change. Things between all of us—me, you, the Alpha Brotherhood—it will all change. We're going to be settling into our new roles as Kings and Queens. We won't get to spend so much time together, as we'll all be living in different kingdoms."

"I'm sure we'll all still visit each other often," I commented. The truth was, I hadn't even considered how much all of us residing in separate kingdoms was going to complicate *everything*.

"It's not just that, Lena. Our kingdoms are all going to rely on us. And the three of us who you don't choose are going to need to get married. I'm not sure about the others, but I haven't even considered who I might choose to be Queen if you don't choose me. I've just been thinking this entire time that it will be me and you in the end, but..." His golden-brown eyes locked on mine. "What if it's *not?*"

I hesitated, not wanting to say too much. "Everything is going to work out in the end."

I could tell from the look in his eyes that he was disappointed by my response, but it was all I could give him at that point in time.

"What was Shere Khan talking to you about?" I asked him.

"He wanted to offer me his condolences," Damon explained. I waited for him to elaborate on the rest of their conversation, but he didn't.

"That's it? It looked like the two of you were arguing."

"I wouldn't say that we were arguing, per se. He just had some strong opinions that I don't necessarily agree with."

"Opinions about what?" I pressed.

"He thinks I should leave Shifter Academy right now. He thinks I should ask the Royal Elders for permission to become King early," he explained.

"The Royal Elders?" I questioned.

"The current Kings and Queens who currently make up the Shifter High Court," Damon explained.

"Oh." I'd never heard that term used before.

"Anyway, Shere Khan feels that if I go through coronation early, it will take some of the burden off of my mom."

"And you don't agree with him?"

Damon shook his head.

"Why?" I asked, raising my eyebrows. I was sort of surprised, considering he hadn't even wanted to leave his mom and sisters behind to come to the Tiger Kingdom for the holiday.

"Partly because I don't feel ready to rule the Lion Kingdom yet. I feel that the instruction we're getting at Shifter Academy right now is topnotch. I don't want to miss out on anything that could help me later down the road." He paused for a moment. "Besides, my mom is a strong, powerful woman. She's Queen of the Shifters. She's more than capable of protecting her kingdom, even during a world war." His eyes met mine. "The other reason I don't want to do it is because of you."

"*Me?*" I asked with raised eyebrows. "You shouldn't let me stand in between you and your kingdom, Damon."

"It's not that, Lena. I don't want to be that far away from you," Damon explained. "I don't think I can handle that during a shifter world war. I'm so afraid of losing you, it's not even funny. I also don't want to miss out on my chances with you.

The more time we spend apart, the less likely you are to choose me in the end. I don't want to just give up on that."

Wrapping my arms around his rock-hard chest, I pulled him closer to me. "Damon, nothing is ever going to make you lose your chances with me. You have to do what's right for you."

"*You,*" he said, "are what's right for me."

THIRTY-TWO

When we rejoined the rest of the Alpha Brotherhood, I saw Queen Bria and King Roman for the first time since we had arrived. They were talking to Rafael on the rooftop patio.

Queen Bria's eyes flitted over to meet mine.

Shit. I had been hoping she wouldn't spot me.

To my surprise, she grabbed Rafael's arm and began to lead him and King Roman in my direction.

The last thing I wanted to do was have a conversation with Raf's parents. The only good news was that he was there, and he at least knew who I was now.

Plus, the rest of my mates were there to protect me if they should try anything. It was going to be okay.

"Hello, Lena. How nice it is to see you again." Queen Bria shot the phoniest smile at me.

"Hello, Lena. I don't think we've ever formally been introduced. I am King Roman." Rafael's dad offered me an equally phony smile.

"It's nice to meet you," I replied.

"Did you ever learn what your shifter race is, dear?" Queen Bria asked.

"Yes, actually, I did," I told her.

"Oh? What is it?" She leaned in closer to me. "Actually, let me guess. Are you a Serpent?"

No, everyone just seems to think I am, I thought to myself.

"I'm a werebear," I told her.

"Oh, thank goodness. This is incredibly good news." Queen Bria's eyes were full of relief as she glanced over at Rafael. "There's no way you can be with Lena now. She's not a tiger shifter. She's not even a cat shifter. So even *if* she entered the Marriage Lottery, her application will be discarded."

"Actually, Mom, Dad... There's something I've been meaning to tell you." Raf glanced over at his parents. "I'm not going to go through with the Marriage Lottery."

"What do you mean you're not 'going to go through with' it?" His mom looked pissed. "Of course you're going through with it! Parents don't just start a Marriage Lottery for their child to back out."

"I don't want to marry someone who's drawn for me at random," Rafael explained. "I want to marry someone I love— my mate." His emerald green eyes shifted over to meet mine. "I want to marry Lena."

"There is no way this girl is your mate." Queen Bria sounded appalled by the idea that I could possibly be his mate... probably just as appalled as I felt about her being my mate's mom.

"She is my mate, Mom." He glanced over at them. "But it's a little more complicated than that."

Oh, no. Rafael was about to drop a bomb on them that I didn't think they were ready for.

"Lena is *all* of our mates." He motioned to Damon, Harden, and Ezra. "She is the one that the prophecy is about—the one about the chocolate brown-haired, honey brown-eyed future Queen of the Shifters who will end the shifter world war."

Queen Bria gasped and just stared at me. "It's about *her*?"

"Yes, it is about her," Shere Khan said from behind me. "Do you have a problem with that, Bria?"

"N-no, sir. It's just hard to imagine someone like... *her*... being the one who the prophecy is about."

"What is it you're trying to imply about Miss Falcone?" Shere Khan asked.

Glancing over at him, I was surprised to find that he looked genuinely offended by her dislike of me. It was strange to have a Legend come to my defense so strongly.

"She became a shifter so late in life," Bria responded. "She hardly seems like the powerful Queen of the Shifters she's said to be."

"Well, I will have you know that Lena receives incredibly good marks at school. She is one of the brightest students we have. She's also doing amazing in her Advanced Weaponry class, I hear. I have high hopes for her." He paused for a moment before adding, "I am also convinced that she will be a much better queen than you have ever been or will ever be in the short amount of time you have left to reign."

Queen Bria rolled her eyes and huffed, obviously offended.

King Roman remained silent, to my surprise. I half-expected him to say *something* in his wife's defense, but it seemed quite possible that even *he* knew she was being ridiculously judgmental of me. It was either that or he was afraid of pissing off Shere Khan.

"So, we're supposed to just let our son marry this girl?" Queen Bria asked.

"I hate to inform you, Bria, but Rafael is already an adult. Legally, he can decide who he wants to marry. And you should feel *lucky* if Miss Falcone chooses to take him as her husband."

"Lucky?" She laughed. "What in the world would be lucky about that?"

"Your son would be the King of the Shifters," Shere Khan replied. "That would be the luckiest thing to ever happen to your family, considering the tigers are not at the top of the hierarchy and Rafael was not born into this position."

Queen Bria stared at him evenly. "I would hardly consider it lucky for this girl—this *werebear*—to taint our family's years of breeding and lineage. I find it absolutely atrocious that you are in support of such a thing, considering the Khan family descended from *you*."

"Bria, times have changed. There is no reason to prevent your son from being with the girl who he loves—his *mate*—and denying him the privilege of becoming the next King of the Shifters simply because of some tainted blood. Personally, I find it to be *absolutely atrocious*"—Shere Khan made air quotes with his fingers— "that you don't want your son to have the life he may be destined for, the life he wants to live. I cannot even imagine what it would have been like if my own mother, may she rest in peace, hadn't supported all of my life choices and endeavors."

Queen Bria rolled her eyes at him one last time and then turned away from all of us in a huff.

I stared after her, not even bothering to hide the smile that took over my face. It felt like I had won my battle—all thanks to Shere Khan.

~

Later that night, Rafael and I laid in his bedroom together. It felt so strange to be there again, given what had happened the last time we had spent the night together. Well, the last time we had *planned* to spend the night together, until someone had apparently tried to frame Shere Khan when they swapped bodies with Raf.

But this night was different. I had a good feeling about this night.

Damon might have felt negative about the new year, but I actually felt the opposite way.

He was right. Everything *was* about to change, and some of those changes weren't going to be easy. But I was pretty sure that there were going to be a lot of good changes, too. It was just a feeling I had deep in my gut. My shifter intuition was kicking into high gear.

"It still makes me sad sometimes, you know," Rafael said, interrupting my thoughts.

I glanced over at him. "What does?"

"The fact that I can't remember everything." He sighed. "I wish I could remember our first kiss, and the first time we really met. I want to remember it *all*."

I sighed. "I wish you could remember, too."

I knew then that it was time.

Climbing off his bed, I walked over to my bags and pulled out the vial.

I crossed the room and handed it to Rafael. "Drink this."

"What is it?" His confused green eyes locked on mine.

"It's a potion that *might* bring back your memories." I chose not to disclose the fact that it would take at least six months. I didn't want him to feel discouraged. It just seemed better for him to not know a potential time frame.

"Where did you get this from?" Raf asked.

"Shere Khan."

"Wow. You guys have been holding out on me." He

unscrewed the cap. Bringing the vial to his lips, he downed the potion in one swig.

"It's not always effective, but it might be," I explained.

"Let's hope. If I could get one wish, it would be to remember you completely, Lena." His eyes met mine.

"I would wish for that, too," I replied.

Leaning in closer to me, Rafael brought his lips down on mine.

His kiss caught me completely off-guard. There was something about it that was less frantic than usual, something more sensual.

Grabbing a fistful of his hair, I pulled him closer to me, deepening the kiss.

As he continued to kiss me slowly, he began to peel off the silky light pink nightgown I was wearing. He tossed it to the side.

Dropping his hand between my legs, he ran his fingers underneath the lacy materials of my panties.

As he pushed his fingers inside of me, his eyes widened at how ready I was for him. I was soaked.

Sliding my panties down my thighs and over my legs, his eyes met mine. "Do you want to do this?"

"Yes." I kissed him again and pulled his boxers off.

He pressed his hardness against my pelvis.

Wrapping my legs around his waist, I pulled his body closer to me.

"Princess...," Rafael groaned as he slid inside of me.

He brought his lips down on mine as he moved in out of me, slowly at first. Waves of pleasure passed through me as he hit every single never ending, some of which I never even knew existed.

He slid in and out of me until I could feel myself tightening at the core.

As we came undone together, the scent of jasmine and orchids mixed in with watermelon and orchids filled my nostrils.

I could smell Rafael all over me.

We were mates... at last.

CHAPTER

THIRTY-THREE

R eturning to school after the winter break wasn't easy. I also couldn't help but question the fact that I had completed the Mate Bonding Process with not just one but *two* of my mates over the break.

I had wanted to hold off with Rafael until his memories returned, but I knew there was no guarantee his memories would *ever* come back. Plus, the prophecy stated:

She will become mated to one Alpha from each of the shifter races,
   But it will be up to her to decide which of the four Alphas to
marry.

To me, the prophecy implied that I needed to become mated to each of them *before* I decided which mate I wanted to marry. Technically, I could probably complete the bonding process with Ezra now that he would be the last. But I knew that my body wasn't even ready to become officially mated to a fourth mate yet.

Completing the Bonding Process with two of them in such close proximity to one another had taken a huge toll on me from a physical standpoint. My heart constantly felt like I was being pulled in three separate directions, at times. This pull was so intense that it became overwhelming at times. I wasn't just consumed by one mate like normal shifters; I had *three* mates constantly occupying my mind.

I knew that the other students at school were probably beginning to grow suspicious. I had three marks on me—the scent of not just one but *three* mates. I was pretty sure all of my classmates were about to figure out that I was the one the prophecy was about, if they hadn't figured it out already.

"I can't even *believe* how much homework we're getting lately," Alexis commented as we were hanging out in our dorm room one Wednesday night in late February.

"Me, either," I agreed. The amount of homework and exams we'd had lately was grueling. Between my schoolwork and my Saturday tutoring sessions with Shere Khan, which were just as intense, I barely even had time for my best friends anymore. Ever since we'd returned from the winter break, I had been spending most of my time at the Alpha Brotherhood's penthouse. It was hard for me to be too far away from my mates now.

Not only did my heart want me to be around them as much as possible, but the truth was that I often worried about them. It was all because of the necklace Gretta had told me to wear. It was weird to have to text them to get in touch throughout the day. It made me feel so... *human.*

"Frankly, I'm over it," Katerina said with a sigh. "But there *is* something I'm excited about."

She grabbed two gold-embossed envelopes from her bag and handed one to both me and Alexis.

"Is this a wedding invitation?" Alexis asked as we opened our envelopes.

"Yes!" Katerina grinned. "The wedding is in just one month from now."

"One month? That's, like... soon!" Alexis said.

"Um, you guys. I have a problem. I don't know who to bring as my date," I commented. That was one of the biggest downsides to having four mates. I never knew who to bring to events with me.

"Don't worry, love. All four of your mates are invited, and you'll be sitting at the same table. You can have them all," Katerina assured me.

I breathed a sigh of relief. "Thanks."

"So, you'll both definitely be there?" Katerina asked us.

"Absolutely," I replied with a nod.

"I wouldn't miss it for the world," Alexis said.

"How is everything going between you and Sean, by the way?" I asked her. "You haven't said much about him since your vision. Is the marriage still on?"

"Yeah, it's still on... *for now*," she replied. "Maybe my vision was wrong. Maybe it won't actually happen. But I've had a really bad feeling about it ever since. I'm just trying to take it day by day."

Katerina nodded. "That's really all you can do for now. Cross that bridge once you get to it."

"*If* you get to it," I added.

"Exactly," Alexis agreed. "So, what's going on with you and *your* mates, Lena?"

"I can smell Harden and Rafael all over you," Katerina added.

"Ugh. Is it really that noticeable?" I smelled my wrist, knowing the answer was yes.

"Extremely noticeable," Alexis confirmed.

"Now I can't help but wonder, why don't we smell Ezra on you, too?" Katerina asked.

"We haven't officially completed the Mate Bonding Process yet," I explained. "He wanted me to save him for last. Since he was the first one who I ever kissed, he wanted to be the last one who I have sex with."

"Aw, that's sort of sweet," Alexis said. "Save the first for last."

"It is sweet, I suppose," Katerina agreed. "But don't you find it strange that he hasn't just found a way to shag you already?"

"That's true," Alexis agreed. "Sean and I couldn't wait to jump each other's bones."

"Ezra is just incredibly patient," I explained. "Actually, *all* of my mates have been extremely patient."

I had known Damon for a year and a half and Rafael and Harden for two years before we'd crossed that line. It was sort of crazy to think about.

"Well, that's because they love you," Alexis said.

Katerina nodded. "There's no truer sign of real love than patience."

"In that case, my mates must *really* love me," I commented. "They're all patiently waiting to find out who I'm choosing."

"Have you made a decision yet?" Alexis asked.

I nodded.

Katerina's eyes widened. "Who is it, love?"

"I'm not ready to share that with anyone just yet," I told them. For now, it felt like this secret was meant to stay between me and Gretta.

THIRTY-FOUR

One rainy afternoon in early March, Princess Kaa and I agreed to meet up at the new on-campus coffee shop.

As we sat at a table, we stared at each other awkwardly for a few minutes. What did you even say to someone who you barely knew and had virtually nothing in common with? But I had to say *something*, since Professor Kaa felt so strongly about us needing to form this alliance with each other.

"So, are you looking forward to the Royal Change of Hands?" Princess Kaa asked.

Not really. But I wasn't about to tell her that. I couldn't show any signs of hesitancy or weakness... and especially not fear.

"Yeah, I'm pretty excited about it. How about you?" I asked.

"Well... sort of. I'm excited and nervous. But it's also sort of weird for me, considering I never thought I would be Queen. It's just another reminder of Cobra being gone. And Rattlesnake obviously won't be there to see me on coronation day, either."

I shot a sympathetic glance in her direction. "When is coronation day?"

"I'm not sure. It used to be on the same day as the Royal

Change of Hands Ceremony, but my dad mentioned that the rules are different this year."

I wondered why they had changed.

"What kingdom are you about to reign over, anyway?" Princess Kaa asked.

I realized then that there was no way I could tell her without telling her about the prophecy. Even though I didn't trust the girl, I also knew that she was going to find out the truth in just two months from now anyway at the Royal Change of Hands.

"I'm about to become the next Queen of the Shifters," I informed her.

"Oh." Her gold eyes met mine. "You're Damon Crowne's mate?"

I realized she was asking that because she thought I was only about to become Queen of the Shifters because I was going to marry him. It was easier right now to let her believe that than to tell her about the prophecy, so I nodded.

"Yeah, Damon's my mate." It wasn't even like I was lying. "How about you? Do you know who you're going to marry?"

It was a rule that all Kings and Queens had to be married before the coronation. But I had never seen Princess Kaa spending time with any guy on campus.

"I'm choosing not to get married," she replied. "I obviously need to get permission from the Royal Elders, but that's my plan. Times have changed. It's such a barbaric rule."

"Well, I *do* think it's a stupid rule," I agreed. "But what happens if they don't agree to your request?"

"I'm not sure," she admitted.

"Why don't you want to get married? Have you not met your mate yet?"

Princess Kaa shook her head. "No, I haven't. There are no eligible bachelors around our age from any of the Serpent families," she explained. "So that makes it a little impossible for me to meet my mate."

"Well, have you thought about dating outside of your shifter race?" I asked her.

"Absolutely not." Her gold eyes looked completely disgusted by the suggestion. "I could never taint the Draco bloodline."

"But what if your mate is someone from another shifter race? What if he's a bird or a wolf or a cat shifter or something?"

"Then we can't be together, anyway." Kaa shook her head. "You don't get it, Lena. It's not acceptable to my family to date someone from another shifter race."

"It's not acceptable to *them*? Or to *you*?" I pressed.

Her facial expression became stony.

"You said yourself that times have changed," I pointed out. "I think a lot of the Royal Elders are open to us choosing love over shifter races."

Well, it might have been about fifty-fifty, given my mates' moms. Half of them seemed to approve, but the others not so much.

"I can just be alone forever." Kaa shrugged. "It's no big deal."

"You would want to be lonely forever?" I asked her. "That doesn't really seem like the happiest life."

"Power is more important than happiness," Kaa replied. "Protecting my kingdom is what matters most."

"Wouldn't you want to have children of your own someday? Someone to pass your legacy to?" I asked her.

"Well... yes."

"You should really consider trying to date outside of the Serpents. You never know. You might fall in love."

"It's not that easy, Lena. Even *if* I was willing to taint my family's bloodline, there's also the fact that most shifters would never want to date a Serpent. We're too sneaky."

"I'm sure there's *someone* out there who would date you, regardless of your shifter race. Plus, if your mate happens to be another type of shifter, I'm not sure that he could refuse you, even if he wanted to."

"I guess." She shrugged and began to sip her cappuccino again.

I realized then just how lucky I was. Even though it was challenging as fuck to have four mates at times, I could have been Princess Kaa. I couldn't imagine what it would have been like to feel like no one would give you a chance because of your shifter race.

There was *way* too much stigma against the Serpents. Even though I obviously hated the King of the Serpents for killing my parents, I didn't think all Serpents were bad.

I decided then that one of my first duties as Queen of the Shifters was going to be to end the stigma against them. I wasn't sure how I would do it, but I would.

THIRTY-FIVE

"Good afternoon, class," Professor Kaa said Monday afternoon. "Today, I am going to teach you the deadliest poison known to shifters. It's called the Lethal Weapon. Before we get into how to make this potion, I should forewarn you. Getting caught using this poison comes with a hefty prison sentence. It is the most illegal poison you could ever use."

A hand shot up at the front of the class.

"Yes, Christopher?" Professor Kaa asked.

"If this poison is so illegal, then why are you teaching us how to make it?" Chris, a werewolf, asked.

"Ah, that is a very good quesssstion." It sounded like she had hissed as she spoke. "Even though it might be smarter to avoid teaching a generation of students *not* to use it, I feel that it's very important for you to know how to create it. You see, throughout history, the Lethal Weapon has often been used to kill Royals. Even though most attempts haven't been effective, the majority of Kings and Queens have received the Lethal Weapon at some point in time. Once you have seen the potion, you will know what to look out for."

Professor Kaa's eyes fell on me, and I wondered if she was trying to let me know that this was something she had seen for my future.

"After we have created the poison, I will then teach you how to create the antidote. In order to save yourself or someone else who has drunk this poison, you will need to consume the antidote in no less than twenty-four hours. Unfortunately, even that isn't always enough time to prevent the poison from taking hold on someone's life. It's best to consume the antidote within three hours, which is how suddenly this poison can take effect."

She glanced around the room. "While we will be disposing of the poisons that you create, you *will* get to keep the antidotes. I highly suggest that you hold onto them. There is a chance that you or someone who you care about may need it one day." She paused. "Now, I have set out the ingredients we will need for this poison at the back of the room. Be *very* careful when you handle the wolfsbane."

As I rose to my feet and fell into line behind the other students, something happened then.

A vision began to play out in my mind.

King Ari took a sip of his morning coffee. He wrinkled his nose at the foul flavor, and then set the cup aside.

Somehow, I knew that the vision jumped forward a few hours.

King Ari was taking his morning stroll when a weird feeling took over him. He suddenly began to feel nauseous.

He was making his way back towards the palace when he collapsed.

His shifter form began to take over.

Once he had transformed into a lion, he struggled to breathe for a few moments. Then his body went still and lifeless.

He was gone.

About ten minutes later, I stumbled upon him and began to scream.

I walked over to Professor Kaa. In a low voice, I asked, "Can the Lethal Weapon be identified by a coroner?"

"That's a complicated question. The answer is *sometimes*," she informed me. "Sometimes, the poison can be easily detected. However, dark magic users can seal it, the same way they can seal a spell, to make the poison undetectable. They can also use dark magic to make the creator of the poison undetectable. This is most often the case, considering how illegal the poison is to create. No one wants to get caught as the creator." She paused for a moment. "Why do you ask?"

"Because," I replied, "I'm pretty sure that whoever killed King Ari used the Lethal Weapon to murder him."

∿

"How could my dad be so foolish?" Damon asked as I told him about my vision later that day. "How could he just drink the Lethal Weapon without realizing it? All Royals are warned about it as children."

"He must not have suspected it," I replied. "Whoever gave him his coffee must have been someone he trusted."

Damon paused for a moment, realizing what this all meant. "That means that whoever killed my dad was on the palace grounds that morning."

"Yeah." I paused. "So, who was on the palace grounds who wasn't actually supposed to be there that day?"

"I didn't notice. I should have paid attention. I should have done an inventory to find out who all was there." He sounded so disappointed in himself.

"It doesn't matter. Even *if* you had taken an inventory of everyone who was there, it doesn't guarantee that you would have found the person, anyway. There's a chance that they could have used an invisibility spell or something to remain hidden."

"You're right, but still. I should have done better that day, and I didn't." His golden-brown eyes locked on mine. "I have to find my dad's killer, Lena. I have to. If I don't, I will have failed him."

I hugged him, pulling him close.

I wasn't sure why, but I had a feeling that this crime wasn't going to be an easy one to solve.

I was in the middle of my Ruling a Kingdom class one afternoon when I could feel it happening.

The pain started in my core before radiating through me.

I just knew that I was about to shift.

"I gotta go," I told Shere Khan as I ran for the Girls' Room.

I couldn't even make it into a bathroom stall as the pain ripped through my entire body.

I quickly pulled my uniform off, right in the nick of time. I had barely pulled my skirt over my ankles when my bones began to twist and bend.

I groaned as I found myself on all fours.

Glancing down at my paws, I noticed they weren't covered in black fur like I expected them to be.

No, they were gray.

I stared at myself in the bathroom mirror. When I saw my own reflection, I did a double-take.

How the hell was this even possible?

I wasn't just a werebear.

I was a werewolf, too.

THIRTY-SIX

The shift lasted for about fifteen minutes.

As I pulled my clothes back on from inside one of the stalls, Jake's grandpa Tom's words about the curse kept echoing through my mind.

"It stated that you would be able to shift into multiple shifter races, so you would constantly be at war with yourself. This would complicate your life forever."

So, apparently, the curse was true.

I really was more than one type of shifter.

⁓

When I returned to Ruling a Kingdom, the other students were reading quietly from our textbook. I headed straight for Shere Khan's desk.

"I need to talk to you."

His green eyes met mine. "Okay. My office hours are between five and six tonight."

"No. I need to talk to you right now... in private."

I noticed my mates glance up at me from where they were sitting. Katerina and Alexis were watching me, too.

"Okay. Class, please continue reading." Shere Khan rose to his feet and led me out of the room, closing the door behind us. "What is it, Lena?"

"I just shifted."

"And your point?" He looked mildly annoyed. "This happens sometimes. You are a shifter."

"I have shifted into a werebear several times," I informed him. "But this time was different. This time, I shifted into a werewolf."

His emerald green eyes widened. "Really? A werewolf?"

I nodded. "There's a curse surrounding me. Have you heard of it?"

"I've heard it was only rumored. I guess the rumors are true. You are a multi-race shifter. This is quite interesting." His eyes met mine. "Kaa will be interested to know about this."

Even though I wanted to believe that they were wrong, that there was no way I could be part Serpent... Well, I had begun to have my doubts.

"You mustn't tell your mates about this. Not just yet. We need to find out first if you're a Serpent or not."

"Okay. But they're going to want to know why I had to talk to you right now."

"Tell them you had to talk to me about the exam I handed back to you this class period," Shere Khan replied. "You were very upset to receive an A-, and you wanted to see what you could do to rectify it. Your mates all know you well enough to know by now that you are quite the perfectionist."

"Fine. That sounds believable enough," I replied with a sigh.

The truth was, I hated keeping a secret from them. As of right now, I didn't even see the point in keeping it from them.

I was a werebear and a werewolf. There was no crime in that.

But I wasn't going to go against what Shere Khan was saying, either. He was a Legend, after all, which should have meant that he was wiser than me.

"There's one more thing I would advise, Miss Falcone." Shere Khan's eyes met mine. "It would be in your best interests if you don't shift in front of your mates or anyone else, for that matter. You should do it alone at all times, just until we can be sure of what, exactly, you are."

I knew he was right.

My shifter race—err, *races*—had to stay a secret from everyone.

THIRTY-SEVEN

Before I knew it, Katerina's wedding day was already upon us. She had chosen to forego a bridal shower *and* a bachelorette party, both of which Alexis and I had been pretty disappointed about.

Nevertheless, I was so excited for my best friend to get married to the love of her life, her mate, her future King.

It made me feel excited for my own wedding. I knew it wouldn't be much longer before I would say "I do."

The morning of the wedding, Alexis and I traveled to the Bear palace, bright and early. We got there around six a.m.

The Bear Kingdom was absolutely beautiful. The palace looked like something out of the Disney movie *Frozen*.

The palace had some sort of magical effect to make it look like it had a silvery blue shine on the outside. It sat on a snow-covered hill, overlooking the frozen ocean below.

It was absolutely gorgeous.

"It's so cold here," Alexis commented.

"It is chilly," I agreed as I knocked on the front door of the palace.

A few moments later, Patrick opened the door. "Hey, ladies. Come inside."

As we entered the palace, I glanced around. Everything was done in silver, blue-toned shades of gray and white, from the white and gray marbled floors to the silver grand staircase.

"Katerina is getting her hair done in her dressing room right now," Patrick informed us. "It's upstairs, the second door on the left. I would take you guys to her, but she keeps reminding me that it's bad luck for the groom to see the bride on her wedding day. We all know how superstitious Kat is."

"I actually didn't know she was superstitious," Alexis said.

"Me, either," I agreed.

"No? Well, if you ever happen to come across a black cat, I would highly recommend doing everything in your power from letting Kat see it," Patrick replied with a laugh. "And don't ever let her break a mirror. She broke a compact one day over winter break and then cried for days because she's afraid it will bring her seven years of bad luck."

I couldn't help but think how cute it was that Patrick knew so much about Katerina. The two of them felt like a match made in heaven.

"Anyway, good luck with her today. I'm sure she will be quite the bridezilla," he warned us. "And be sure to take lots of pictures."

"We will," I assured him.

"Oh, and the guest room is the fifth on the right. You can put your things in there. Your bridesmaid dresses are in there, as well."

"Thanks," I replied as Alexis and I headed up the stairs.

When we reached the top, I could already hear Katerina saying, "I don't know if I like this updo. Maybe we should try doing my hair half up, half down."

Alexis and I quickly dropped our things off in the guest

room.

"Hey, girl," Alexis said as we entered the room.

"You've made it!" Katerina said with a wide smile. "Philomena, these are my two best friends, Alexis and Lena. Philomena has been my hair stylist since I was a little girl. She'll be doing both of your hair once she's finished with me."

"Hi, ladies." Philomena gave us a little wave before glancing back at Katerina in the mirror. "Are you *sure* you want to do half up, half down?"

"Yes. I'm positive," Katerina said with a nod.

"Okay." As Philomena began to unpin her honey blonde curls from the top of her head, there was a knock at the door.

I glanced behind me to find a tall woman with blonde hair and gray eyes standing behind me. "Hello, ladies. Welcome to the Werebear Kingdom. I'm Katerina's mom, Queen Alexandria. You must be Alexis."

Alexis nodded. "Yes. It's so nice to meet you."

"Likewise." She turned to me. "And *you* must be Lena Falcone."

I nodded. "Yes. It's nice to finally meet you."

"I am thrilled to meet you." Her eyes stayed on mine. "I have heard so very much about you, Lena."

I hadn't even thought to ask if Katerina had told her mom about the prophecy, but she must have. I wasn't sure why else her mother would have been so interested in meeting me.

"I've heard a lot about you, too," I said, unsure of what else to say.

"I hope that my daughter has only told you good things."

I might have been overthinking it, but I could have sworn that Queen Alexandria almost looked *nervous* that Katerina had told us bad things about her.

"The best things," I replied with a smile.

"Good." She glanced over at her daughter with a look of

relief in her eyes. "So, tell me more about yourself. Are you looking forward to the Royal Change of Hands ceremony next month?"

"Yeah, I'm excited about it," I replied, even though it was still a lie.

"You must be looking forward to getting a kingdom of your own to reign. That comes with a good deal of power. Who doesn't want power?" Queen Alexandria smiled at me.

"I guess." I shrugged. "I'm hoping to actually help the shifter world. I think there are a lot of things we can improve on."

"Oh? Like what, dear?"

"Well, it would be nice if we could all live in harmony," I replied. "I want to help reduce some of the prejudice that exists between shifter races, and—"

"Lena, you don't have to tell her *all* of your future plans," Katerina interrupted me.

"Sorry. I wasn't trying to get all political," I apologized. "Today is about you, anyway. What are you doing for your makeup?"

As we began to move onto Katerina, I couldn't help but notice that Queen Alexandria kept watching me out of the corner of her eye. I might have only been imagining it, but it felt like she was studying me.

Why was this woman so fascinated by me?

Alexis and I had just changed into our bridesmaid dresses and returned to Katerina's dressing room when I felt it happening.

Holy.

Fuck.

I was shifting.

But something about this shift felt... well, *different.*

It felt like every muscle, every nerve ending, in my body was being stabbed with a hundred knives.

"I'll be back," I muttered, even though no one was really paying attention to me as the stylist did Katerina's eye shadow.

Running to the end of the hall, I slipped into the guest room and closed the door behind me. I had just managed to slip out of the gold dress and hung it from the closet door before I felt my bones twisting in ways that I had never felt them move before.

I fell on my knees to the floor, and my body began to transform.

~

Once all was said and done, I used every muscle in my body to lift my head high into the air.

I stared at myself in the floor-length mirror that stood before me.

I took in my yellow and white markings.

Staring into my black beady eyes for a moment, I opened my mouth.

I watched in the mirror as my pink, fork-shaped python tongue darted out of my mouth.

Apparently, Queen Bria and Kaa had been right.

I really *was* a Serpent.

THIRTY-EIGHT

S o many emotions washed over me.

How the hell was this even possible? How could I have been a Serpent?

I didn't even know my lineage, but I wasn't sure that it even mattered. It all came down to the curse. The stupid fucking curse.

I glanced up at the clock. Katerina's wedding ceremony was in twenty-five minutes. I had to figure out a way to shift back into my human form *and* make my hair and makeup look at least half-decent again in time for the ceremony. The guests, including our mates, would be arriving any minute.

No. Freaking. Pressure.

At that moment, I heard the sound of footsteps in the hallway outside the door.

Shit.

A realization hit me then.

I couldn't let anyone see me like this. It would have changed everything.

Now that I was a serpent, it meant I couldn't be the next Queen of the Shifters. It was against the law.

But it would only be a problem if anyone found out.

I wasn't even sure what would happen if my *mates* found out. I knew they wouldn't rat me out, but it would be a big secret for them to keep. That also wasn't to mention the fact that they would see me differently.

Everyone would see me differently.

Everyone would think I was sneaky like a snake.

No, word couldn't get out about this to *anyone*, friend or foe. Shere Khan was right. I had to protect my secret at all costs.

A knock at the door interrupted my thoughts then.

"Lena? Can we come in?" Queen Alexandria called from the other side.

Shit, shit, shit.

I glanced around the room, trying to figure out a way to conceal my python body.

Finally, I decided to slither beneath the bed. I had just managed to fit my entire body far enough underneath it to remain unnoticed when I heard the sound of the door opening.

I saw champagne-colored heels as the Queen entered the room.

She stood there in the doorway for a moment before saying, "That's unusual. I could have sworn I saw her go in here. I guess I was wrong."

"She must have gone downstairs or to the loo. We've probably just missed her," Katerina replied. She stood before the mirror. "Do you like this lip color, Mother? I'm not so sure about it. It's so ordinary. Maybe I should go with something bolder— red, perhaps."

"Red makes you look washed out. It looks fine, dear." Queen Alexandria seemed to be only half in the conversation. "Isn't that strange? Lena isn't here, but her *dress* is here."

"I'm sure she'll be ready in time, Mother. I've known Lena long enough to know that she's never late to anything."

"Lena is not at all what I expected. All of these years, I thought she would be... *different*," Queen Alexandria murmured. It almost seemed like she was talking more to herself than she was to Katerina.

"*All of these years?* Mother, you make it sound as if I've known her forever," Katerina said with a laugh as she continued to stand in front of the mirror.

"Sometimes it feels like we have."

"Well, what, exactly, *were* you expecting?" Katerina questioned.

"I thought she would be more like me," her mom replied.

"More like *you?* What in the world ever gave you that impression?"

"I just figured she would be a little more... elite. Noble. Aristocratic."

"So, uppity? Conceited? Self-important? Is that what you're really saying?"

Queen Alexandria hesitated for a moment. "Well, yes. I suppose." She paused. "Meanwhile, she seems to be completely the opposite. She's certainly very kindhearted, but she just isn't what I imagined she would be. She seems very confident in her own skin."

Just not in my own scales, I thought, eyeing my newfound snake skin.

"She also seems like she's a bit of a free spirit. A wild child, if you will."

Katerina snorted. "Did you really just call my bridesmaid a 'wild child'?"

Queen Alexandria ignored her question. "Where do you think all of those qualities of hers come from?"

"How should I know? Her upbringing, I assume. It's not like she was raised as a Royal like we were. She wasn't even raised in the shifter world. She grew up believing she was a human."

"Her parents did a very good job convincing her of that," her mom replied.

"I suppose, but I can't imagine why they wanted it to be such a secret. The poor thing ended up with such bad culture shock." Katerina sighed. "Anyway, enough about Lena, Mother. This is *my* day—mine and Patrick's, of course. I'd rather not spend it analyzing my best friend's upbringing."

"Yes, dear. I'm sorry to have this discussion with you on your special day. How silly of me." Her mom didn't sound even the slightest bit apologetic.

"It's fine. But we had better head down to the dressing room. It's time to put my veil on. I'm sure we'll probably find Lena waiting for us down there."

"Yes, of course. Let's head down there now."

As they left the room, I wondered, yet again, why Queen Alexandria seemed to have taken such an interest in me.

THIRTY-NINE

Somehow, I managed to shift back *and* pull myself together, just in time to walk down the aisle with Patrick's brother Cody.

Alexis and Patrick's other brother Nate followed down the aisle after us.

Patrick came down the aisle next, grinning from ear to ear.

I glanced out at my mates, who were seated in the third row. All four of them were staring at me.

I smiled at them.

At that moment, Katerina made her grand entrance. Everyone in the room rose and watched her walk down the aisle.

Her long, flowing white gown made her look like the Princess she was.

As her father handed her off to Patrick, she handed her bouquet to me.

The wedding officiant began to perform the ceremony.

Out of the corner of my eye, Queen Alexandria continued to stare at me. I couldn't help but find it strange that it was her daughter's wedding, and it wasn't her who she was staring at... but me instead.

∼

"Are you okay?" Damon asked me as we slow danced that night to an Ed Sheeran song at the wedding reception.

I met his gaze. "Yeah. I'm fine. Why?"

"You just seem a little... on edge," he replied with a shrug. "Anxious or something."

If only he knew.

"I'm fine. It's just been a really long day."

"Okay." His eyes met mine. "Today has really gotten me thinking."

"Oh? About what?" I asked.

"About how badly I want this to be us." Damon's eyes continued to linger on mine. "I want you to make whatever decision will make you happiest, Lena. I want you to choose who you feel is best for you. But I just want you to know how much I want it to be me who you spend eternity with."

Staring into his eyes, I decided not to say anything at all. Instead, I pressed my lips to his and kissed him. Right there in the middle of the dance floor, I kissed him with everything I had, hoping that he knew I didn't want this to ever end.

CHAPTER
FORTY

"Are you ready, Lena?" Dolly asked me as I got ready for the Royal Change of Hands ceremony in May. The school year hadn't even officially ended yet, but the ceremony day was already here.

The truth?

I felt far from ready.

Mostly, I felt like I was going to puke.

I did a once-over of myself in the long-gold-framed mirror as I stood before it. My chocolate brown hair was done in long curls. I had chosen a long, gold princess-style gown to wear. Even though I never would have chosen this gold gown for myself, it was exquisite. It reminded me of Belle's gown from *Beauty and the Beast*, just with way more sparkle.

I had tried to go as natural as possible with my makeup, opting for only a pinky nude lipstick and mascara.

"I think so." I turned to face Dolly. "Do I look okay?"

"You look hot... in the next Queen of the Shifters sort of way." She smiled, glancing in the mirror at her own light pink gown. "My mother wants me to take you to meet her before the ceremony begins."

"Okay," I agreed with a nod.

Dolly led me out of the dressing room. As we reached the staircase, I found that all of Damon's sisters were standing in a line on the landing. Kylene wore a burgundy gown, while Elsa's was a lipstick red in color. Megan had opted for a burnt orange gown with a leg slit, while Catherine wore a bronze mermaid gown.

All of their gowns gave me lioness vibes.

As Dolly and I reached the landing, all of Damon's sisters bowed before me.

I smiled at them. "You guys do *not* have to do that."

"Nonsense, Lena. You're about to become the next Queen of the Lions—which is huge, by the way," Elsa said.

"So huge," Megan agreed. "Pre-congratulations."

"Thanks." It was strange to me that most of Damon's sisters *still* didn't know the truth about me and the prophecy.

Well, they were about to find out. Them and the rest of the shifter world. It was sort of nerve-wracking that this whole event was freaking televised.

"I have to take her to see Mom," Dolly told her sisters as she continued to lead me down the long hallway.

Finally, we reached a door on the left. "She's in here. Just knock."

"Okay. Thank you." I hugged Dolly.

She gave me a tight hug. "Good luck."

"Thanks." I needed it more than she could ever know.

As she walked away from me, I knocked on the door.

"Come in, Lena," Queen Kiara said.

I twisted the door handle and entered the room.

I took her in. Her long, light brown hair was in a beautiful updo. It stood out against the gold crown adorned with rubies that she wore on top of her head.

She wore a long gold gown, similar to my own, with sequins at the bust. It looked striking against her golden skin.

"You look beautiful," I said.

"As do you, my dear." Her pink lips formed a natural smile. "I just wanted to wish you luck out there today—and give you my blessing."

I shifted in my high heels uncomfortably. I hadn't actually told her if I was planning to choose Damon or not.

Had she just assumed I would choose him, because he was born to be the King of the Shifters? Maybe she thought it was the smartest choice I could make.

In a lot of ways, it *was*.

"One of my shifter abilities is seeing the future," Queen Kiara continued. "I already know the decision you're about to make. I just want you to know that I support you."

"Will the other Royal Elders support me?" I asked her.

A faint smile hit her lips. "You must fight for what you want, Lena. You can do this."

I swallowed hard. Her response made me think this was all going to be okay in the end—somehow, some way, it was all going to work out. But I had a feeling it wasn't going to be an easy road until then.

"Shall we head down to the ceremony?"

I nodded.

As Queen Kiara and I headed out of the room and down the hallway, all of Damon's sisters fell into line after us.

With every step I took towards the hall where the Royal Change of Hands Ceremony was being held, the knot in my stomach began to tighten a little more.

Everything was about to change: my life, the shifter world as we knew it... *everything*. In just a matter of minutes from now, I would be announcing my decision in front of the Royal Elders and on live television.

I was about to open a whole new chapter. And right now, that was scary as fuck.

~

When we reached the Hall, everyone was already there. All eyes fell on me and Queen Kiara as we entered the room. It was as though they had been waiting for us.

My eyes flitted around the room. There were so many spectators in the audience. Towards the center of the room, the Royals from our generation were lined up.

Alexis was standing next to Sean.

Katerina stood next to Patrick.

The Hellcats were lined up. Anastasia met my eyes and shot me a small smile as I walked past her.

That was when I approached *them*—my mates.

I walked past Ezra. He had on a light gray tuxedo with a deep blue tie that made his blue eyes look even more striking than usual. A small smile tugged at his lips as I passed him.

Harden wore a purple tie with his black tuxedo that was so deep in color, his violet eyes took on an almost pinkish hue. He nodded at me as I passed him.

Rafael was next. His orange tie popped against the black tux he was wearing. His emerald green eyes found mine. He winked as I moved past him.

Damon was last in line. His golden-brown eyes locked on mine. He held my gaze with so much intensity; it felt like he was piercing straight through my soul.

I drank the rest of him in. His tie popped against his black tuxedo. It was orange... like fire.

"Let us begin," Queen Kiara said as she stood at a podium a

few feet away from me. "Today, we celebrate the past one-hundred years that we, the Royal Elders, have reigned. Under our rule, our kingdoms have grown. For the most part, they have thrived, even in spite of the events of the past year." She shot a sad smile at the audience. I knew she was talking about the shifter world war and the many losses it had brought to every kingdom, including King Ari.

"Of all of our many great achievements, we have all birthed children—children who have prepared to take our places," Queen Kiara continued. "Our first-born children or grandchildren will rule each of our kingdoms for the next one-hundred years, during which point *their* children—our grandchildren—will take their places and reign."

She glanced around the room. "In other words, today is a momentous occasion that marks the ending for us and the beginning for our children. Our doors will close so theirs can open. It is a bittersweet day, one that will forever go down in history." Queen Kiara paused. "Before we begin with the official Royal Change of Hands ceremony, I would like to remind you all of a new policy that has been introduced this year. Whereas past Royals were required to be married by the date of the Royal Change of Hands, each King or Queen to be has twenty-nine days *after* today to take a husband or wife if they haven't already. On the thirtieth day, each of the Kings and Queens will go through their official coronation."

A few of the Royal Elders whispered, and I couldn't help but think they seemed unhappy about this policy change.

"Now I would like to introduce all of you to someone very special." Queen Kiara turned to me. "Lena, please join me."

As I walked over to her, I knew that just about every pair of eyes in the room was on me. It was unnerving, but only because of what was about to happen next.

My decision, my choice, would be out there in the world.

"Lena Falcone is a third-year student at Shifter Academy, but she is so much more than that. Today, I would like to introduce her to you as the next Queen of the Shifters."

A pin-dropping silence filled the room. It was followed by whispers.

"Lena was not born into this role."

Wrong, I thought. *If only I could set them all straight...*

"She is the one who the prophecy is about," Queen Kiara informed the audience. "If you'll all recall, the prophecy states: 'She will become mated to one Alpha from each of the four shifter races. But it will be up to her to decide which of the four Alphas to marry. The marriage will break her bond with the other three Alphas, and it will also determine which shifter race will rule the world.' Lena is currently mated to my own son, Damon Crowne, as well as Rafael Khan of the Tigers, Ezra Gray of the Wolves, and Harden Swift of the Jaguars. It is now up to Lena to make her decision." She turned to me. "Who do you choose?"

I glanced around at my mates. I wasn't sure how any of them were going to feel about what I was going to say next, but that was okay. Queen Kiara had already given me her approval. I just hoped that the rest of the Royal Elders would agree. I turned my attention to the long table at which they were sitting.

"Your Majesty, I wish to go against the prophecy. Instead of marrying only one of my mates, I would like to request your permission to marry all four of them."

"You wish to marry *all four of them*?" King Roman was the first to speak.

"Is that even allowed?" Queen Bria asked quietly.

"We *do* set the rules," Queen Kiara replied. "We can choose to allow this."

"But why *would* we?" King Aloysius, of the Birds, asked, narrowing his beady little eyes at me.

"What would this mean for the hierarchy?" Queen Bria questioned.

"I would like to keep the current hierarchy in place," I explained. "Damon and I would be King and Queen of the Shifters, but I would also act as Queen of the Wolves, Tigers, and Jaguars."

"I know this change will be a large one, but I think it is something we should give some consideration to," Queen Kiara told the other Royal Elders.

"I highly disagree," Queen Bria said, shaking her head.

"How would all of this work out logistically?" Queen Maya questioned. "There needs to be a Queen in place in every kingdom at all times."

"I would travel from kingdom to kingdom regularly," I replied. "The portals make that easy enough to do."

"It seems so... complicated," Queen Alexandria commented.

I swallowed hard. I knew this was my *one shot* to try to convince them.

"This would be a complicated arrangement," I admitted. "But the thing about this prophecy is that it's made my *entire life* extremely complicated. I didn't ask to fall in love with all four of my mates, but now that I have... Well, I can't imagine a life without any of them. So, I want to ask you all to please consider allowing me to spend the next one-hundred years with all four of the guys I love."

"Thank you, Lena." Queen Kiara's eyes locked on mine. "Please give us an hour so we may deliberate," she announced into the speaker. "Once we have come to a resolution, we will call all of you back."

I nodded.

At that moment, many of the shifters began to leave the room.

Shere Khan glanced over at me from where he was sitting, with the rest of the Legends, in the first row. He nodded at me as he rose to his feet.

I knew he was going to try to talk the Royal Elders into letting me do this. I hoped they would listen to him. If anyone could convince them, I was pretty sure it was him.

My mates walked over to me then.

"Lena, I can't believe the decision you've made," Ezra whispered. "I'm not entirely sure how I feel about it."

"I'm not sure how I feel about it, either," Harden admitted.

Damon remained silent. He was quiet and brooding.

"Princess, there's something I need to tell you," Rafael informed me.

"What is it, Raf?" I asked.

"My memories just came back right now. I remember *everything*. I remember you, and I remember the night of the switch." Rafael's green eyes met mine. "Lena, I know who switched bodies with me!"

"Who?" I asked, just as I heard the sound of the door click open. I watched, completely shocked, as Ella Gray entered the room. Her icy gray eyes locked on mine as she walked towards the rest of the Royal Elders.

What was *she* doing here? I couldn't believe she had the audacity to show her face here. The Legends would finally have the chance to get rid of her, once and for all.

Well, the Legends and *me*. And I was far from ready for this.

"It was my brother, Lena," Rafael whispered to me. "Ricky is the one who switched bodies with me."

A nervous knot twisted in my stomach. Well, that's what I thought it was... *at first.*

But then I felt it happening: a sharp pain cascading through my spine before radiating throughout the rest of me. It was followed by the sound of my own bones twisting and snapping.

Fuck. This couldn't have been happening—not right now, of all times.

Gasps filled the room as I slithered onto the floor.

Glancing into the faces of my mates, I couldn't help but think that they looked completely horrified to see this side of me.

My worst nightmare had come true.

Everyone knew I was a Serpent now.

TO BE CONTINUED

in the fourth and final installment:

Shifter Academy: Year Four

Printed in Great Britain
by Amazon

21299442R00180